A WORLD OF SONG

Sharon Webb's blue-green world of Aulos is a stunning creation: a culture whose customs and offices, festivals and folklore are all pervaded by the harmonies of music.

RAM SONG is Webb's most powerful and moving novel, a soaring portrait of a planet caught in the throes of cultural change. It is the tale of four lives intertwined by a mysterious cosmic force: an untried nobleman, a brilliant woman doctor, a wild young dancer, and an ageless immortal who must leave his long isolation to save Aulos from destruction.

Novels by Sharon Webb

THE ADVENTURES OF TERRA TARKINGTON

EARTHCHILD

EARTH SONG

RAM SONG

RAM SONG

Sharon Webb

BANTAM BOOKS
TORONTO • NEW YORK • LONDON • SYDNEY • AUCKLAND

This low-priced Bantam Book
has been completely reset in a type face
designed for easy reading, and was printed
from new plates. It contains the complete
text of the original hard-cover edition.
NOT ONE WORD HAS BEEN OMITTED.

RAM SONG

A Bantam Book / published by arrangement with
Atheneum Publishers

PRINTING HISTORY
Atheneum edition published October 1984
Bantam Spectra edition / October 1985
The map of Porto Vielie and the illustrations
of the "Diagram of the Composition" were done
by Thomas Dietz.

ISBN 0–553–25168–6

Published simultaneously in the United States and Canada

Bantam Books are published by Bantam Books, Inc. Its trademark, consisting of the words "Bantam Books" and the por-
trayal of a rooster, is Registered in U.S. Patent and Trademark
Office and in other countries. Marca Registrada. Bantam
Books, Inc., 666 Fifth Avenue, New York, New York 10103.

PRINTED IN THE UNITED STATES OF AMERICA

H   0 9 8 7 6 5 4 3 2 1

For Ted
and
Jayne Sturgeon

Acknowledgments

I would like to thank these people: Thomas Deitz for taking my scrawls and transforming them into handsome maps and illustrations; Jean Karl for her editorial advice; Wendy Nesheim for throwing a lifeline when I took my floundering dip in the genetic pool; Bryan Webb for everything else.

I would also like to offer my appreciation to this silicon life-form: Algernon Apple III for his masterful typing and editing and especially for his startling and serendipitous revision.

SHARON WEBB

Music, Artisan of *Abbr.* AM. The highest degree. One who has knowledge of all the disciplines of the Composition. After study of all sectors of the Composition (illus. below), and an arduous internship, the candidate must complete an Etude of Synthesis after which the degree is conferred and the recipient is appointed to a Conductus. As Conductus, the artisan assumes command of city or national government and mediates all disputes between subordinate officials.

Music, Composition of The unifying field in the affairs of humankind. In the Composition, Music encompasses the four quartals of Canon Law, Mathematics, Esthetics, and Medicine, and their connecting disciplines, the conjuncts of Ethics, Science, Communication, and Spirit.

Diagram of the Composition

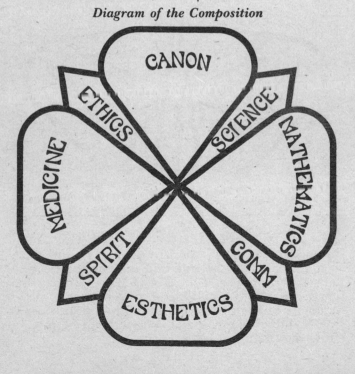

Music, Field Practitioner of *Abbr.* FP. A technician trained in a quartal or conjunct. One who practices under the supervision of a monodist or quartalist.

Music, Monodist of *Abbr.* MM. One holding a degree with a specialty in one of the four conjuncts. A monodist studies at the conjunct and its two adjacent quartals. EX: A MM/SPT studies at the conjunct of Spirit and draws from the quartal of Medicine knowledge of physical derangements which affect spiritual health and from the quartal of Esthetics appreciation of the beauty of the human spirit.

The Trigon of Monody, Spirit

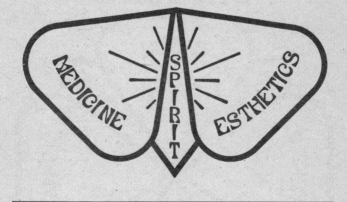

Music, Quartalist of *Abbr.* QM. One holding a degree with a specialty in one of the four quartals. A quartalist studies a quartal and its two adjacent conjuncts. EX: A QM/MED studies the quartal of Medicine and its two conjuncts, thus moderating treatment of the body with laws drawn from the conjunct of Ethics and consideration of psyche from the conjunct of Spirit.

Polytext of Aulos
Introduction to the Composition,
2d rev. ed., Baryton, Anche, AU 1937.

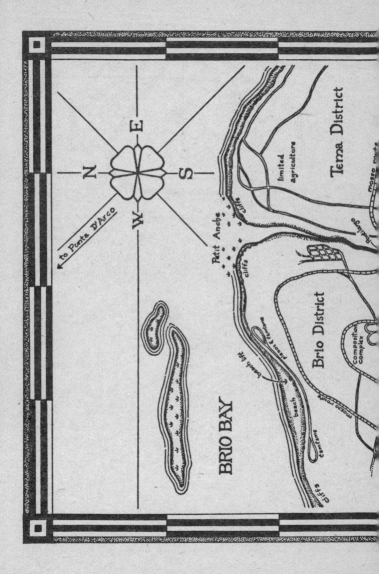

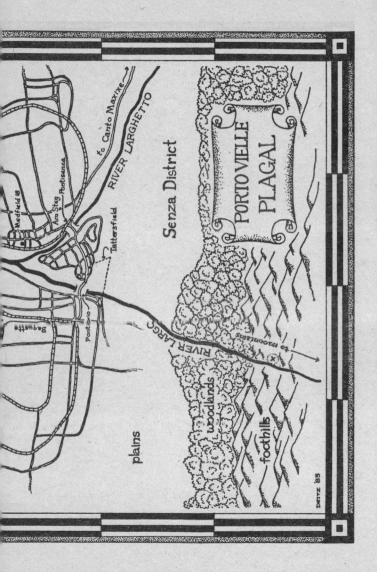

Prologue

The creatures stood at the far reaches of time without knowing that they did this. They stood at the far reaches of time and felt the universe shudder like a live thing at the approach of another.

Impingement . . .

The breach in space-time was minute. The rift sealed instantly. The captured wave of energy from the alien universe was no more than a ripple growing from an infinitesimal point.

The creatures turned anxious, slanting eyes toward the instruments of their starship and saw the wave echoed there.

The wave was a stormtide.

Cataclysm . . .

A tag-end of the universe turned in upon itself. Flesh pulsed into energy. A billion thoughts spilled free to swirl like flotsam on an alien tide rushing backward in time.

Chapter 1

The Ram sang in the night of space. As she circled the blue-green world beneath her hull, she sang of another place and another time.

She spoke to the stars and the lonely reaches between them, telling of her origins in metaphors of light, mapping her genesis with whispered infrasound and ancient cadences.

And as the starship sang, she listened as she had for ten thousand years for the answer that had never come. Instruments catching the subtle rhythm of the stars probed and analyzed, storing data within the Ram's vast memory. Yet there were minute changes that the ship could not detect. Not until the fabric of space and time began to warp.

Within the shell of the Ram the lights on the wide control console flashed a warning.

The man spoke to the heart of the ship. Again the warning. His eyes met the woman's next to him. "He'll have to be called."

She looked away. "I don't like to."

"What choice do we have now?"

"I don't like to." She turned from him and a thousand tiny crystals on her cap danced around her ears with the motion. "He's on retreat," she added needlessly.

The man raised an eyebrow. "I know that."

She had no choice, not really, but still she hesitated. Foolishly, she told herself, yet a part of her

1

stood in awe of the man they called Kurt Prime. She looked back at the console. The man was bending over his instruments now, his brows beetling. The yellow and amber warning lights reflected sharply from his cap and she narrowed her eyes.

"The effect is increasing," he said. "You can see that yourself."

She nodded slowly. "We'll do it then."

He straightened. "We should go now."

Again the hesitation. She looked up as if she could see through the ceiling, as if she could see the lake many kilometers above her reflecting like blue sky on the village beneath. "We'll have to bring the interface. He'll need it."

The immortal, Kurt Kraus, walked alone through the ancient subtropical forest ringing Sky Lake. Brushing a thick, dark lock of hair from his eyes, he looked up at the tangle of branches silhouetted in the brilliant light of midday.

He had begun to see the woods with new eyes now—not a static grouping of leaves and bark, but instead a slow-moving war dance, a frozen battle for supremacy. There a giant mahogany fought with another for the light from a bogus sun. On a slight rise above him a young gumbo limbo, springing from the rotting remains of its parent tree, methodically starved its spindly siblings. But even as it prospered, the gumbo limbo carried the instrument of its own death: the dark green leaves and clinging aerial roots of a strangler fig showed in the young tree's crown—another cycle beginning.

He moved to the shore of the shallow lake where five brown ducks broke formation and waggled their tails at his approach. Across the wind-riffled water ancient liveoaks marked the edge of the Ram's mortal colony. Once it had been called New Renascence. Now it was simply Renascence—or The Choice.

At the juncture of far shore and woods stood a small group of young men and women in their mid-teens. Children really, he thought. Poignant young new lives. He watched as one by one they stepped forward. It was time again for the choice—the Final Decision. He had seen it come a dozen times during his retreat. Though he could not hear their voices, though he had heard no voice except his own in the five years of his isolation, he knew what it was they said.

That one, the girl with slim brown legs straight beneath her short garment and eyes raised to meet the interrogator—she would choose to deny immortality. But the next? Not that girl. Her head was thrown back a trifle too high, her chin thrust out too far. Kurt imagined that he could see the flash of defiance in her eyes, though the distance was too great. That one would choose with a bright smile on her face. She would choose immortality, he thought, and later, in the privacy of her tiny cabin, she would weep at her loss.

Each time he viewed the ancient ceremony of Renascence the memories replayed, and again he wondered how he might have answered. The question he had never been asked spoke in his mind: How do you choose, Kurt Kraus? And what if he had denied his immortality? What if, instead, he had chosen his music, his creativity?—a blaze of being gone in a flash of time, a tiny sun gone nova, then dark? A firefly? He tried to peer into the dark well of distant memories and wondered if the spark of what he might have been could still be seen after ten thousand years.

He looked across the shallows once again. The ring now. They placed it on the finger of the first girl as if she were a bride. He could see her looking at it, and a bit of the wonder crept into his heart. A simple ring of ancient design, the golden lazy eight of infinity, broken, vanishing into black, and then the words: "For Art."

Cycles.

It was strange about memories, he thought. Strange how something could stay in his mind in tiny protein coils for millennia while other things could

vanish without a trace. No, not without a trace.
Vague thoughts glided in and out of his mind—
incomplete hints that lay just beyond his grasp. They
seemed to be dreamlike echoes of things he almost
knew, things he should know. But just why he should
know them, he could not say.

At the beginning of his retreat these shadowy,
fragmented thoughts tormented his dreams, and he
would waken in the dark to feel the cold sweat
gathering on his body.

Coming to consciousness like a man anesthe-
tized, he tried to validate himself with the memories
that would not come. He had to remember. Had to.
He tossed on his narrow pallet and struggled for a
hold on the cloudy shards of his mind. Then, as
surrogate winds blew over his sweaty body and chilled
him, he wrapped himself in a robe and listened to
the faint sounds of lake and woods until at last he
could sleep again.

Now, although the fragments still lodged in his
brain, they seemed less important, less threatening.

The midday winds were beginning, riffling over
the silver blue lake, tossing the leaves of the trees,
sending tiny seeds and pollen on currents of air to
renew the forest and the fields. The wind was cool
on his face and pleasant. As it rose, it sang in the
leaves and brought with it another sound. Voices.
Closer than they had come in the five years of his
isolation.

He could see them in the distance: five of them
cresting a low hill. They moved purposefully, and
when they saw him, they lapsed into silence.

He felt a wrenching pang of regret. They had
come for him. But it was too soon. Too soon.

One of them, a woman, stepped out of the
group toward him. He stared at her. She seemed
familiar, but he could not call her name.

She held a small bundle in her hands, but made
no move to open it or offer it. She seemed apologetic, and it was obvious to him that she desperately

wished she were somewhere else. "I'm sorry, Kurt Prime," she said at last. "There's trouble."

He tried to gather his thoughts. "Trouble?"

"With the Ram. Communications with star drive are garbled. Our instruments are showing an echo effect, but nothing registers on sensory."

He stared at her. "Where are we?"

"Off Aulos, the second planet of Cuivre. The mortal colony from Renascence," she prompted. "Most were musicians."

When he said nothing, she went on. "There's something else. We've lost contact with one of our skimmers. We're sending a homing beam, but we can't read the skimmer's position." She hesitated, then said, "Alani was on board."

"Alani?" His little girl? Alarm tracked through him. "Does Liss know?" She had to be told.

A puzzled look came into the woman's eyes. "Who?"

"Liss. Her mother. . . . My wife."

Her eyes widened, then dropped, and she refused to meet his gaze again. Instead, she thrust the little bundle toward him.

It opened in his hands. He stared down at the iridescent helmet. Its crystal tendrils spilling through his fingers glittered as they moved in the wind. He looked at the little group, first at one, then another, finally the woman. At her faint nod, he lifted the cap and put it on.

It was soft and light. Its tens of thousands of tiny crystals, woven intricately together, covered his hair completely; its faceted tendrils hung to his shoulders. He felt the helmet mold to the contours of his head, and as it did, he knew that it was his alone. He sensed rather than felt it interface with the circuits hidden beneath his hair at the base of his skull; and as he did, the flood came and he staggered against its intensity.

Alani. Not a little girl. Not a little girl for ten thousand years now. And Liss? Gone for a thousand, left by her own choice on a watery world half a galaxy away. No more than frozen memories.

He looked evenly at the woman whose name he knew was Kiersta. He was Kurt Prime now, and in his mind he carried the glittering memories of the Ram's ten-thousand-year voyage. He nodded sharply. "I will come at once."

Chapter 2

A crowd of vacationers pushed aboard the skimboat and jostled one another as they headed up the curving ramps of her tower. The ship sat high in the water, and the view from her lofty observation deck was magnificent. Shoreward, the southern coastal city of Punta D'Arco sprawled at the point of the low peninsula like a scattered tumble of children's blocks. To either side of the city, vast stretches of the tall musical reeds, the Anche, that gave the major country of Aulos its name, tossed in the afternoon wind, but their song and the high-pitched cree of a wheeling flock of blue-backed harks was lost in the distance and the hubbub of the crowd.

The vacationers' bright, loose clothing reflected their festive attitude. They were about to leave the quartals of civilization for the mezzo and adventure.

A young couple, obviously newly duet, strolled hand-in-hand toward the railing. In a burst of exuberance, the man hoisted the girl to his shoulder, where she steadied herself with one hand around his neck. "There it is. I can see it."

"No, you can't," he said. "That's just an offshore

island. The mezzo lies that way." He squinted at the brilliant reflections from the choppy gulf and flung and arm toward the horizon.

The peninsula pointed like an arrow toward the Plagal, the strip of land that formed the mezzo between the north polar country of Anche and the torrid, almost uninhabitable continent that lay beyond. The girl gave a shiver of excitement. "Is it really as wild as they say?"

The young man affected a look somewhere between sophistication and boredom, but it was lost to the girl who stared eagerly toward the mezzo. "It's safe enough," he said, "as long as you're with me. Safe enough in the city at any rate, but you wouldn't want to leave Porto Vielle." He gave her a mischievous look. "The Tatters might get you."

With a vibrant hum, the skimboat came to life. The girl gave a breathy little shriek and clutched the young mans neck as the ship rose on its cushion of air. A moment later it began to accelerate.

They skimmed across the gulf like a great white pebble skipping across a pond until at last the pale cliffs of the Plagal came into view.

Spilling from the skimboat like bright flowers, the vacationers scattered through Porto Vielle. Some, succumbing to the insistent call of vendor's gongs fashioned of scraps and flotsam, shoppped for trinkets at the native tam-tams that lined the whitewashed streets and drove what they took to be hard bargains. Others strolled along the bluffs overlooking the blue-green waters of the harbor and watched the kitesingers perform for small coins and the occasional hoped-for quarter note.

By early evening the lowering sun, Cuivre, set the sea on fire, and the tourists gathered in twos and fours in the open-air plenos by the gulf to dine on fresh fruits and the specialty of the Plagal, sea harp broiled in its nest of feathery nettles. When the moon Presto began to show a crescent low in the sky and the first sign of Allegro gleamed over the horizon, the visitors smiled and nodded to one another. There would be two moons for Festival tonight.

Porto Vielle perched on the flat plane of the broken and fissured Plagal Plateau. It was a city divided by its terrain, its three sections connected only by the sculpted lace of suspension bridges. Far below them, the river Largo and its tributary the Larghetto crept through twisting beds toward the gulf.

Beyond the city and its seasonal fringe of bright tents and banners, the Largo ran swifter as it fell from the foothills. Here open woodlands touched its banks, and far above the river silent waterfalls tumbled in clouds of mist.

A boy of about eighteen sat leaning against a giant boulder overgrown with blue-gray moss. Staring with serious dark eyes at the leaping water, he held a primitive reedflute to his lips and played a song as liquid as the river at his feet, but he played without thought. His mind was still in Porto Vielle.

It had taken him nearly half a day to come here from the city. At first he had walked, but his steps quickened to a lope and then a run as if Hexen pursued him. Finally he collapsed, his ragged breath searing in and out of his lungs. After that, he paced himself with long, lean-legged strides until he reached the foothills.

The river ran clean and cool here. He stripped off his clothes and scrubbed away the city's dirt, watching as the cloud of brown swirled away from his body and ran downstream, knowing that he would meet it again when he returned to his family and the crowded tents of the Tattersfield.

As he played his flute, he stared absently at the river. A shoal of stretchscales broke the surface, bodies gleaming silver in the sun, but he saw only his mother. He saw her eyes, pale gray and strained in her gaunt face; he saw her thin hands clutch at her swollen, knotted belly. Her pains had begun before dawn. While his sister kept the smaller girls, Shawm ran for the midwoman of the stave.

Grudgingly, the old woman consented to come, but not before she had her breakfast. He waited while she blew the coals of her stove to a glow and cooked her meal. She ate it slowly, squatting on her haunches in front of her tent. But still she wasn't done. With growing impatience he watched as she licked each drop of fat from her fingers with greedy darts of her tongue. At last, when Cuivre blazed over the horizon, she rose and followed him to his mother.

Crimping her lips in a pinch of a smile, she unfolded her pouch and, kneeling at his panting mother's side, drew out her instruments. They were made of metal touched here and there with rust or streaks of dried blood, he could not tell which.

She drew out a vicious curving probe and set to work.

Shawm stared down in an agony of fear at the gush of fluid stained with blood. At his mother's strangled cry, he pulled at the midwoman's arm. "Stop. You're hurting her."

The midwoman spat at him. "Get out."

"No."

But his mother blinked and pressed his hand. "Go, Shawm."

He stood then, hesitating, staring at his mother. When she nodded faintly, he turned and strode out of the tent.

Outside, his sister Clarin sat with the two little ones in the shade of the family jig, her back pressed against the shaft of the two-wheeled cart. She looked up at him with anxious eyes. He started to speak, then shrugged and turned away with a catch of his breath. It seemed to him that if he stayed, the city would smother him with its press of people and its dirt.

He turned toward the distant mountains where he had been born and began to walk. Soon he was running.

                    *   *   *

Cuivre was low in the sky now. It was time to go back to Porto Vielle.

Kneeling, he gathered the small bundle of gray-brown mimeset tubers that he had dug from the riverbank. The scentsinger would pay well for them, and they needed the money. He thought of a new child in the crowded tent and scowled. Another belly that would need filling. The twisting stab of resentment grew. Maybe it would die. Maybe it would be dead. The intensity of the hope washed over him, and he felt both defensive and ashamed.

It was time to go back to the city, yet he hesitated, drawn in the other direction. Only a day's walk more and he could be in the high mountains. He could be home again to stay. He wouldn't leave again, he told himself. He'd never again follow his people to towns and cities scattered over the Plagal; he was sick of wandering. But what was the use? It was time to go back to Porto Vielle.

Not moving, he knelt in the crumbly soil at the river's edge. A tiny jailor carrying its mate on its back crept along the ground near Shawm's knee. He stared at the insects. The male had trapped the female in a curving mass of upturned legs that had grown together now. She thrust stalklike eyes through the trap. He could see her swollen egg sac. For the rest of her life she would produce young, shedding them like dust through the bars of her cell. His fingers itched to free her, to tear apart the flimsy, chitinous prison, but he knew if he did she would die. "Maybe you'd be better off," he said aloud.

The answering voice was as shocking as a splash of icy mountain water—a girl's voice speaking a barrage of gibberish.

Startled, Shawm scrambled to his feet, but there was no one there. Nothing but woods and water and a tiny cloud of golden darts hovering over a bank of sweetset.

Another string of phrases. This time he caught a meaning from one of them: "Calling. Calling."

He whirled around; he saw no one.

"Answer, please," the voice insisted.

Feeling foolish and a little uneasy he said, "Who's there?"

There was a pause. Then the girl's voice came back, accented, but intelligible. "Good thanks. I was afraid you wouldn't." Then, "Say something else so I can connect your dialect."

He stared in what he took to be the direction of the voice. "Where are you?"

"Oh . . . sorry. There."

Suddenly Shawm was looking into the blue-green eyes of the most beautiful woman he had ever seen. She was sitting in the shade of a bitterbole by the riverbank, sitting gracefully on what seemed to be nothing at all. Bewildered, he said, "Where did you come from?"

Her eyes met his. "The Ram." Her eyes were as deep and blue as the gulf. "I wanted to see your world again, so I took out a skimmer." Her lips quirked in a rueful smile. "Now I seem to be lost. I'll have to triangulate a distress."

Completely confused, he stared at the girl and tried to place her accent. It was as lilting as his, but the intonation was reedy as a tourist's from Anche and her carriage was proud. An upperstave, he was sure, yet her pale hair was nearly covered with a shimmering cap and he had never seen clothes like that before. Puzzled, he watched as her hand shot out, fingers moving in a tapping motion. Suddenly she vanished.

Before he could blink, she reappeared, teetering in the edge of his vision. Horribly startled, he reached out to steady her, but instead of touching flesh his fingers raked through thin air.

Her eyes widened slightly. "Oh. I guess you didn't know. I'm imaging. See?" The solid planes of the girl faded to mist and shadows. The ghostly curving lines of the river showed through her body. He took a slow gulp of air to quiet the pounding of his heart. Just another gadget of the upperstave, he told himself, or an illusion. He sniffed tentatively at the air, testing for the telltale scent of guilefly, finding nothing but fresh clumpweed and the sharp odor of the mimeset tubers.

The image grew solid again. "I've frightened you, I suppose."

Shawm's chin went up at the insult.

"I didn't mean to. Some people can hold image when they go into synchor, but I don't do this often enough to be good at it."

The quick rush of adrenalin put an edge to his voice, "What are you talking about?"

"I told you. I'm lost. I can't find the Ram. My instruments are telling me the ship is hopping all over its orbit. I can't get anything but echo patterns." She glanced down quickly, then gave a little gasp. "And there's another!"

She caught her lower lip between her teeth and narrowed her eyes in concern. "Well, if I can't find them, they'll just have to find me." She looked up at Shawm. "I'll have to stay in synchor until they do."

"Stay where?"

She sighed faintly. "I've confused you again. Sorry. Synchronous orbit. If they're going to find me, I have to make it easier. Otherwise they'll tractor dust."

As a blank look trailed across his face, she looked at him sharply. "You do know about the Ram, don't you?"

Puzzled, Shawm stared at her. Then he nearly laughed when he realized that she meant the silver egg, the fabulous silver egg that had brought them to Aulos. Folklore. A fable. It was said that the upperstave actually believed in it, but then they believed in all sorts of foolishness, and a good thing too. If they didn't, his people would go hungry during Festival. Then it occurred to him that she must think he was stupid. "I'm not ignorant. I know all the stories."

"Good. It's been so long, I was afraid you people might have forgotten us." In answer to his questioning look, she added, "It's happened before, but only with the mortal colonies, of course. The people of

Escher thought we were gods. Some of them wanted
to build a shrine in our honor." She laughed ruefully.
"Doom that project. They finally decided we were a
hideous menace from space..." Her voice dropped
to a conspiratorial whisper; her brows rose in mock
horror. "...awful aliens with the power to cloud minds.
You can believe we were lucky to get away."

He met her smile with set lips.

"You don't believe me, do you?"

His eyes darkened, "You think I'm a fool, a buffo."

She seemed surprised, "No. I don't." A look he
could not read came into her face. "What must you
think?" she said. "What must you think of me?"

A smooth answer sprang to mind. Instantly he
compressed his lips as if to hold it in. She expected
flattery, he thought. Deference. They all did. They
wanted to be humored like small children. Easy
enough to do; he had learned the trick of it when he
was very young. He looked at the woman before
him—the image of the woman, he reminded himself.
At that moment she was very beautiful and very easy
to hate. "I think you're playing with your clever
toys." He spoke deliberately, meaning to insult her.
"I think you're a child."

To his amazement, she laughed.

He felt himself stiffen.

"I'm sorry. It's just that it's been a very long time
since anyone thought that." Her smile swept away.
"Of course you couldn't believe me. You need proof.
Let me show you." Hands moved quickly, her fingers
tapped out a strange pattern. Then she was holding
something toward him.

He hesitated, not knowing whether to take it or to
show his independence. Yet he could not help but stare
as a swirling golden speck hovered in the air between
her outstretched hands. Intrigued, he took a step closer.
As he did, he felt—or heard—a faint pulsing.

Suddenly the dancing, golden speck flared into
a giant, boiling sun.

Gasping, he fell back. The image of it burned
into his eyes, blinding him. Then he heard it. He felt

its song as a throbbing deep inside his body. In a spasm of fear he flung himself away, but still it grew until each bone and sinew pulsed with the turbulence of the yellow sun. The ground under his feet convulsed. He swam in flowing fire and felt his body explode in tongues of flame.

Then, quite strangely, he was not afraid.

At the center of himself he felt the star's vastness, its clean white fire, its churning power. He breathed, and his breath was a flare burning into blackness, his heart a pulsing inferno, his blood great streaming flames. He stood at the center of himself for an eternity, then suddenly, abruptly, he was cast out in a spiraling pinwheel of fire.

He spun in an uncontrolled, headlong flight into cold blackness. In vain he turned his face toward the warmth of the sun, but it whirled away until it was nothing more than a distant blazing globe.

Eons passed, and he felt himself cool and darken. Darken.

Eons passed....

Then the tiny light of a single thought pierced the darkness. There was something he needed to do... Something nagging at his mind....

"Move. Quickly."

Something....

"Get out of the beam. Jump!"

Chapter 3

The dark-haired immortal bent over his console, brow furrowing, smoothing, furrowing again as he rechecked his equations. Kurt Kraus stared at him and thought, how young he is—too young even to need a cap. He was surprised at the thought; he had never really thought of the gulf that separated him from so many of the people now. And this man? He was still in his first specialty, but he knew his work well. For thirty years he had been the Ram's chief Technologist of Communication, star drive; for thirty years he had done his job without a flaw. Now he raised troubled eyes toward Kurt and shook his head.

"Still no response?" Kurt asked.

"No, Kurt Prime," said the Comtech, quickly adding, "Nothing that means anything. I'm getting tronic debris from star drive now, and not much else. Let me show you." He touched a featureless segment of the console, and the flat plane dissolved to a stage. "Plot Starpoz," he commanded.

Instantly the stage darkened and a tiny three-dimensional sun, the star Cuivre, glowed against a star field. Near the point of light that represented the Ram, a bank of numbers formed in a cluster. "See that?"

Kurt nodded.

"According to Star Drive, that's our position. Perfectly accurate. The only trouble is, the information's 28 ramins, point 08299 seconds slow."

"You mean that's where we were, not where we are?" said the woman Kiersta.

He nodded.

Kurt narrowed his eyes at the display. "Is the aberration consistent?"

"No. It fluctuates. Look." He touched the companel that communicated directly with the heart of the ship's star drive. "Plot retrorbs 2 RamZ to StarPoz."

Together they stared at the stage. Instead of the ordered increments of their last two orbits, the point of light blazed into an erratic streak that curved back onto itself.

"Smear," said the Comtech. "And it's increasing."

Kurt stood silent for a moment, staring at the stage as if he could see beyond it into the churning heart of the Ram's drive. "Is there compensation?" he asked slowly.

The Comtech's hesitation was just for a moment. Then he said, "Yes."

Kurt closed his eyes. The image of the blue-white smear still danced before his retinas. For a moment he imagined he could see the Ram's drive engaging and disengaging its warps at lightning speed in a desperate attempt to compensate for its erratic data. "Then you've shut down the drive," he said irrelevantly. He knew, of course, that they had. Anything less and the Ram and its passengers would be pulled and compressed to strings of jellied pulp.

The Comtech nodded, then with a quick check of his figures, said, "With warp out, we're down to .00069 Light capability."

"I need Jacoby," Kurt said to Kiersta, "and Poetson."

"Poetson? From Renascence?" she began.

When he nodded, Kiersta opened her mouth as if to say something. Instead, she turned and spoke to an undertech. A moment later she stepped up to Kurt, "We've sent your call. Jacoby is close by. He's on his way."

Kurt caught the warm musk scent of her and felt an old sensation return. The suppressants he had taken during his retreat were beginning to wear off. Not now, he thought, looking at her. Not now, but soon. He straightened and said briskly, "Tell me the rest?"

"This way," she said.

He followed her to the bend in the horseshoe-shaped console where a small group of people clustered near Station 4. As he approached, they fell back, and he stepped up to the panel.

The Probetech turned quickly toward Kurt and nodded in deference. The crystals on his cap glittered with the reflection of the amber and yellow warning lights of the display. "We're in the edge of some sort of field, Kurt Prime," he said, running name and title together so that they sounded like one word. "We're getting an echo effect. I've never seen anything like this before."

"Can you give me visual?"

In answer, the man touched the panel of number sequences. A thin gray cloudy area sprang on the stage. "I'll enhance with 10Cyan."

The cloud deepened to shades of blue. As Kurt watched, the mist swelled, receded, swelled again. Cyan pulsed into touches of gray-bleached blue streaked with indigo and flowed out again. A curling plume of cobalt melted into a swirl of ice-blue smoke.

"Interesting," came a voice just behind Kurt. It belonged to his oldest friend, Jacoby.

Turning, Kurt clasped the man's shoulder warmly and said in greeting, "More's passed."

"More will." Jacoby caught Kurt's hand in his. "They tell me you need a Jack of Trades." Then he grinned. "Into the breach with Omni John."

A smile traced Kurt's lips. Jacoby had sampled so many occupations, had followed with unending curiosity so many specialized disciplines, that he had long ago ceased to be a specialist in anything. And the very lack of specialization had turned him into something of more value: a generalist, a man with the ability to see the forest from a very dense thicket of trees.

"What have you heard about this?" Kurt indicated the banks of instruments.

"A little here, a little more there. You know what they say: nega-news travels at Light Nine." His eyes searched Kurt's "I heard Alani was missing. Any word?"

Kurt shook his head. "Nothing yet. We've sent out a scanner."

Jacoby turned to the Probetech. "Give us a walker." When the man handed him a hand-sized console controller, he snapped it to his belt and said to Kurt, "Let's talk." With a quick nod, he indicated the door.

"They told me you'd asked for Poetson," said Jacoby as they turned the corner and stepped onto the hemichute.

Kurt nodded, then looked up sharply. There was something in Jacoby's voice....

"Poetson's dead. Almost three years ago now."

Kurt touched the railing, broad fingers with neatly clipped nails grazing the smooth gray surface underneath. Outwardly he gave no sign, yet the sinews of his hand tensed, relaxed, tensed again. Another one. Another mortal gone from a life that seemed as brief as the blinking of an eye. Kurt thought of the old man: Poetson. One of the most brilliant physicists ever to come out of Renascence. The man who had brought a new design to the Ram's star drive over forty years ago, one that used the very fabric of space for its ends.

Every man's death diminishes me, he thought, blinking at the words he had stored in some forgotten niche millennia ago. Even now he was not free of the quick stab of guilt that had come each time. He had never been able to forget that he was the one who had given death back to the world, that he was the one who had brought its dark seed to the stars.

The path of the hemichute veered, and it slid to a stop. When they stepped out, Jacoby swung onto a waiting floater. Kurt followed and the floater's gate clanged shut, enclosing them in a round cage studded with handholds. At the floater's soft but insistent demand, they clipped on the safety harness it presented. "Where are we going?" asked Kurt.

"Out to catch a squirrel," said Jacoby. "Ooberong. She's out here every day about now."

Zeni Ooberong: Poetson's protégé. She was rumored to be up each day and hard at work while most of the Ram still slept, and her workday never ended until long after everyone else's. So this is what she does in between, thought Kurt, an hour or two of flight instead of a meal.

Quickly gaining momentum, the floater slid silently along its tunnel. Then, with a final burst of speed, it shot through the terminus and with a sighing rush of air extended four long dragonfly wings.

As they broke through and sped toward the

center of the Ram, Kurt squinted against the sudden dazzle of the ship's sun. Kilometers away, the Ram's inner layer curved around them like a gigantic blue glass bowl furred with the dark green of its forests. In what passed for overhead, sky-lake reflected back the blue-roofed city below it.

"They used to think that bumblebees couldn't fly either." Jacoby patted the floater's frame in admiration. The motion threw him off balance in the rapidly decreasing gravity, and he steadied himself by gripping the nearest handhold.

"SLOWING," warned the floater. Then reversing, it slowed again until finally it hovered like a giant, ungainly insect slowly swaying in opposition to its minute correcting jets.

To starboard a red bud blossomed, then shattered, as a dozen young Renascence squirrelers ended their aeriallet and glided apart in twos and threes. To port, a group of young children tumbled with awkward delight to the amusement of the more experienced, who gave the cluster of orange-finned learners a wide berth.

Jacoby touched the band on his wrist with two quick taps. Responding to his call, a figure in deep red banked and with a long, lazy circle turned toward them.

Her hands and feet were spread, stretching the webbing of her suit into a thin magenta membrane. The stabilizing fin along her back arched in bright blue spines. She took the air in such swimming curves that it seemed to Kurt she was more fish than flying squirrel—an exotic tropical circling in a giant bowl of blue-green glass.

A final curving arc, a slow bank as if she were reluctant to end her flight, and Zeni Ooberong reached out and expertly caught the tether Jacoby threw to her. Clinging to it with one hand, with the other she reached up and touched her left shoulder. The blue spines collapsed and the stabilizing fin molded itself to her back. As she swung through the open gate, the floater swayed and hissed in compensation.

Without speaking, she stared at them, and Kurt thought that he could see the curiosity of a child in her frank gray-eyed gaze. It had been five years since they had spoken. With regret he saw that she was getting old now—regret overlaid with faint surprise, because somehow she had seemed different, somehow he had believed the youth that glowed from her eyes would always serve her. Close to sixty, he guessed, and beginning to gray in silvery waves that softened the firm line of her jaw.

With a tug at her waistcord, she drew the flight suit up between her legs and in at her waist until it resembled a pair of harem pants topped with a loose cape. The thin material served to reveal her compact and still quite shapely body. When she caught Kurt's stare, she said with a quick smile, "Not very fashionable, I suppose. But it's better than tripping over the folds."

He caught her hand in greeting. Trapped in his, her hand seemed no larger than a child's, and fragile, as if it might break in his grip.

As if reading his mind, she said, "I suppose you think it's time I clipped my wings, but I'm not feeble yet." Her keen eyes caught his. "Someday I'll tell you why I fly. Now I want to know why you called me, Kurt Prime."

"We need your help."

She listened, nodding quickly at times, narrowing her eyes at others. Then interrupting abruptly, she said, "Let me see this cloud."

Jacoby touched the little console controller, and swirling vapor filled the stage.

With her head cocked and a fingertip resting on her teeth, she stared at it without speaking. Finally, she said, "Give me the walker." With a few quick stabs, she enhanced the display. Frowning, she enhanced again, then quickly called a series of equations.

The stage changed. Kurt stared at it. Now instead of an amorphous cloud, it showed a collection of rapidly undulating shapes that looked like squat cylinders pinched in the middle with fat, curling rope.

"Do you know what these are?" she demanded. Before Kurt could answer, Jacoby said, "Twistors? There?"

She nodded. "The fabric of space." Then to Kurt, "The Poetson star drive defines and accentuates a gravity field. When the twistors react to it, we have a warping of space. All the Ram has to do is follow the path they make at sublight speeds. Just like thread following a needle." She nodded toward the stage. "The cloud is matter—created by twistors. Each twistor can create a subatomic particle. Two twistor combinations produce electrons, three can create protons and neutrons, the building blocks of atomic nuclei. Higher combinations, and you see the creation of every known particle."

"Then the cloud was caused by the star drive?"

"By the original effect, I think," she said. "The smear. When the drive began to compensate by toggling warp, the cloud formed."

"Then the cloud has to be expected," said Kurt. "It happens every time the Ram goes into warp."

"Every time, certainly," she said, "but this?" She stared at the stage for a moment longer. Then she switched it off. "Twistors travel at the speed of light. The cloud should have dissipated instantly." She stared at Kurt, then at Jacoby. "This twistor field is in stasis, in some sort of tension. There's no force in the universe that can cause this effect."

Chapter 4

Dorian Rynn's cool gray eyes widened at the probationer's words. He blinked slowly, partly in astonishment, partly for effect, and said in the clipped tones of the upperstave, "What did you say?"

Picardy Medfield stared down at her patient, a small boy of four sitting apprehensively at the edge of the shabby examination table. Dirt and tears streaked his face, but not enough to hide the flush of fever that touched his cheeks. Both his knees were hot and red, swollen with arthritis. She brushed a stray curl from the boy's forehead and smiled at him before she raised her dark eyes to meet Dorian's. "I said, I don't think incision is indicated." Her fingers gently touched the boy's knees. "There's no sign of suppera-tion."

Dorian blinked again and curled his lips in a pinch of a smile. Self-satisfied little fielder, he thought. It had never occurred to him that a lowerstave Plagal field practitioner would dispute his diagnosis. She wasn't even fledged yet, just a probationer, and no more than nineteen if she was that. He straightened and looked down at her from his full height. Her head barely came to his shoulder.

She stared back evenly. "I've seen a lot of cases like this. He can be treated with sharps—subsonic two." Picardy reached over her shoulder and, by practiced touch, extracted the silver sharp she needed from the quiver on her back.

At the sight of the long, thin needle, the little boy gave out a wail.

"Sh—sh," she said gently. "This one won't hurt. It sings." Twirling the sharp between her palms, she set it to humming, and then touched the blunt end to her temple. She cocked her head. "Yes. I can hear it now," she told him. "Would you like to try?"

The boy stopped crying long enough to stare suspiciously at the sharp for a moment. Then he nodded slowly and held out a grubby hand.

She placed it in his palm. "It tickles."

He looked down at the vibrating thing he held and then in imitation placed the nub on his fore-head. His eyes widened as the bones of his skull carried its song into his head. He listened gravely for a moment, then handed it back to Picardy, who twirled it between her palms again.

Dorian looked down at the girl. The motion she made rounded the muscles in her small arms. His eyes traced the swelling curve of her upper arm as it disappeared under a short cap of sleeve bearing the red and gray clef of her trade—the ancient treble clef with the backward S-curve ending in a serpent's head. She was shaped like a dancer, he thought. Pretty in a common sort of way, but the Plagal slur in her voice marked her as a hopeless lowerstave. And then there was the undisciplined way she let her hair curl in short dark twirls all over her head. It was disconcerting. He wanted to reach out and smooth it down. Instead, he raised a palm and slicked down his own pale hair and, with a little laugh that verged on condescension, said, "You didn't understand me, of course. According to all the authorities, incision is the only cure for Gli's Syndrome."

"So it is . . ." then with a pause, ". . . for Gli's Syndrome."

Leaning closer to her shoulder, Dorian reached across and grasped the child's bare thigh in a movement designed to show off his bright blue sleeve, a reminder to her that he wore the artisan quartals and the fifth year stripe of the Polytext. "But then," he said, "your view is quite limited."

"Yes, it is," she said pointedly, "so if you would just move your arm . . ."

He drew back. "I mean, your outlook on medicine is limited to the Plagal."

"Not entirely. I studied for ten measures in Anche," she said. "But look at the marks on his neck. This boy has been bitten by scoreflies. I know you don't have them in your country, but they're common enough here."

For the first time, he noticed the puffy little spots on the boy's throat. Plagal Fever.

"But we can call the quartalist." Picardy reached for the battered red button below a thin scanner panel.

Startled, Dorian gave out a quick, "No." He had forgotten they were being scanned. And Picardy was a probationer; it wasn't just a random scan—it was constant. There was a record of everything they had done and said, and he had forgotten it! A hot flush began to creep up his neck. He could imagine in frightful detail the scorn of the quartalist, the curl of his lip and the hardness of his eye when he reviewed the records.

Dorian managed a smile that was astonishingly assymmetrical, "Of course, uh, I was just testing you." He cleared his throat, "Uh...Plagal Fever is often compared to Gli's Syndrome. Why, just the other day I was reading about it and, uh..." His voice trailed away when he realized that in spite of the throat-clearing it sounded strange. Pinching his lips together and blinking once again, Dorian backed off two steps and watched as Picardy deftly inserted the tip of the sharp at sound-point eleven.

She was impossible, really. Even fledged fielders back in Anche showed more respect, he thought darkly, choosing to ignore the fact that most of the respect had been directed toward the professors and not the Polytext students who trailed after them.

"There," she said to the child. "Just one last thing, and then you can go home." She pulled another sharp from the quiver. This one was a sonic, transparent with a cylindrical base. She turned a dial on the cylinder, and the sharp began to hum: a low sustained note that stopped as abruptly as it began. Satisfied that it was sterile now, she flipped a small container from her treatment belt and inserted it into the cartridge. Fluid ran through the sharp, turning it to pale blue. A drop glistened at its tip.

"Now, poco," she said taking the child's arm in her hand, pressing with her thumb to raise the vein, "this is going to hurt. But only a little. Only for a moment. Will you be brave?"

Catching his lower lip between his teeth, the little boy stiffened his arm and stared at her with big, dark eyes. Before he could react further, she quickly inserted the tip of the sharp and the blue fluid began to glide down its shaft. A moment more and she was done.

Giving the boy a quick kiss, she called him brave and opened the door to his anxious mother, who scooped him in her arms and took him away with promises to bring him back in a quarter measure to be seen again.

When the door whisked shut, Picardy leaned against it. "A dozen still waiting and another just coming in." She sighed. "We might have a very late supper."

Dorian glanced at the time. With relief, he saw that his period was up. "You'll have to manage without me until tomorrow," he said quickly. "I have other quartals to do, you know," he added for the benefit of the scanner.

She picked up the transparent sharp and, touching its lever, ejected the thin inner sheaf. "Of course."

He watched as she plunged the needle into a long cylinder and drew in a fresh sheaf. There was something about the way she looked, the curve of her neck with the dark curls spilling over smooth, olive skin. Again he wanted to reach out and smooth her hair.

She leaned over and absently massaged her calf as she often did to prevent the cramps that came from standing too long in one position.

Dorian stared as the curving muscle of her calf swelled with the pressure of her fingers. Like a dancer, he thought again. He moved toward the door and then, remembering all the work he left her with, said defensively, "After all, I have to balance my etude."

When Picardy looked up at him, she kept her lips solemn, but she couldn't hide the laugh that danced into her dark eyes. "I'll try very hard to manage without you."

Dorian walked past the cluster of waiting patients and, with a quick, final glance at them, opened the door in relief.

Most of his medical knowledge was theory. So was his training in the other quartals and the conjuncts—until now. His etude had thrust him into a grubby reality that he had never known back in Anche. There, sheltered by the homogeneous atmosphere of the Polytext, he had moved through the streets of his native Baryton confident of his position. There he had worn his student artisan quartals with pride, and he never forgot that they set him apart from the others. Only an artisan could know all its parts. Only an artisan could synthesize.

He had done as well at the quartals as the other students in his concord: better than some in Medicine, less well in Canon—the density of the body of Aulosian law confused him at times. As for the other two quartals, he had shone in Esthetics and dimmed in Mathematics, but where the two overlapped at the conjunct of Communication, he felt comfortable enough.

Dorian stepped into the street and drew a quick breath. The image of one of the waiting patients stayed with him, a poco no older than three. The face of the child hung in his mind: her pale blind eyes ran with purulence; her face was thin and pinched around the lips.

He shuddered.

The patients made him nervous, all of them. They refused to stay in neat categories. They presented with a jumble of complaints mixed with ignorance and dirt—always dirt. He had never seen dirt on a Baryton patient. In Baryton the sick were organized into precise modalities: livers this measure, lungs the next. He had fallen into the rhythm of it easily; he had done well. But here ...

A frown slid over Dorian's face. It was frustrating to have to work with the sick of Porto Vielle. And what was the point? It was a skill he'd never have to use once he became a Conductus.

As if in answer, he remembered the words of his advisor: "You are raw—all of you. Unfinished. You think you know so much, but in truth you know nothing at all. You are about to begin your etude, and yet you question the wisdom of it. A waste of time, you think. And yet I ask you, How can you expect to mediate a dispute between two officials when you have no practical experience in their fields?

"As you enter this last phase of your training, remember this: Your internship was not designed for your amusement. Your work in all the disciplines will not be with the Augments or even the quartalists in charge; you will work with lowerstave field practitioners—in Canon Law and Medicine, in Ethics and Science—and you will learn from them. Not the least of what you will learn is humility. Only when you have learned that lesson, and learned it well, can you call yourself Conductus."

Sighing, Dorian tried to imagine his dour advisor afflicted with humility. He sniffed at the ludicrous idea.

Just then his internship seemed intolerable. He'd been in Porto Vielle for only a quarter measure and it seemed like a year. Four measures to go at Medfield 18 and then his etude turned to Canon and Mathematics. He tried to take comfort in that, until the uneasy thought came that his poorest work had been in Canon.

The prospect of the next fifteen measures was dismal: Practicum in the quartals, then Synthesis. Only the specter of failure kept him from throwing it all away. The burden of the upperstave, he thought. A catch phrase, but wasn't it true? Didn't the integrity of the government depend on his kind? The lowerstaves were like children. Imagine a government run by quarrelsome, greedy children. It would be so unstable, so corrupt, that society would crumble to bits.

Sighing again, he contemplated the weight of his burden. It won't be forever, he told himself. It only seemed that way. This time next year he would get his appointment. Just an assistantship at first, but

some day his own Conductus. Not in Baryton—
nobody's first Conductus fell there—but maybe near-
by. Or maybe one of the small towns along the north
shore where a real winter came. Deep in thought, he
imagined himself at his first official meeting. In his
mind's eye the man who was the Augment of Canon
became his grim advisor from the Polytext, but now
the tables were turned. The stern old man meekly
outlined his problem—one that lay at the conjunct of
Ethics and concerned a disagreement with the Augment of Medicine, a small woman who looked strangely
like Picardy. The answer was clear to Dorian, of
course. His was the broader view, after all.

He was half-delivered of his brilliant imaginary
Synthesis when the angry bleat of a rumbling mosso
frightened him half out of his wits. He leaped aside
as the open vehicle deviated from its programmed
route and swerved to avoid him, causing its load of
tourists to lurch against one another.

He caught his breath and glared. He would
never get used to Porto Vielle, or any part of the
Plagal for that matter. With a pang, he realized that
he was homesick. Just then he wanted to see the
familiar, ordered streets of Baryton more than he
had ever wanted anything.

He blinked and drew a long breath. At least the
rest of the day was his, with no tiresome field practitioner of Esthetics to worry about. Esthetics he practiced on his own.

This section of Porto Vielle's Tema District lay
near the juncture of the other two districts. At first
he turned north. In the distance he could see the
Pontilargo. The great bridge swayed gently, its cables
straining with the seasonal press of people and vehi-
cles. Beyond it lay the Brio, the section the tourists
seldom left. Far beyond the bridge he could see Brio
Bay sparkling in the afternoon light, its blue-green
waters dotted with white skimboats.

He began to walk toward the Pontilargo. Then
he stopped. It was the first day of Festival, and there
was something he wanted to see. Turning, he retraced

his steps and headed south toward the smaller bridge that led to the Senza District.

Near the Pontisenza, the pale, square buildings thinned and gave way to the Am Steg. The open market flamed with yellow and orange awnings. Vendors squatted underneath and peddled their goods from the relative cool of the shade.

At Dorian's elbow an old man hawking leathery strands of dried seaskips began his syncopated jazcant, a throaty monotone accented with thrusts of thumb and knee against tuned stretchskins. Just beyond, a seller of sweets took up the cry with a rhythm of his own, punctuated with a high-pitched warbling. Thinking that the cants could be useful in his etude, Dorian pulled the tassled string of his packbelt and started a tiny recorder. Then, as his nose was assaulted with the odor of something both fried and offensive, he moved quickly on.

The dusty heat and a sudden thirst drove him toward an old woman selling twists of chilled tash. She held a three-quarter-filled cone toward him. "Fresh. Cold" Then an obsequious bob of her head, a shrewd glance veiled with half-closed lids. "Only a semi for the Artisan."

Flattered by his promotion, Dorian fished out a handful of coins, half Plagal money, half Anche. He found Plagal coinage confusing, another example of the chaos of Porto Vielle, he thought. Nothing sensible like the note system of Anche. Giving the woman the triangular semi she'd asked, he took the drink and wondered vaguely if he'd been cheated.

The first few swallows gave him the lift he wanted. He tossed a small coin to a dull-eyed poco tardo and then expansively followed it with another. The little beggar stuck the coins in a little pouch and extended his dirty palm again, its single crease showing white against the filth.

Just ahead stretched the Pontisenza. He took the pedestrian way and stepped onto the swaying bridge. Halfway across he stopped. Far below, the Larghetto, caught in its stone canyon, rolled toward its rendez-

vous with the Largo. Along the sheer sides of the
cliff narrow steps cut out of rock zigzagged down to
the river's narrow shore, where a group of women
on the Senza side spread brilliant strips of rinsed
skeinlyn to dry in the sun.

They must be Tatters, he thought. The skeinlyn
strips looked like narrow ribbons from this height:
ribbons of rich purple and crimson interlaced with
golds and greens.

They would wear the costume tonight—the
bariolage of the Tatterdancers. He had never seen
the Hexentanz, the infamous dance of the witches.
In fact, he had never seen any of the Tatterdances.
In spite of himself, he felt a growing excitement, and
he raised his eyes toward the far shore.

In the distance he could see the edge of Tattersfield, the packed cluster of tents where the nomadic
dancers lived during Festival. Overnight its banners
had grown vivid with seasonal and transient paints.
From the center of the cacaphony of colors rose a
tall structure. Shading his eyes, Dorian stared at
what he had come to see.

The Fiata hung between the scaffolding like a
giant crimson kite suspended by invisible strings.
Each scalloped sail was tasseled in fringes of gold.
High above it, horns curving toward the sky, yellow
eyes glowing like twin suns, rose the awesome mythi-
cal beast, the Ram.

Tonight the Fiata would roll across the Pontibrio
toward the bay. At full dark, when the night wind
began to blow from the distant mountains to the
gulf, he would hear the Ram's song and Festival
would begin.

Dorian waited at a street stile near the Am Steg.
When the approaching mosso sensed his presence
and slowed to a stop, he dropped a coin in the stile
and stepped on. There was a single empty place next
to a couple whose small child held a Tatterdancer
doll-on-a-stick. He swung into the seat as the mosso

clattered around a corner on its perpetual figure-
eight loop. Now they were headed toward Brio Bay.

At the pinch of the figure eight the mosso
turned onto the Pontilargo's public car tract and
clacked over the swaying bridge. The mosso's top
was retracted, and the breeze from the bay felt fresh
against his face.

The child at his elbow began to whine nonsense
syllables in a singsong voice, punctuated with sharp
jabs at his thigh with the toe of her shoe. Dorian
gave her a strained smile. The poco worked a dili-
gent finger into her nose and stared up at him.
Then, abandoning her kicks, she thrust the doll-
on-a-stick in front of his face and giggled as the
bright tatters, fluttering with little snaps of the wind,
slapped at his nose.

When the mosso stopped at a Baguette Street
hotel, to Dorian's relief the trio crowded past him
and got off. A block further, the street widened and
the buildings thinned. The Brio bluffs stretched out
ahead. Beyond them, the bay glittered like shards of
glass in the late afternoon sun.

Squinting against the light, he swung off the
mosso as it reached the bay end of its loop. A cluster
of open-air plenos shaded straggles of tash-drinking
vacationers too indolent to join the swimmers on the
beach far below them. A breeze whipped his hair
and filled his nose with the smell of the gulf. He
smiled. This was the only part of Porto Vielle that
Dorian liked.

He walked along the bluff toward the old public
beach lift that creaked in protest as it raised and
lowered its incessant cageloads of tourists along the
face of the cliff. A kitesinger was working the crowds.
As the conveyor raised each group of sun-scorched,
wind-burned bathers, the boy, with a twitch of a
string, sent his hexen-kite swooping.

Dorian watched in admiration. The kitesinger's
timing was perfect. Out of sight of the tourists, he
waited at the top, kite flying above him. When the
rising lift hit a certain pinging note as it scraped an

outcrop, the kite swooped low with an angry hum. Another series of twitches changed the angle, and the wind blew a plaintive sob through the kite reeds— just enough to rouse curiosity in the rising group of bathers. Then, as their heads rose over the cliff, he gave a half-twist to his line, and the witch-faced kite rushed them with a fearsome cackling shriek. They invariably shrieked back and fell against one another in disarray. Then laughing as the witch fluttered its straggly gray hair and alternately crooned and cackled, they began to reach for small change. With one hand the kitesinger scooped up the coins as the lift started down again. A minute more and his kite was soaring and ready for the next load.

Dorian recorded the song of the hexen-kite and then stepped onto the lift. It creaked downward along the face of the cliff and deposited him on the sand. The beach, wide now at low tide, stretched pale curves toward the bay. As Cuivre sank lower in the sky, the water began to take on the pinkish tones of evening. His steps quickened then. If he wanted to record the petit anche, he had to get to them before the wind changed.

Farther down the beach a solitary blueveer glided slowly overhead and scanned the surf for silver helmets. The powdery white sand began to show streaks of ocre, curving lines of dark gold river mud sculpted by the tide. As he rounded an inward-curving cliff, he could see the fan of the Largo's delta stretching into the bay. The sand was brownish now, and sticky underfoot. He stopped and tried to hear the song of the distant reeds.

At first, the soft lowing of the reeds was scarcely louder than the whisper of the surf. The petit anche grew in the brackish, ankle-deep mud that was exposed at low tide. The reeds he sought were different from the anche of his country. These were smaller, and reddish in the backlight of the sinking sun. Dorian flipped on his recorder. As he drew closer, he realized that the song of the reeds varied with each puff of breeze. As the wind skittered through the swaying rushes, he heard them sob. Like a child, he thought. Like a sick child, he amended, seizing the opportunity to meld Medicine with Esthetics—a nice touch for his etude. Very nice. But, what else? He thought of the canon of the surf—the inexorable law of the tides and the currents—but immediately rejected it as a cliché.

A new sound, a low-pitched hum, blew across the mud flats from a patch of reeds that stood alone, separated from the rest by a narrow rivulet. Dorian's splashing advance startled a tall brown limberdip, which fled on awkward reed-legs to the safety of another islet. The humming seemed louder now. But it wasn't louder, he thought. Not really. The sound was the same, but now he could feel it. It started as a low thrumming deep in his chest, a slow vibration that pounded like a second heart. Curious and a little wary, he took two steps more.

The ground began to boil beneath his feet....

Hot...red hot...

He plunged into a sea of molten lava. Liquid fire swirled over him. In an agony of fear he felt his flesh erupt, his blood hiss into bubbling gas, his bones dissolve and flow in streams of mercury. He heard a scream and knew it was his own.

Chapter 5

"Get out of the beam!"

Without thought, Shawm leaped. A moment more and he found himself sprawled in a patch of clumpweed.

"Are you all right?" There was a sharp edge to Alani's voice.

Disoriented, he blinked at the image of the girl and looked around as if the woods and the river were an alien landscape.

"Are you all right?" she demanded again.

He tried to speak, but it seemed impossible over the drumming of his heart and the rasping hiss of blood in his ears. Fingers outstretched, he touched the ground tentatively, as if it might give way beneath him, as if it were no more than a thin crust, a single layer of tiny boulders held together by nothing at all. Carefully scooping away a bit of soil, he looked down expecting to see a hole into nowhere.

Surprised, he found it quite solid, quite convincing to his touch, but in his mind he saw it for what it was—illusion. With eyes widening, he looked up at Alani.

She was staring at him strangely. "Shawm?"

She was an illusion too—nothing more than a clever, insubstantial image—yet she looked real, as real as the ground. He reached out and, with a nod, saw his hand move through her body. Nothing was real.

Something was... The blood rush in his ears hummed with another sound. He turned toward it. He could see nothing, but that was only illusion again—a trick. The magnetic humming tugged at his mind. Scrambling to his feet, he moved toward it.

"Stop!"

He paused.

"Don't. Please!"

Shawm shook his head as if to clear it. He narrowed his eyes at the girl. She was trying to trick him.

"No."

He shook his head again. Suddenly he was struck with a dizziness so overwhelming, so disorienting, that he fell to the ground in a heap. His stomach clenched into a cold fist that sent its chill rippling through his body. "Sick... going to be sick...."

Clutching at the ground, his nails raked furrows in the soft soil.

The sharp, sweet odor of crushed weeds stung his nose and he was violently ill. Through his shuddering nausea his brain registered only two things: A voice saying over and over, "I'm so sorry," and a faint, insistent sound that hummed and tugged at his soul.

"You're sure you're all right now?"

Shawm stared up at Alani and nodded weakly, "I think so." He turned his face toward the riverbank. The beam was invisible, but he could hear it humming faintly over the rush of the river as it leaped from stone to stone. He shook his head. It was more than hearing; it was something calling like a lost part of himself. "What is it?" he asked her. "What's in there?"

"The Earth Song," she said. "The Ram is broadcasting it—but something's wrong. I shouldn't have done it. I shouldn't have tried to connect while my instruments were reading echo patterns." Distress furrowed her brow. "I was so worried . . . I never saw anyone react to it the way you did. I kept calling, but you didn't seem to hear me. And the look on your face—" Frowning quickly, she caught her breath. "I tried to shut it off, but I couldn't. It's still broadcasting along my triangulation signal."

"The Earth Song?"

"From the world we left a very long time ago." Alani looked away for a moment as if she were lost in thought, then she said, "I've never seen Earth, but I always felt as if I knew it. I suppose that's because of the infrasound. It works below conscious level."

"I don't know what you're talking about."

"I'm sorry. I'm not making any sense, am I?"

The answer was written on his face.

She tried again, little lines furrowing her wide brow, smoothing, furrowing again as she talked; Shawm frowning too as he tried to imagine an unimaginably distant world locked in a piece of music.

Infrasound: too low for the ear to register, too
subtle for the senses—yet somehow his whole body
had responded to it, and his soul.

They had all come from a star called the sun,
she said, and he knew the star; he had felt it, seen it,
been a part of it. They had come from a planet
called Earth, and he knew it too, for he had felt the
movement of deep rock and the shift of tide, the
thrust of mountains and growing things.

They had all come from the sun, each molecule
of them, and he could feel it now in his own body as
he looked at hers, slim, with long, smooth curves—a
girl's body. Immortal.

"I've always loved the Earth Song," she said,
finishing. "I wanted you to know it too, so I patched it
through the Ram's signal. But something went wrong."
The trace of a rueful smile flitted across her lips. "…as
if I needed anything else to go wrong today."

Standing very still at the center of himself, buffet-
ed by a turmoil that felt like storm winds, Shawm stared
at her. Though she kept on talking, her words ceased
to reach him. He wanted to deny what she had said. He
wanted to call it a lie—the Ram, this woman, all of it.
It's not so, he told himself. It couldn't be so. No one
could live forever. It was a myth; it had to be. But the
Earth Song, echoing in his head, resonating in every
sinew and bone of him, spoke with a stolen part of his
soul: It was true. It was all true.

"…my real father wrote the Earth Song," she was
saying. "I never knew him, but I feel as if I did. It gives
me a sense of myself—of who I am.…"

And it pleased her. It obviously pleased her. She
found it very pleasant to know who she was, what
she was, he thought with a growing rage. She was
going to live forever. Wasn't that nice? Wasn't it fun
to be rich and play with little toys and gadgets and
talk about a childhood ten thousand years ago?

"Do you know who I am?" he demanded with a
vehemence he could not control. "I'm a Tatterdancer.
I won't be going to the stars. I can only go as far as I
can pull a cart. They don't let us own animals to pull

our jigs. That's because we're thieves, and thieves might steal draft animals." He thrust out his jaw and glared at her with mingled pain and anger. "But we travel a lot—just like you do. That's because they don't let us own land, so we have to keep moving."

He began to tear at the dried fan of a large oilnut growing by the river, wrenching and tugging at it as if he fought a human adversary. When the large frond came loose, he clutched it like a shield and stared at the image of the silent, stunned girl. "I don't have a father, either." And snatching up his little bundle of mimeset tubers, he threw the frond into the river and jumped after it.

Scrambling onto his improvised raft, he caught the current toward Porto Vielle. As it moved him swiftly downstream, he heard her calling, "Stop... please...stop...." until white-foamed rapids drowned out her voice and the spray of the river mingled with his tears of rage and shame.

The rapids gave way to a rippling current as the Largo broadened and deepened on its way to the bay. A warm breeze began to dry the clothes plastered to Shawm's body. The river was slowing now, and soon he would have to paddle.

He had drowned the surface of his rage in the river's rapids. What was left now was a deeper turbulence that sucked coldly at his soul. He thought of the things he had said to the girl—stupid, revealing things that he had never said to anyone before. He tried to focus on the words. If he could think only of the words, he wouldn't have to think about what was swirling just beneath them.

Rolling over on his back, he stared up at the sky. The underside of a thick cloud grew pink with sunset. "God's blush," his mother always said. Her God was a human God, able to laugh and cry or rage and frown like any of his children. "Why else do we? We're in his image."

He had never thought about it much. He had never bothered to examine the beliefs he had been

brought up with. They were simply there, like a
comfortable old garment. If he had thought about
them at all, it was to consider them gentle myths that
lent a pattern to his life. Now he saw them for what
they were: sharp-edged truths glittering in a tangled
web of dance and story and tradition—and the web
was a lie.

He could hear its gray whispers in his head:
Chosen. Chosen by God. Chosen to wander the
world with His message of paradise. And the message was death.

Shawm pressed his fingers to his eyes until brilliant needles of light stabbed at his brain. He had
thought it was a myth...a way to explain the
unexplainable: The Ram—the great silver egg. They
escaped it just in time, said the silken whispers of the
web, for it held the growing beast, the curved-horned
devil that tried to lure them with its song.

For a time, they thought they were safe, but the
beast's influence was great and it sent seductive
witches to entice the people with the poison of eternity. But eternity was bondage, and the chosen knew
this. So they stole the poison from the beast—the
hated process that made life interminable—and gave
back paradise to the world. For this, they were cast
out from society. For this, they were reduced to rags
and tatters and made to wander without home or
property. And yet they had never ceased their
vigilance—they never could—for at night when the
moons cast shadows of ink, hexen danced and the
song of the beast could be heard in the wind.

Not a myth, he thought in despair. Not a myth.
The poison was real: not poison at all, but a gift of
life. And his people had stolen it, destroyed it,
destroyed the chance of it forever.

The thought crept into his mind that the woman
of the Ram was an illusion. For a moment, he imagined that he could see her as a witch, luring him,
laughing at his discomfort, hiding the horror of
what she really was behind a mask of eternal youth.
But he knew in his heart that what she told him was

true. He had heard the voice of the beast, and the Ram's song had spoken to his soul.

"We all have to die," whispered a final echo of belief. "It is God's will."

Do we? he thought grimly. And what about the people of the Ram? Do they? Does God? After all, came the mocking thought, we're in his image....

As the thick cloud overhead grew pinker with the dying rays of the sun, he felt an emotion erupt that he couldn't control. "Damn you," he said aloud with a vehemence that sickened him. "Damn you."

The knowledge was a cold stone inside him. He had cursed his God—and there was no one to hear. No one at all.

The gentle current of the Largo rocked him. Exhausted, he lay on his back and stared up at the sky, and in his mind he heard the Ram's Song. He felt its call in every cell of his body and somehow he knew he always would.

Chapter 6

"Let's have the current status on Aulos," said Kurt Kraus, frowning slightly as he looked at the stage in the contact room.

"Beginning, Kurt Prime." The robot system clicked on, and its stage cleared and darkened. A blue-green planet swam in space beneath a silver egg-shaped Ram. A spawn of tear-drop colony ships rained down on the planet. "Descent of the mortals," intoned the system in its mellifluous Entertainment Mode.

Jacoby stared in disbelief as the system continued in a burst of eerie, ancient music:

"...Having made their vows to mortality, an intrepid band of Renascence musicians choose the unknown as they leave the Ram forever to establish the artist colony of Aulos—"

"Intrepid band!" Jacoby snorted. "Who set up this thing?" Ignoring the remote, he stalked across the room and, with a quick stab at the inner workings of the robot, reset the system to Briefing Mode.

The lights rose along with the robot's voice, which assumed a businesslike tone: "Aulos, second planet of the G2, Cuivre: Ready. Do you want astronomical data?"

A system scanner noted Kurt's negative hand signal. "What information, please?" asked the robot.

"Current data, all areas."

"Current data is incomplete. Band interrupt prevents a read."

"Fill, then."

"Current data is incomplete," complained the robot. "Repeating: Band interrupt prevents a read."

Muttering increasingly inventive epithets under his breath, Jacoby plucked loose the midsection of the robot and inserted a hand. A moment later, the chastened mechanism burped once and said, "Override attempt successful. Reading to band interrupt..." A moment later it said, "Current status, planet Aulos: Human colony. 7.45 million inhabitants plus-or-minus error of 200,000, 86.6 percent on the north polar continent of Anche; 12.2 percent on the island, Plagal; remaining 1.2 percent distributed along northern border of the desert continent, Rock—"

Kurt interrupted the flow of statistics, "Hostility status."

"Impossible to determine to more than 43.0287 percent accuracy. Destruction of Ram Beacon believed to be from extensive planetquake in the first century of the colony, prevented usual communication for last 1829 Ramyears. Read to present band interrupt indicates rudimentary nuclear in delimited area, Anche, possibly experimental. Limited laser, status unknown, possibly non-weapon. No Particle. No C- or T-wave weaponry. Rudimentary rocketry. No artificial satellites."

"That translates to a forty-three percent chance that the twistor field hasn't got anything to do with Aulos," said Jacoby.

"Or a fifty-seven percent chance that we're wrong," said Kurt. It seemed completely improbable that the Aulosians could be the cause of the star drive disruption, but the memory of the isolated Escher colony was strong. And even though they had taken the Mouat-Gari process with them, none of the original Aulos Colony were immortal; no one was alive there with firsthand memories of the Ram. Couple that with no communication with the ship for centuries, and the situation was totally unstable. The people of this planet were Aulosians now—completely—with no ties at all to the Ram.

"Based on this data, it's impossible for the effect to be caused by Aulosians," said Jacoby.

"Based on my data, nothing in the universe can cause the twistor effect," said Zeni Ooberong from across the room. "Obviously," she added wryly, "one of us is wrong."

"Read alert status," Kurt said to the robot.

"No alert noted."

"Do they know we're up here?" asked Ooberong.

"No airwave recognition noted," said the system.

"The Ram's shields are up," said Kurt. Even a suspicious mind would have to reject the idea that Aulosian technology could penetrate them.

"What about the skimmer?" asked Ooberong. "Isn't there a skimmer lost?"

"It's shielded, too," said Jacoby.

"But its distress signal," she persisted. "Isn't it likely that it triangulated a distress?"

They stared at each other for a moment. Then Kurt spoke rapidly to the robot: "Correlate twistor effect with missing skimmer. Realtime."

"Correlating," said the machine. Its stage darkened

and the image of a tiny skimmer appeared. Next to it, the stage split to show a depiction of the Ram. Suddenly the skimmer disappeared. Less than a minute later, a pulsing graphic cloud enhanced with 10Cyan engulfed the Ram.

Jacoby's eyes moved toward Kurt, then back to the stage. His eyebrow rose in a question. "Coincidence?"

"Maybe," said Kurt uneasily.

Chapter 7

The flaming orange of the setting sun had muted to purples streaked with grays by the time Picardy helped her last patient up from the examination table.

The old man wheezed with every breath. He rose slowly, steadying himself with one hand on the table, the other gripping Picardy's shoulder. His shoes were split to accommodate the swelling of his feet. The pale flesh bulged, blunting his ankles into doughy lines.

In the waiting room, the man's daughter took his arm and questioned Picardy with a look.

"It's bad again. He needs to see the quartalist."

"The hospital, then," said the woman.

Picardy nodded. "I'll tell them you're coming."

The woman leaned toward her and said in a low voice, "Will he get better?"

Picardy nodded and said, "Yes," but she left unspoken, "... for a time, for a little while." The parasite that invaded his heart had been destroyed long ago, but not before its work was done. Now the spongy walls of his heart were failing again.

After they had gone, Picardy notified the hospital. Then wearily rubbing the calf of her leg with one hand, she tapped out her field number with the other. When communications answered she said, "I'm closing Eighteen now."

"You've been working late again," observed the comfielder.

"When have I left early?" She sighed, then added, "Going on portable."

"Right." She heard a faint tone as he switched to her offtime frequency. Then he said, "Hope I don't have to call you."

"Strange how we think along the same lines."

He laughed, said "Good Festival," and clicked off.

She snapped the portable communicator onto her treatment belt and hoped for a quiet night, or failing that, at least a grave malfunction of the portable. Vain hope, she thought; it never malfunctioned. Its voice had regularly penetrated her meals, her baths, her dreams, but at least it would be quiet tomorrow. Tomorrow was her off day, and she was going to spend it sleeping: the first half curled in her bed, then a late breakfast and a long nap on the beach. And after that—delicious thought—home to bed.

She switched on the old sonic and began to run its sterilizing sweep over the examination table. The wand vibrated in her hand and burbled self-destructively. The sonic was obsolete and subject to incipient failure like everything else in Field 18—except for the portable communicator, she thought ruefully. Only her sharps and belt were as good as they should be, and they were hers, issued to her by the Field Conservatory when she entered at fifteen.

Her training had begun long before that though. Picardy was barely nine when she began to help her parents run the Medpost in Canto Maxixe. She stacked supplies, folded and sterilized dressings, and with a consuming curiosity observed the treatment of the sick. By the time she was twelve, she was a valuable assistant with a sharp bent for diagnosis. By then her calling was obvious, and when she was accepted to the Field Conservatory as one of the youngest students, she decided to train her little sister Kithera as replacement assistant. But Kith had ideas of her own. The pretty little girl's only interest in the Medpost was a fascination with the sharps, and once Picardy found her playing tunes with them, completely absorbed in the sounds they made and oblivious to the hole the cautery beam was burning in the wall as it hummed its enchanting deep bass note.

It was obvious that Kith's talents didn't lie in medicine. And just as obvious that her own fell outside of teaching, Picardy thought with a quick grin. But her smile was touched with a sharp wistfulness, and just then, she wanted very much to see Kith and give her a hug. In spite of her efforts to control it, once in a while she still felt a rush of homesickness for her family and the pretty little Plagal village where she was born, but not often now—there just wasn't time.

The sonic's complaining hum was so loud that the boy was at her elbow before she knew he had come in.

Startled, she took a quick step backwards and instantly scolded herself for not locking the door. A quick look at the boy's face made her feel ashamed of the thought. He was probably younger than she was, but the strained lines around his mouth and eyes made him look very old just then. She snapped off the sonic, and it shuddered to a stop. "What is it?"

He gasped for breath as if he had run a long way. "Come quick...my mother."

"What's wrong?"

"The baby. The baby came and—She's worse." He tugged at her arm. "Please. Come."

Picardy reached automatically for the portable

obstetric pack and slung it over her shoulder. "What's your name?"

"Shawm."

"Have I seen your mother?"

He shook his head. "Please. Come quick."

"Where?"

"Tattersfield."

She stared, hesitating only a moment before she followed him out the door.

Picardy was glad to have an escort through this part of Porto Vielle. Her area of Tema district was fairly safe. Even the Am Steg was—in daylight. But when the shadows of evening began to creep, the boundaries between Tema and the Senza district blurred, and it wasn't wise for a girl to walk alone in the market near the bridge.

Without speaking they moved swiftly through the Am Steg, Shawm striding just ahead with frequent glances back as if to make sure she still followed. In the shadowy press of stalls and people, jazcant wailed over the thrum of drum and gong, and the smell of cooking mingled with human musk.

Even with Shawm near and the last pale glow of twilight still in the sky, when the market thinned and the dark lines of the Pontisenza stretched ahead, Picardy's hand unconsciously went for her sharps and the reassuring feel of the cautery's nub at her shoulder. She had reached for it more than once on dark, lonely streets, and though she had never been forced to use its beam for self-defense, she felt safer knowing it was there if she needed it.

The bridge's pedestrian way was splashed with yellow puddles of light that served to make the shadows deeper. Far below, the black Larghetto lapped against its charcoal banks. Ahead, in the calm that fell before the nightly change of the wind, the darkened sails of the Fiata sagged in its tall scaffold and the vague outline of giant, curving Ram's horns brought Picardy disturbing memories of early childhood dreams.

To banish the thoughts, she made herself think of the boy's mother. They were Tatterdancers. That meant inadequate care, if any. She'd probably been delivered by one of the stave's midwomen. Picardy began to review all the possible post partum emergencies. Surely not infection—not yet, not if the baby had just come. Hemorrhage then. She had seen the horror show of ignorant midwomen before—young girls crazy with toxic fevers after abortions, women bleeding from birth lacerations, and once the appalling sight of a woman's uterus turned inside out after someone had stupidly tried to dislodge the afterbirth by pulling on the cord.

Beyond the bridge crouched the darkened, crumbling buildings of Senza District's oldest section. At the edge of her vision, something moved. Then a purring voice: "Codetta? Ten semis for the codetta." She caught the quick scent of the drug, as they moved quickly by. Guilefly, but with a subtle edge to its odor that told her it was probably laced with shak. If she was right, the unwitting buyer might get more than his money's worth. Instead of the little death, he'd be buying the big one, the final one: coda.

"This way," said Shawm.

She had to approach a run to keep up as Shawm's strides quickened. At a break in the buildings, Tattersfield stretched ahead. Threading quickly through a confusing maze of tents and flickering campfires, Picardy was acutely aware of the curious stares that traced her steps. Outsiders were rare here—and not too welcome, she thought uneasily.

As they approached Shawm's tent, a dark-eyed girl of not more than twelve or thirteen opened the flap and looked out anxiously.

"How is she, Clarin?"

The girl shook her head. "Hurry."

Shawm brushed past her, and Picardy followed.

A woman lay in a splash of yellow lamplight. Against the stretched wall crouched two wide-eyed little girls, one holding an infant wrapped in a scrap of crimson cloth.

The sturdy drabskein tent was large, but poorly ventilated, and the air was hot and close. Catching her breath, Picardy knelt by the sparsely stuffed mattress. The woman was barely conscious. As she fought for breath, her fingers plucked aimlessly at the rough gray cloth that covered her. Each quick, sucking breath thrust her thin shoulders upward; then, sagging briefly, they struggled up again as if they operated a bellows. With dismay Picardy saw the bluish discoloration that traced her lips and spread over her nose. "Help me lift her."

Shawm knelt quickly on the other side, and together they raised his mother's head and shoulders. "We need something to prop her with."

Clarin ran to the far wall and rolled her own thin mattress into a pillow and slipped it behind her mother's shoulders.

"That's to help her breathe." Picardy stared anxiously at the woman. The blue receded a little. Not enough, she thought. Not enough. She reached for her treatment belt, snapped off a cylinder, and held it to the woman's face. When she pressed a tiny lever, a mask sprang out with a hiss and molded itself firmly to her nose and mouth. With a sinking feeling, Picardy knew that the oxygen wouldn't help much; there was a look in the woman's eyes that Picardy had seen in other faces.

She flung back the cover. A pool of blood soaked slowly into the mattress. "Press here," she said to Shawm, "like this. Then rub." Her hands traced a circular movement on the woman's belly. After a moment, she felt the uterus firm slightly.

Awkwardly, he imitated her.

Picardy's hand flew to her shoulder quiver. By touch she drew out a thin sharp and held it to the woman's chest. A quick turn of the dial and the sharp began to transmit rattling lung sounds. Squeezing her eyes shut, Picardy listened intently, then shook her head. Pulmonary edema.

Picardy was afraid she knew what was wrong. Quickly keying her communicator for help, she

drummed her fingers against it anxiously until the
quartalist on call answered. In a low voice she told
him what she had found. Holding the comset close
to her ear, she listened intently and then stole a
quick, grave look at the woman. She had seen only
one case like this when she was a student in Anche,
and there was so little they could do. Finally she
clicked off and looked up at Shawm and his sister.
"It's amniotic fluid embolus."

They looked at her without comprehension.

Picardy hesitated and then drew out another
sharp. When it came on with a high-pitched hum,
she inserted its tip at sound-point five. "The waters
around the baby got into her bloodstream. It's gone
to her lungs." Filthy fluid, she thought, filled with
cheesy vernix from the baby. It probably carried hair
and meconium too—deadly little emboli that clogged
the tiny pulmonary vessels.

She pulled away the sharp and quickly felt the
woman's uterus. It was firm under her hand, contracted by the massage and the powerful action of
the sharp. "You can let go now," she said to Shawm.
"The bleeding's stopped."

"She'll be all right then." It was a statement, not
a question.

Picardy drew a subsonic from the quiver. She
found sound-point twenty-one and inserted the tip,
knowing that it was too late for it now, knowing that
she was only buying time to answer him. Finally she
raised her eyes to his, "It's very bad, Shawm."

"How bad?"

She looked down at the sharp, feeling its tingle
as it vibrated in her hand. She stared at the sharp
and said in a low voice, "They almost never recover."

She heard the sharp intake of his breath, followed
by a little gasp from Clarin. Shawm caught her arm.
She looked up and saw how pale he was.

His lips pressed tightly together for a moment.
"It's that woman's fault. The midwoman."

And was it? Was it her ignorant manipulations
that caused it? Picardy stared at the sharp as if it

totally absorbed her, but she was thinking, what if it
was the midwoman? Would telling them help? Or
would it only make them feel guilty. Besides, no one
really knew. "Sometimes these things happen," she
said, knowing how trivial the words sounded, saying
them anyway because they were all she had.

Shawm couldn't speak for a moment; when he
did, his voice was husky, "There's no hope? At all?"

She shook her head.

Clarin stepped out of the shadows. Her face was
pale, her dark eyes huge and shadowed in the flickering
lamplight. She looked down at her mother, whose
breathing grew increasingly agonal; she caressed her
hair. Then she turned and touched Shawm's shoulder with a hand that was hesitant, almost tentative,
"We have to prepare her. We have to speak for her."

He jerked his face away as if she had slapped it.
"No."

Shawm's only movement then was the slow
clenching of his fists; they closed tightly, more tightly
yet, until his knuckles were white as the bone beneath. A look of such anguish came over his face
that Picardy felt a pain in her chest as if his clenching
fingers closed around her heart.

He stood like this for a long time, not speaking,
not moving. Finally, he gave a short nod, turned, and
walked like an automaton out of the tent.

Clarin followed him with her eyes. Then, turning, she spoke briefly to her little sisters in a voice so
low that Picardy could not hear what she said. The
children, eyes wider than ever, huddled against the
wall, the oldest clutching the baby to her chest.

Suddenly Shawm strode back into the tent. He
carried a dark pouch. Silent, he handed it to Clarin.
Her eyes met her brother's. Without a word, she
took the pouch and opened it.

Not knowing what to do, Picardy sat back on her
heels and watched as Clarin unrolled the dark wrappings. The pouch stretched into a long, heavy length
of webbed cloth with handles at each end. Inside lay
a tight roll of purple cloth, a shallow clay basin that

held three bottles, and a small nagarah. The nagarah was unlike any Picardy had ever seen; the little drum was two joined ovals, the smaller nearly touching the larger, the stretched soundskins silver in the lamplight.

Setting the bottles in a row, Clarin opened the largest. With both hands, she held it up to the lamplight and gave a soft keening cry that repeated once, then twice, then again with a variance of rhythm. Startled, Picardy suddenly realized that what she was hearing must be the coronach—the ritual deathcant of the Tatterdancers. She had never heard it before; she wished she were not hearing it now. It made her feel furtive, as if she had crept in, uninvited, to spy on their pain.

As the clear fluid trickled into the basin, Clarin began a low melodic chant.

"I bring you water from swift mountain streams."

She opened a tiny bottle.

"I bring you scents of cool winds and growing, living things."

As Clarin sang and slowly poured the dark essence into the bowl, Picardy caught the scent of deep woods like those she had known at home and thought of her little sister who was so much like this girl.

Blinking a quick, bright tear away, Clarin reached for the last little bottle. It held a bit of powder. When she shook it over the basin, it glittered silver in the light.

"I bring you guile for sweet dreams."

Moving the basin and the little nagarah aside, Clarin unrolled the length of purple cloth. It was as long as the black webbing of the pouch and three times as wide. She spread the cloth over the webbing. In the center lay four small cloths of gold, crimson, purple, and green.

The girl took away the gray spread that covered her mother and gently pulled off the blood-stained garment she wore. Shawm stood by, silent, his eyes bleak. From the shadows came the baby's fretful cry.

Clarin took the thin red cloth in her hand and

dipped it in the basin. She held it to her mother's face and then stopped to stare in distress at the oxygen mask. She looked questioningly at Picardy.

The mask moved erratically with the woman's ragged breath. She was profoundly unconscious now; her skin was cold and clammy. Picardy raised her eyes toward the girl. Why not, she was thinking. The oxygen was no use to her anymore. Picardy reached out and stripped away the mask. It came free with a little hiss, and she shut it off.

Clarin began to bathe her mother's face, and in a high, sweet voice sang:

"You are touched with the blood of martyrs."

She laid aside the crimson cloth and moistened the gold one in the basin. With long, gentle strokes she washed her mother's limbs.

"Touched with the light of belief."

Then the green cloth, darkly shining with water, moved across the woman's body.

"Touched with the growing truth."

When she finished, Clarin looked up at Shawm. He stared away for a moment then awkwardly knelt and cradled his mother's head and shoulder. The two tried to lift the woman onto the length of purple, but the girl was not strong enough. She raised pleading eyes to Picardy and whispered, "Help us, please."

Feeling like an intruder, Picardy quickly helped lift the woman, and the three moved her to a new bed of purple cloth.

Shawm silently rolled the empty, stained mattress and carried it outside. When he came back, his lips were white and his eyes and nose were touched with red.

Clarin wrapped the deep purple cloth around her mother, drawing it around her face and hair.

"Now evening clothes you, and the night is near."

The interval between the woman's breaths grew until, once, all three were sure it was over, but then another shuddering gasp escaped her.

Clarin took the little drum and held it toward her mother's face:

"I give you the two moons to light the darkness."

Then she handed the negarah with its silver drumskins to Shawm and took the last small length of purple cloth in her hand. Kneeling, she wrapped the cloth around her own shoulders. With a quick, anguished look at her mother, Clarin caught her breath. When she found her voice again, it was a fragile quaver that sounded very young and very alone.

"I speak for my mother who has no voice."

She looked up at Shawm and gave a faint nod.

At the slight, almost imperceptible tapping of his fingers, the little tuned drums vibrated with a faraway sound that slowly swelled into a throbbing distant thunder.

With hands trembling on her knees, with eyes lifted upward, Clarin began the final halting words in a voice that wavered like a slim reed tossed by storm winds.

"Creator of all ... reach out to me,
for I am mortal and I hear
the growing cadence of the coda...."

And Shawm's hands moved with the quickening drumbeat until his mother breathed no more.

Chapter 8

Zeni Ooberong set down the walker, aligning it precisely with the edge of the table as if for emphasis. "You can think of the universe as an invisible fabric—a sort of net—held together with twistor energy. The net is expanding at the speed of light."

"And it can't stop," offered Jacoby, "but something's holding it back."

Ooberong narrowed her eyes in thought, absently locking her gaze on the sector map that served as a wall. For a long moment she focused on the glowing starpoints scattered on deep black, as if she could see beyond them to the edge of the universe. "It isn't stasis, of course," she said abruptly. "It's more of a dynamic equilibrium."

"And the cause?" asked Kurt.

Her lips quirked in a wry smile, "If we knew that, we'd know a lot, wouldn't we?"

Jacoby sprang to his feet with the energy of a man distrustful of inactivity and began to pace. "Twistor space isn't uniform; it gains energy here, loses it there. We're inside an amoeba of a universe. It can expand in all directions, but it can't stop. There isn't anything to cause that equilibrium."

"Flying..." Ooberong said softly.

Both men looked at her expectantly, but she seemed lost in thought. A minute passed in silence, then two before she said, "An extension here, a retraction there. Just a cock of the arm can give a flyer control over the air currents. Control and balance."

They looked at her blankly.

"That's what an amoeba does. It flies in its tiny drop of water, doesn't it? Always balancing against the currents, always controlling them with its movement." She looked first at Kurt, then Jacoby. "Don't you see?"

Ooberong popped upright, and her chair hummed in protest as it adjusted to her body. "Turbulence. Sudden turbulence throws it off balance."

"From what?" asked Jacoby. "There's nothing else in that hypothetical drop of water."

"Unless there's another amoeba," said Kurt in a low voice.

She looked at him sharply. "Not just any amoeba would do, would it?" She reached for the walker

again and spoke quickly into it. A moment later, its
stage darkened and a series of three-dimensional
plot positions showed in shades of amber. "That's
the Ram's current position according to the ship's
instruments," she said. "If we enter independent
data, here's what we find:"

A set of blue figures superimposed themselves
on the stage. "Discrepancy equal to +8 remains
28.0933 seconds," said the walker.

"According to the ship's instruments, the Ram
thinks it's here," Ooberong pointed toward the graphed
display. "But by our calculations, it won't reach that
orbit point for another eight ramins. We said the
ship's instruments were malfunctioning. Maybe we
were wrong."

"You think our calculations are off?" asked Kurt.

"No," said Ooberong, "I think they're right."
She looked at him evenly. "I think we have to consider that the Ram may be right too."

His eyebrow quirked in a question.

In answer, she spoke again to the walker. Then
she said, "Let's take a look at how this started." In
moments, a three-dimensional band of color appeared
on the stage as the machine began to correlate the
two sets of data from the beginning of the disturbance. "Here's what we expect to see," she said
pointing to an interlocked band of blue and amber.

As they watched, the edges of the narrow band
of color wavered, then widened slightly. "There,"
said Ooberong, "it begins." She spoke again to the
little machine.

"Correlating data to present," said the walker.

They stared at the stage. The band widened,
then narrowed to a thread and began to change
shape. Suddenly it was a bizarre ribbon of blue and
amber light, a shallow, rippling sine-wave that bulged
and thinned and bulged again until it seemed to
Kurt like two live things locked in each other's coils.
Yin and yang, he thought and wondered why he
thought it.

"The wave . . . It's deepening," said Jacoby with a questioning glance at Ooberong.

The woman was gazing at the stage as if she were hypnotized by it. Finally, she raised her eyes toward Kurt. "A very special amoeba," she said at last. "It travels faster than the speed of light."

Kurt stared at her. His mind was a jumble of thoughts: Another universe? A universe that was somehow impinging on this one? He tried to frame a dozen questions that began "How?" a dozen more that asked "Why?"—when suddenly a flaring red alert light flashed from the walker:

"MALFUNCTION . . . SHIELD FAILURE . . . MALFUNCTION . . . SHIELD FAILURE"

Jacoby's eyes pinned Kurt. "They'll spot us now."

But Kurt was quickly calculating their position in his head. Bad, he thought, but not too bad. From Aulos, the Ram would be no more than a point of light—another star in the sky.

The rippling blue and amber ribbon vanished from its stage as an override came on. This time the walker spoke in the woman Kiersta's voice, a voice stretched taut with urgency:

"Come at once, Kurt Prime. To Observation. Come at once."

The hemichute sped its passengers outward through the onioned layers of the ship, past Agriculture and its programmed temperate weather, past Earthplace with its tiny mountains and its small false sea. The pull of the ship's gravity grew stronger as they neared the Ram's outer skin.

Kiersta met them as they stepped off the bright blue car. Tension lines traced the corners of her eyes. "Come with me, please." Kurt swung in beside her, followed by Jacoby and Zeni Ooberong. At the end of the commonway, a wide door slid open and shut silently behind them.

As he moved through the antechamber, Kurt's eyes gradually accommodated to the dimness. The faint glow of hidden lights played over rocks and crystals culled from diverse planetary systems, here reflecting from a blue-green amorphous mineral, there glimmering through a clear yellow decahedron.

Kiersta touched the entry panel, and a heavy door glided open. "We don't know what we're seeing. Sometimes the instruments read it, sometimes they don't."

The dark of the observation gallery was just ahead. Kurt instinctively reached for the railing as they rounded the curving passage. The view of open space after the confines of the inner Ram often led to a short-lived sense of disorientation. A step more and they were in the transparent bulge of the dark gallery.

Below him, Aulos hung in the blackness like a blue-green jewel swathed in white. Her smaller moon, Presto, lay to starboard, its white, irregular ellipse shadowed with the gray of hills and crators.

Kiersta's hand sought the controls, and the bulging observation gallery began to turn obliquely, gliding like the lens of a giant, blind eye. Finally it hissed to a stop. "There," she whispered.

Kurt's eyes followed hers.

It was disk-shaped and bright. Brighter than the glow from the thousand stars that spread before him. He stared, squinting at its brilliance. What was it? Kurt touched his thumbnail with the tip of its neighboring index finger; the distant, glowing disk seemed no bigger across than that. He felt a welling excitement, and suddenly the old hope was back, burning into his brain, glowing with dark fire from his eyes. Was it contact? Finally?

Almost instantly the reaction came, and fingers of ice gripped his belly. For ten thousand years the Ram had sent its Earth Song into deep space. For ten millennia it had listened for an answer that had never come. All their probes had returned only silence; all their explorations had found nothing more than lower forms of life. Now something was out there—something unknown and irrevocable.

He felt a sense of unreality, a detachment, as if he stood somewhere just behind and above himself. The irony of his reaction struck him then: They had hoped for this moment for centuries. Now that it was here, he knew all their plans and strategies had been nothing more than intellectual exercises. For better or for worse, what they had invoked had come and there was to be no turning back.

A sound came from beside him; a sighing, stretched-out sound as if a last breath formed it: "Yes..."

Zeni Ooberong stared at the disk, its light glittering strangely from her eyes. Again the ragged, sighing, "Yes..." as if a vision had come to her alone. She didn't move when she spoke again; she didn't raise her eyes from the sight before her. "An eddy..." she whispered. "A whirlpool..."

"What?" he said, distracted by the look on her face. "What?"

She stared straight ahead. "Our alien amoeba is a clever one. He travels faster than light. He travels backward in time." Her hand reached out; her fingertips touched the clear shield between them and the black of space. "Out there," she said. "It's the Ram."

Chapter 9

Stumbling with the weight of the dead woman, Picardy helped Shawm and Clarin carry her to the jig outside the tent. Small muscles tensing with the strain, she raised her burden, and together they laid the body in its purple shroud on top of the little cart.

Picardy steadied herself with both hands along the rough edge of the jig. Waves of fatigue laced with guilt threatened to drown her. Had she done everything she could? She wanted nothing more than to go home and crawl into bed, but she knew that no matter how tired she was, sleep wouldn't come until her brain replayed every treatment in minute detail and held it up for scrutiny. Now there was the new baby to see to.

Firelight flickering from torch and campfire sent deep shadows to dance on the shroud of the woman. Her thin body was almost as long as the jig. A man wouldn't fit, thought Picardy. Did they use extenders of some kind for a man? Or would he just hang over the edge? And which part? Head? Feet? Both? The dilemma suddenly struck her as hilariously funny. Part of her wanted desperately to giggle; the other part recoiled at the inappropriate emotion. She knew it was only a defense, a way to release tension, yet knowing didn't help to keep it under control.

Then suddenly she lost all desire to laugh. Shawm had begun to sing. It was a lilting ripple, only a phrase, a snatch of music, yet to her it was incredibly beautiful. She raised wondering eyes to Clarin.

The girl blinked away a quick rush of tears. Then she said, "It's my mother's call. Her 'I.' We each have one. It's given to us when we're born. Our living shapes it." Clarin stared at the ground studiously, as if it were an anchor to her control. "We won't hear it again. Ever." After a ragged breath or two, she said, "The people are listening now, inside their tents. They hear my mother's I in Shawm's voice, and they know she's gone."

It was true, thought Picardy. A hush had fallen over Tattersfield as the call repeated again and again in the early night, until now there was only Shawm's clear voice and the hiss of campfires to break the stillness. Her I, she thought. And suddenly the dead woman wasn't a stranger anymore. The joyous cry of a young girl rang in the call. She could imagine her running through the high hills, singing, reveling in the touch of cool wind against her skin. She was like me, thought Picardy; and in wonder, she felt tears sting against her eyelids.

Suddenly the call stopped, and Shawm turned and strode toward the tent. Stooping at its flap, he pushed it away and stepped inside. Before Picardy could wonder what to do next, he was back, carrying the baby boy.

He stood, holding the infant, looking away from it as if he could not bear to see it. Then, slowly, he brought his eyes back to the baby. He searched its tiny, red face as if he sought someone else there. And with a long, slow breath, he cupped its little head in his hand and gently drew a wisp of its dark hair through his fingers.

Shawm began to sing again, softly, tentatively. It was a short, sad phrase, a minor whistled interlude, then the phrase again.

The baby's I, thought Picardy. Born in sorrow with no mother. Born in the dirt and grime of a Tattersfield.

And then the call was over. Turning abruptly, Shawm handed the baby to Picardy and opened a small door at the side of the jig.

The infant squirmed in her arms and thrust a tiny fist in its mouth. He'll have to be fed soon, she thought. Picardy stole a glance at Clarin. She could use her sharps on the girl if she had to. They would fool her body into producing milk for him. She looked at the slim young girl and tried to imagine her small breasts enlarged and hot, springing with milk. Too young, she thought. Not physically, but Clarin wasn't any older than her sister Kith. Too young to have to care for a baby.

Shawm straightened, holding a pouch in his hands. He slammed shut the little cabinet, turned, and began to walk away.

"Where are you going?" asked Picardy.

He looked at her evenly. "I'm going to dress with the men of the bariolage."

"What do you mean?"

"It's the first night of Festival, isn't it?" His lips thinned, then he said bitterly, "A time of joy—" He turned away again. "I dance tonight."

Picardy looked at him with amazement. "You can't. Not tonight. What about them?" She nodded toward the two little girls shyly peeking out of the tent. "They need you."

With eyes narrowed, he turned on her. "What do you know about need? Would that feed them? If I stay here, will someone bring us food?"

She recoiled as if he had slapped her.

He glared at her and then suddenly thrust his chin away as if to hide the look of pain that tracked across his face. "I'm sorry," he said in a low voice. "You tried to help." His eyes met hers just for a moment, then they dropped to study the inky shadows that crept along the ground. "Too many things died today," he said at last. He laughed—a short, humorless, self-deprecating laugh. "I stood in a beam I couldn't see and I heard the Earth Song. It's driven me a little mad."

Puzzled, she stared at him, wondering what he meant.

"God help you if you hear it, too." He gave a short, tight smile as if he had said something bitterly funny and turned abruptly to stride away.

"But the baby—" said Picardy.

He didn't look back. "I'll send someone." And then he was gone in the twisting maze of tents and jigs.

A tall girl of about sixteen raised the flap of the tent and stepped inside. When she moved haltingly toward the little clutter of pots and dishes near the center of the tent, Picardy noticed that her left foot was clubbed. The girl tossed a coin and a smooth white pebble into the little open pot at the tent's center post. "I've come for the pocos," she said and reached down to take the baby from Picardy's arms.

"Who are you?"

The girl laughed and turned toward Clarin. "This one is the stranger and she asks 'Who?'"

Clarin said quickly, "It's all right, Picardy. This is Burla."

The girl laughed again and scooped up the baby. "Call me Zoppa. You will, you know."

Picardy blinked and shook her head.

"Ah, but you will. Who doesn't call a cripple, Zoppa, huh?"

"Will your mother have milk enough for him?" asked Clarin with a nod toward the baby.

Again the laugh. "Milk enough for him? She has milk enough to fill the Largo." Clutching the baby with one hand, Burla reached out another to the little girls. The smaller caught hold of it. The larger child followed, and they crowded through the tent flap and were gone.

Strange girl, thought Picardy. Not one word of regret about Clarin's mother. "Is she always so cheerful?"

"It's her way," said Clarin, scanning Picardy's face for signs of disapproval. "Her way is good enough."

"I didn't mean that it wasn't," Picardy answered quickly.

"Zoppa bears her dishonor well," she said defensively.

"Dishonor?"

Clarin looked up in surprise. "The dishonor of her foot. She can never dance," she added as if that explained everything.

"It's very important to you, isn't it? To be a dancer, I mean," said Picardy, thinking how little she really knew about these people.

Again the look of surprise, then a matter-of-fact, "It's what I am."

There didn't seem to be anything left to do or say, yet Picardy didn't want to leave. She was tired enough, that was sure, and very hungry, but she hesitated. Somehow it seemed wrong to leave Clarin alone just now.

"I have to dress," said the girl. "It's time." She was staring down at the little pot and the single coin and pebble that Burla had tossed there as if she were hypnotized by their glow in the flickering lamplight.

It seemed like a dismissal. Not knowing what else to do, Picardy got to her feet. "Is there someone who can stay with you?"

She shook her head. "No one can tonight. Everyone is dressing now for Festival." Clarin looked up then. Her dark eyes were clouded with grief. "She would have dressed me tonight. She always dressed me the first night of Festival."

Picardy reached out and caressed the girl's shoulder. She hesitated for only a moment before she said, "I can help you."

The girl caught one hand in the other and stared at the floor. She sat like that for so long Picardy thought she had not heard her. Then Clarin raised her eyes and the look in them was both pleading and apologetic. "It's thought to be an act of love," she said, "to dress a dancer."

Picardy's fingers brushed through the girl's dark hair. "I'd like to try," she said softly.

Clarin's eyes searched hers, then she nodded faintly and slipped through the flap of the tent. In a few moments she was back. She carried a dark pouch. Kneeling, she began to draw out its contents. "On the first night of Festival, the bariolage has to be made up," she said, pulling bright, tightly rolled bundles of narrow cloth from the pouch.

When the girl began to lay them in precise patterns, Picardy realized that she had become part of a ritual. The bundles of cloth were grouped by color and by width: a circle of gold and green to the left, another of purple and crimson to the right. The circles filled with bundles of rich color until they formed a vivid figure eight.

Clarin reached into the pouch again and pulled

out a small bundle. It opened to reveal two bags made of purple, a wide roll of matching cloth, and a tiny undergarment. She looked up at Picardy. "Hold your hands out, please."

When Picardy did, Clarin shook her head and turned her palms upward. "Like this." Each bag hung from a strip of purple ribbon. The girl slipped one over each palm and transferred them to Picardy's.

They were surprisingly heavy. Wondering what was inside, Picardy looked at the little pouches. They were narrow—much longer than they were wide—and held together at the top by thin circles of metal that looked as though they might spring open at a touch.

Clarin undressed, stripping off her clothes quickly, laying them in a pile on the floor of the tent. She was slim. Her breasts were still hard buds, little cones with barely the suggestion of sexual maturity. She stepped into the purple undergarment. It was tiny, barely covering her sex, scarcely reaching the bones of her hips. Picardy noticed it was covering with matching loops of purple. Clarin quickly undid the roll of purple cloth. With a single twist in the middle, it covered her breasts and tied at her back.

Taking one of the bags from Picardy's hand, Clarin clipped it to a metal loop at her hip. Then the second. The bags hung snug to her thighs and ended a little distance above her knees. While Picardy was wondering what they were for, the girl reached in the figure eight and began to unfurl long strips of brilliant skeinlyn. Within a few moments, dozens of them hung from her outstretched fingers.

Perplexed, Picardy stared at them.

"Thread them into the loops," Clarin prompted.

She took a strip from Clarin's hand and pulled it through a loop on the undergarment. Divided, the strip fluttered in two long ribbons that reached almost to the girl's ankle.

"Once more to anchor it."

Picardy drew the strip through the loop again, forming a soft, flat knot. Then she began to loop the next. When she had finished, the girl stood in a soft, flowing skirt of ribbons that hid the pouches completely.

Clarin began to braid the remaining purple strips. Each twist of the braid captured the knotted end of a long ribbon. When she was done, Clarin settled the braid over her shoulders and the loose ribbons cascaded in a brilliant shawl of color that reached to her hips.

Fingering one of the ribbons that fluttered from the braid, Clarin said, "They have to be weighted now." Taking out a little package from the pouch, she opened it. Dozens of small, polished river pebbles spilled from their wrappings. "These are mine," she said shyly. "From the stream near my birthplace. When a baby is born, everyone brings a pebble and a coin. Soon there's enough for the bariolage." She leaned toward Picardy. "It's done like this. See?"

She took a strip of shining gold, and with a twist a little stone disappeard in a knot a third of the way up from the loose ends of the ribbon.

Picardy knelt, and catching up the trailing end of a gleaming scarlet strip, tried awkwardly to tie it around the pebble. At first her knots were clumsy, but then her fingers learned the rhythm of the task. "There," she said as the last smooth stone disappeared into its knot of green.

Clarin threw back her shoulders, and the cascade of strips parted with the motion. She gave a quick, whirling turn, and the weighted ribbons splayed out. With a movement so quick that Picardy couldn't follow it, the girl ran her hands through the strips of her skirt, fluttering them in a billow of color. Another turn and she faced Picardy again, but this time her hands were full of bright bells and clappers.

"How—" Picardy began. Then she sat back on her heels and grinned at the sleight of hand. Somehow Clarin had whisked them from the twin pouches that now hung concealed under the strips of skeinlyn. Of course, she thought. The Tatterdancers were pickpockets. She must have learned the ancient craft when she was tiny.

In a bright flutter of skeinlyn, Clarin knelt on one knee and began to bind a circlet of bells around her ankle, tying them with a bit of purple cloth. The other ankle came next. Suddenly she rose, twirled again, and spun to a stop on one knee. She held out her hands toward Picardy, fingertips touching, but this time a heavy gold ring gleamed on her finger.

Picardy shook her head in amazement and then took Clarin's hand. The yellow lamplight glinted on the deep purple stone. "It's beautiful."

"It was my mother's." Clarin's voice was suddenly very small. She stared at the stone without speaking again for a long time. Finally she said, "It's mine, now." She knelt in her flutter of brave colors and stared at the ring with such a look of anguish that Picardy longed to gather the girl in her arms, and yet something held her back, something in the girl's eyes that cried out for privacy.

The silence passed, and Clarin looked up at Picardy with bright eyes. "She taught me how to dance as her mother taught her. She would have taught my sisters. Now they'll have to learn from me." She stood and turned away for a moment. Then she spoke in a voice so small that Picardy had to lean forward to catch her words: "Since I began, my mother dressed me on the first night of Festival. Each time my dance was for her. Tonight it is for you." Suddenly she buried her face into her hands and began to cry as if her heart would break.

Not knowing what else to do, Picardy gathered the girl in her arms and, hugging her close, smoothed her dark hair and made little shushing noises against her ear, until finally the convulsive sobs slowed and stopped.

Finally Clarin's lips wavered in a smile. "I'm better now." The smile disappeared as Picardy's portable communicator squawked on, startling them both.

"Listen all Fields: All-Come. I say again, this is

an All-Come. Quartalist in emergency . . . Brio District . . . at the Baguette. All-Come."

Picardy felt her heart quicken. She had experienced only one other All-Come—the terrible Tema school fire that took the lives of twenty children. She tried to think: The Brio Baguette. She could retrace her steps to the Pontisenza. But no. From here the Pontibrio would be quickest. The message started again, and Picardy shut it off. "Show me how to find the Pontibrio from here."

"This way." Clarin pushed open the tent flap and pointed to her right. "Toward the Fiata. Then right again. You'll see it."

The night breeze had begun. It felt cool on Picardy's skin after the heat of the tent. Here and there women in full bariolage emerged from tents and, clustering in groups of three or four, began to move in the same direction.

As she threaded her way through tent stakes, jigs, and flickering torches, Picardy saw the girl who called herself Zoppa, the cripple. She was standing just outside a shabby tent, clinging to the flap as she watched the colorful dancers pass her by. But now her smile was gone and a terrible look of hunger filled her eyes. Picardy felt a sudden stab of guilt, as if she had been caught prying in someone's soul. She moved quickly past.

A low moaning sound froze her in her tracks. The sound became a wail that sent chills rippling up and down her spine, nightmare chills from something hidden away in her mind. With a relief that left her trembling, she suddenly knew what it was.

Just ahead the tents gave way to a clearing swarming with Tatterdancers. The dark frame of the giant Fiata was black against a sky lightened to charcoal by the two moons. As the mountain-born breeze rolled in, the sails of the Fiata rippled: billowing, emptying, billowing again, then abruptly filling with the night wind. A thousand reeds imbedded in its sails found voice; a thousand more answered.

The people looked up above the low gleam of the torches. Their voices were like one. "He sings..."

With the signal, the dozens of young boys who clung to the giant frame lit oiled wicks, and the Fiata blazed with light and color. Above it, the great Ram stared with yellow eyes of fire and sang an eerie devil's song that echoed to the bay.

Drawn by dozens of men, the Fiata began to move toward the Pontibrio. Spurred by the urgency of the All-Come, Picardy pushed past the mob of people. Taking a side way, she moved quickly toward the bridge. Soon she had left the Fiata behind.

The dark arch of the Pontibrio was just ahead now beyond a narrow cluster of buildings. As she passed them, she heard a sudden scuffling sound. Uneasy, she veered away.

Too late. A hand closed on her upper arm. A harsh breath heavy with the smell of tash blew against her face. "You like the Tatters, don't you, girl?"

And then a laugh...another voice: "We'll see what else she likes."

Chapter 10

"I've set my cap for you," Kurt said to Zeni Ooberong. "Will it hold outside?"

Ooberong looked sharply to the right as if she could see her thoughts laid out there. Then her eyes darted back to his. "I don't know."

And how could she? he thought uneasily. The

Ram's communications were disrupted. No one knew if its calling signal had reached the brilliant disk that hung to starboard. There was nothing left to do but go out there, he thought, see for themselves. With communications out, Ooberong would be their sole link to the Ram, and Ooberong was crucial; she was the one who would feed their data to the Ram's brain; she was the one who would find the answers there.

Would she? came the anxious thought. He brushed it away. She had to. If she couldn't, no one could.

Whether the new compath would function was anybody's guess, but it had to be tried. Jacoby had quickly volunteered himself as the interface. Just as quickly, Kurt had refused. It was his responsibility— his alone.

Again the Ram sent its calling signal. Again it paused and listened. No answer. Nothing.

Ooberong reached for the crystal skullcap she wore, fingertips exploring the juncture of cap and short, graying hair. "I never thought I'd need one of these," she said.

"You don't," said Jacoby. "We're the ones who need you to wear it." The crystals on his own hung almost to his shoulders. The main function of the caps was memory storage. The immortals had learned that over centuries a measurable loss of memory was inevitable without them. The finite human brain, adapting to its immortality, simply erased excess data when it threatened to encroach on processing space. With a cap interfaced, the brain could instead displace data to the crystals for recall when it was needed.

Ooberong's cap was different from theirs. Her's was a sending device intimately interconnected with the Ram's memory. The unit was experimental.

Neurosensory perception wasn't new, of course; various forms of NSP had been used for centuries, but its uses were limited. NSP was a form of intercommunication between technicians interfaced to the same data-core of the ship's memory—and no one liked it. In effect, NSP made the ego subsidiary to the Ram. Each user became a peripheral of the ship. Going on NSP meant an acute, often frightening, sense of depersonalization, a feeling of disconnection from a rapidly-shrinking self. The reaction was often severe, and in extreme cases led to a form of psychosis—fortunately temporary. Because of this, NSP was used only in emergency situations that required almost instantaneous reaction from two or more people.

The experimental cap functioned differently. It was transparent to the sender, who was able to manipulate portions of the Ram's vast memory without any loss of personal identity. The effects on the receiver were an unknown quantity. Initial trials had been promising, but they had been few and short-lived.

"Are we ready to try?" asked Ooberong.

Kurt spread his hands on the table and willed them to relax. An old trick. Control the hands, and the mind and body follow. "Let's begin," he said, looking up, fixing his gaze on the star chart. Its curving walls turned the sector map into a dark, surrogate window into space. A thousand points of light glowed from it—points of light that veered in curving streaks of silver on black when the Ram took warp. Now they were motionless, frozen specks of dust. At the edge of his vision hung the disk. Like Alice, he thought. They were going out there, he and Jacoby, through a looking glass of stars toward the reflection of an impossible ship that somehow wore the guise of their own.

Ooberong turned away. She had not yet taken the time to change clothes, and as she leaned over the console, the blue spine of her flightsuit rose slightly with the motion. She touched a milky panel, and a red light sprang on.

Kurt stared at the ring she wore. Red lights danced on its gold band and glinted from its dark stone with the golden figure at its center. He could

see it in minute detail—the curving lazy-eight, the
sharp break in its pattern of infinity.

The ring seemed to tilt. He blinked and in that
split second felt himself shrink. Then he was sliding
on the slick, burnished planes of a curving figure-
eight and there was nothing else, nothing except the
wide gold plane slanting through a thick blackness
that pressed against his lungs and drove out his
breath. Scrambling, he tried to stop. Instead, the
plane angled again, and he slid faster. Just ahead, he
saw the break. No way to span it . . . no way. . . . out of
control . . . out of control . . . out of control. . . . Cold
blades of nausea touched his stomach.

Suddenly it was over. Ooberong's clear gray eyes
pierced his. "What do you think, Kurt Prime?"

He caught his breath. "Not too pleasant. And,
I'm afraid, not too effective. I was falling. That's all.
I didn't pick up anything from you."

Her laugh was low and soft. "Didn't you?"

He felt a quick flash of irritation at her tone.
"No. I didn't."

Her steady gaze met his. He found himself
staring at her suit—at the lines of the blue-spined
stablizing fin curving along her back, and suddenly
he knew that she had not turned toward him, had
not spoken at all. And neither had he . . .

He felt violated. Trying to silence his mind, he
stared at his hands. An ancient voice came to him—
the voice of an old music teacher to a boy: "Never let
anything harm your hands, Kurt. They're you way to
music." His fingers trembled against the smooth dark-
mirrored table. Fixing his eyes on them, he willed
them to be still. He had clipped his nails close, doing
it himself. Illogical, yet to thrust his hands into a
machine and feel its grasp as it scrubbed and mani-
cured had always made him feel unpleasantly vulnerable. Violated.

Control the hands, he told himself. If he controlled his hands, then his body and mind would
follow.

Chapter 11

Picardy's heart lodged in her throat and threatened to choke her. The man's fingers dug into her upper arm. Twisting in his grip, she threw her weight away from him only to feel his fingers tighten. Someone else grabbed her right arm.

The second man's thumblight flared in her eyes. Her pupils contracted to pinheads in its glare. A thumblight, strapped to a hand that was formless in the dark, glinted on a thin, flat blade. A knife...he had a knife.

The blade swung in a slow arc toward her throat.

Her voice when it came was a strangled whisper. "Let me go."

His low, flat laugh blew the sour smell of tash into her face. She could see the man's face now, streaked with black shadows. A net of scars slashed through an eyebrow over a white, blind eye. The other eye, pale, almost silver in its paleness, flicked over her body and came to rest on her throat.

Breath held, she froze as she felt the knifetip prick her skin just below the angle of her jaw.

"You like to play with the Tatters, don't you, girl? Do they give you a thrill?"

Her pulse pounded against the tip of the knife—pounded, swelled as if her flesh tried to impale itself on the blade.

He gave a low laugh again and with a light, almost caressing touch, drew the blade across her throat. He was playing with her now. She wanted to scream. Instead, she gave out a low moan that was echoed by the wailing cry of the Fiata.

A sound of surprise came from the first man as the second's light flickered on her shoulder insignia. "She's a fielder!" His grip loosened for a moment.

It was enough. With all her strength, she spun toward him, tearing loose from the second man as she did, throwing him off balance. Her freed hand darted for her sharps. The cautery flicked on with an angry hum almost before it was out of its quiver. A twist of thumb and forefinger set it to maximum penetration. The cautery snarled in her hand, and a thin, red line of fire struck him in the left shoulder. Raking down across his chest, it bit his right arm to the bone. With a howl, he fell back and she was free.

With a half-spin, Picardy faced the man with the knife. His light moved, tracking her as he advanced. With a terrible desire for revenge, she aimed the cautery toward his throat, his face, his only eye. Then as he leaped, she suddenly swung the cautery down. Hissing, it burned through cloth and flesh.

With the man's scream in her ears and the smell of singed flesh in her nose, she fled toward the bridge and the devil cry of the moaning Fiata.

Thick clusters of townspeople and tourists lined the Pontibrio's pedestrian way as the giant, wailing Ram, fluttering with crimson sails, flickering with the light of a hundred torches, began its swaying trip across the bridge.

Running on legs that felt like stone, Picardy pushed her way through the crowd of spectators. She ran until a sudden stitch in her side doubled her over with pain.

She found herself supported by a tourist wearing a ridiculous hexen wig and three layers of seaflowers around his neck. He clutched her arms. "Are you all right?"

Recoiling, she spun away. Still holding her, he

followed in a bizarre clasping dance. "Here...lean on me."

With the last of her strength, she broke loose and began to run again toward the Brio.

At the end of the bridge she saw the canoner. The man was vainly trying to keep the crowd in some semblance of order as first one wave of people, then another pressed forward to gain a fist glimpse of the Fiata. Launching herself at him, she caught at his sleeve. "Two men...I was attacked—"

With a piercing take-charge whistle to a partner, the canoner flicked on his Witness. "Keep your eyes on this," he said, indicating the flat lens of the Witness. A white light came on. "Talk now," he said.

She took a long, shuddering breath. Then, with a quick glance toward the canoner, she gave her name at the Witness's prompt. Squinting at the light from its recording scanner, she told it what happened.

"You're not hurt then," said the canoner when she was done.

Slowly, she shook her head.

"Can you work, fielder? There's trouble at the Baguette."

Picardy stared at him and blinked. Suddenly comprehension dawned: The All-Come....The attack had pushed it completely out of her mind. "I think so," she said.

"Hurry," he said, adding kindly, "Don't worry. This is the Brio. You're safe now." Then the torches of the towering Fiata blazed in the distance, the crowd pressed in, and the canoner turned his attention to the mass of people milling toward the bridge.

Safe now.... The thought echoed in her head to the rhythm of her heart. Safe now...safe now....She shivered and found she could not stop the trembling of her muscles. The fatigue that adrenalin had banished came back to turn her legs to putty. Swaying, she reached out and steadied herself against the rough bridge abutment as the waves of people pressed past. She had to get control now. Had to. Had to.

As the crowd thinned, she broke through and began to move toward the Baguette.

Bariolage swirling, Shawm moved to the beat of drums punctuated by the keening night-wind cry of the Fiata behind him. His chest, bare except for the purple braid streaming with bright tatters, glistened; sweat darkened the waist of his loose purple trousers.

The crowd at the end of the Pontibrio pressed against the canoners' boundaries for a closer look at his whirling solo that ended with a series of leaps and a midair split. Panting, he dropped into a kneeling bow, head low, almost touching the ground.

"Pick of the bitch's litter," said a beefy man in admiration. "I'd say he gave the slut a tickle on the way out." The obscene description that followed erupted into coarse laughter.

At the words, cold rage pumped through Shawm's veins. He held the pose as long as he could. When he finally raised his face toward the tourist, it bore a strange smile. He stared at the man. The first trap of the dance, he thought. So be it.

He sprang to his feet and pointed at the man—a hard, thrusting stab of his index finger. At the sight, the crowd howled in delight. This was what they had come for.

The beefy man took the bait. Swaggering a little, grinning self-consciously at his companions, he reached into his pocket, pulled out a coin, and tossed it.

Shawm caught it expertly and spun it into the air. The crowd hushed as the coin flipped end over end. Then he whirled, and the coin was gone—vanished. Palms out, Shawm turned slowly before the delighted crowd, then faced the man again. Hidden in a clever pocket, the coin swung against his thigh. He felt its weight. For a moment it seemed as if the single coin was a leaden weight anchoring him to the ground.

The drumbeat changed to a throbbing, insistent rhythm. Slowly, Shawm began to circle the man. The thickly packed spectators picked up the beat and clapped to the pulse of the drum.

Facing him, the tourist began to move in an awkward imitation of Shawm's step. Grinning, the man slapped twice at his thigh—the challenge: The money's here, boy. Take it if you can.

Shawm raised his right hand, palm outward, toward the tourist's face. The little bag strapped to his wrist gave off silver glints. The crowd stared in anticipation as Shawm circled the man.

Bobbing close, then ducking away in sudden feints, the tourist kept his eyes on the bag, but the advantage was Shawm's; the man's circle was tighter, less maneuverable.

Suddenly Shawm's wrists struck twice together. Startled, the man threw back his head. Too late. As the crowd howled its approval, a thin cloud of silver dust blew into the tourist's face.

The faint, sharp odor of guilefly stung Shawm's nose. Although the widening cloud of dust was enough to befuddle several bystanders, he ignored it. Increasing doses since childhood had made him immune to all but the strongest concentrations of the drug.

With a subtle shift in rhythm the drumbeat changed to a driving beat that inflamed the crowd. Eyes glittering, the tourist stared as Shawm began a slow circling turn. Suddenly Shawm whirled and the weighted strips of his bariolage flew almost into the man's eyes. Gauging his distance carefully, Shawm spun again, stopping, spinning outward, back again, all the while taking a measure of the man's intoxication.

The drug gave false confidence to the tourist. Picking up Shawm's rhythm, grinning, he bobbed and turned as the bright, stone-weighted knots of the bariolage swirled hypnotically before his eyes.

The insistent drumbeat quickened with the high-pitched pip of a tuned nagareh. As it did, the thick braid with its spinning tatters began to swing like a hoop around Shawm's throat. The rhythm drove the muscles of his hips, his thighs in closer and closer passes until the tourist, blinking, dizzy now, suddenly stumbled. Shawm's hands blurred under the brilliant, moving tatters.

The weight of the man's purse swung in the pocket against Shawm's thigh. Without changing his rhythm, he estimated its value. The trap was good. Even after the drummers had their measure, what was left would feed him and his family for the rest of the Festival. The single coin that the man had thrown so contemptuously hung by itself in another pocket. The challenge coin. His alone. He had earned it. The man's casually tossed insult throbbed and festered in his mind, and the coin burned like cold fire against his flesh.

Now, the ruse...Half-stumbling, Shawm reached out. His hands fumbled awkwardly against the tourist's hip. With a triumphant yell, the man grabbed for Shawm's hand, then blinked as it slid away. With a quick backward leap, Shawm landed with perfect balance and shrugged as if to say, "You win."

The tourist was exuberant. Swaggering, laughing loudly, he patted his thigh in triumph. Then a puzzled look tracked across his face followed by a howl of outrage.

Again the strange smile flickered on Shawm's lips. It was replaced almost at once by an elaborate look of innocence and an equally elaborate shrug that played to the delighted crowd. Bowing deeply, he gave a mocking salute to the despoiled tourist and melted into the ensemble of dancers as the next soloist leaped into a series of handsprings and the caravan with its eerie, wailing Fiata moved onward toward the Baguette.

"Help me. Please won't you help me." The girl clutched at Picardy's arm, but her shocked eyes were frozen on the young man. He was sprawled on the ground, head lolling against the lip of a fountain that spewed its spray in jets of red and orange light at the center of the Baguette. His face was raised toward the girl, but he did not seem to see her. His

gaze was fixed on some unfathomable inner vision
that flickered its horror in his eyes.

A crowd of people pressed between Picardy and
the man and then washed back in a tide as a dozen
canoners in riot gear, ear plugs in place, sonic con-
trollers blaring, formed a chain. "Back. Stand back."

Picardy stared, incomprehension in her eyes.
She stood at the swell of the Baguette, where the
wide street opened to an ellipse circled by the curving cantilevered balconies of the Brio's finest hotels.
The street was crammed with a thousand milling
people, some crying, some dazed, others swaying in
a strange, almost ritual ecstasy.

"Back. Stand back."

A woman screamed in terror. Another, squatting in the black shadows of a stalled mosso, plucked
blindly at the darkness. "I see it. Oh God, I see it."
Raising blank eyes toward the sky, she whispered, "It
isn't human."

The blare of the sonics throbbed in Picardy's
brain. She felt suddenly dizzy. With a howl, and old
man pushed her aside and broke through the canoner's
chain.

"Back!"

Picardy stared as the old man leaped. His white
hair flamed red with the light from the fountain. He
whirled. His pale eyes glittering with madness caught
hers, and in that instant she felt ice grow in the
marrow of her bones. Spinning, he leaped again,
hair streaming red, then yellow, stick fingers clawing
at nothing.

He melted into a writhing knot of people near
the fountain. Hands reached for him, pulling him
and the others back, but as quickly as some were
extricated, others took their place.

Fascinated, Picardy stepped closer. Now she could
hear a low humming. The hum grew louder, as if it
modulated of its own accord. And there was something else, something more—a faint whisper just below understanding, a low crooning sound that she
felt rather than heard. Totally absorbed, she strained

to make it out. Somehow she knew that a part of her had been sleeping all her life. And only now had it begun to stir and to listen, to really listen, for the first time.

A hand locked on Picardy's wrist. A harsh, "Back, girl."

She stared blankly at the canoner who restrained her. Then, with a start, she realized that she had pushed through their line. She was only an arm's length from the knot of people at the fountain. Her eyes sought the canoner's. "What is it? What's in there?"

The canoner caught her shoulders and guided her firmly away from the fountain. "What is it?" she said again. When he didn't respond, she realized that his hearing was shielded. He couldn't hear her or the blare of his own sonic; he couldn't hear the faint humming sound that pulled at her mind like a magnet.

Backing away, she stared at the people inside the circle. Flickering fountain-light played on their hair, their faces, their grasping hands. There was nothing else to be seen, but somehow an invisible barrier separated them from the rest.

A young girl moved within the circle, turning slowly, staring at the ground beneath her feet as if she expected it to open up and swallow her. Circling faster, she began to spin, yellow hair whipping in the streams of fountain light.

From outside the circle a cry of anguish came from a woman who fought off restraining hands and dashed toward her child. Stumbling, the woman fell to her knees on the rough white paving stones. Confusion flickered in her eyes. Her hands flew to her ears, pressing, clawing. Then, as slowly as if they moved underwater, her arms dropped to her side and her upper body began to sway, back and forth, back and forth, as narrow ribbons of blood trickled from her knees and streaked the whitewashed stone.

"Fielder," came a cry.

Picardy tore her eyes from the woman and turned toward the voice.

Helped by two other men, a quartalist gripped a struggling boy. Each time the man let go to reach for a sharp, the boy fought with fresh strength. Now, half-free, he clawed toward the fountain. Red light flickered across his face and flecked his eyes with demon glints. Tiny drops of sweat beaded his upper lip. "Fielder!" bellowed the quartalist.

Picardy darted to his side, "Here." Kneeling quickly by the boy, she reached automatically for her sharps. Subsonic twelve would calm him.

As if reading her mind, the quartalist said, "No. Sub five, then four."

Surprise widened her eyes, but she did as he said. Subsonic five vibrated in her hand. Its tip found the sound-point at the angle of the boy's jaw. She held it for the count and then reached for Sonic four.

Why? she thought as the sharp wailed to life between her fingers. Sub five and four was the combination for stimulus—a patch to the central nervous system for patients who hovered near coma.

As the boy struggled against the three men who held him, she grasped his left hand and aimed the sharp at the web between his thumb and forefinger. Then she hesitated, eyes flicking in concern toward the quartalist.

He pressed down hard, pinning the boy's arm into immobility. "Do it. Quickly."

Please don't let me hurt him, she said to herself and thrust the tip of the long needle home.

As the sharp touched his skin, its tone changed. Instantly the boy's muscles began to relax. Amazed, Picardy searched his face. The wild stare faded from his eyes. He tried to form a question but it seemed too great an effort for him. Slowly his eyelids crept shut and he slept.

A dozen questions tumbled in Picardy's mind: What was happening? And why? And the boy? How

could he sleep? Sub five and four should have made
him wilder.

The quartalist looked down at the boy, then at
Picardy. "We don't know why it works," he said.
"Sedation doesn't help. Sub twelve makes the agita-
tion worse."

At the sound of approaching drumbeats, they
both looked up. Some distance away they could see
the flaring torches of the Fiata as the caravan turned
onto the Baguette.

"No," said Picardy in horror. "They'll come this
way... the crowds..."

"We planned it." Sudden relief eased the fatigue
lines on the quartalist's face. "They'll stop soon. That
should siphon off the crowd from this end."

She stared first at him, then at the howling
cluster of people near the fountain. "What is it?
What's happening?"

The man shrugged and shook his head. "We
don't know." He nodded toward the two men still
holding the boy. "Take him inside." With a jerk of his
head, he indicated the entrance to the Nocturne.
Following his gaze, Picardy looked through the wide
glass entry of the old hotel. It was a hospital now. A
half-dozen Fielders moved among hundreds of people heaped like tidefloss on its smooth stone floor.

"Go with them," the quartalist said to Picardy.
"They need you in there."

With an unsteadiness born of fatigue and hunger, Picardy scrambled to her feet. Sudden nausea
struck her and a black curtain slid over her eyes. She
felt herself begin to fall. Then there was nothing but
the wash of indistinguishable voices and the distant
sighing wail of the Ram.

Something was stinging her arm. Picardy brushed
at it in irritation.

"Stop that."

She opened her eyes and looked up at the face
of the quartalist. He held a sharp in his hand. With a
final plunge of its hub, he pulled it away and the

stinging pain in her arm stopped. "Didn't you eat?" he demanded.

She tried to think. Not since morning—or was it last night? With an effort, she managed to shake her head.

Exasperation traced his lips. "You'll have to go home."

Picardy struggled to sit up. "I'm all right."

"For now. But not for long. You need to eat."

"I'll be all right."

His voice was sharp. "Go home, fielder. I have enough problems. I don't need another one."

Horribly embarrassed, Picardy got to her feet. She stared at him mutely, wanting to offer an excuse, knowing that none would do. She was on duty until morning. It was her job to be alert, to be ready—and she had failed.

"Go to bed. But eat first," he added, not unkindly.

She tried to mumble an apology, but he turned and vanished into the crowd.

As Picardy moved through the clotted mass of people, the crowds began to thin. By the time she reached the Pontilargo and began to cross toward Tema district, the streets were deserted. An empty mosso, following its mindless, perpetual figure eight, clacked across the mainway just above her, and the great suspension bridge swayed with its passage.

She was quite alone now, the moan of the distant Fiata no more than a faint echo. Far below the pedestrian way, the Largo, engorged with tide, sucked and lapped at steep stone banks. A smell of salt touched the air. Picardy found herself glancing fearfully at the night shadows that crawled toward the yellow puddles of light. More than once she started at a faint sound. Scolding herself for a coward, she tried to hum, but at the high, tremulous sound of her own voice, she subsided into shocked silence.

Her hollow footsteps on the ridged metal of the pedestrian way seemed unbelievably loud and vulnerable in their singleness. With relief, she reached the end of the bridge and turned onto the narrow street that led to Field 18 and her quarters above it.

Suddenly a hissing sound came from behind. Fingers of ice closed over her heart. Then she was whirling toward it, cautery in hand, its light blade cutting the darkness. The hissing dropped to a low chitter as a dark raggwing fluttered toward its web hung from the eaves of a narrow building. With a pounding heart, she stared at it. The raggwing folded its body into the oval depression of the pale web. Against its body, the intricate web formed the pattern of a single silvery eye—a ruse of nature. The harmless raggwing, somnolent in its web, could fool its predators into thinking they saw its unpleasant and inedible distant cousin.

Only a raggwing, she told herself. Clutching the cautery, she stared at the malevolent pale eye. Like his, she thought with a shiver. She looked at the cautery for a moment, then back at the silver pattern of the raggwing. She found herself trembling and it seemed to her that she could feel the point of the man's knife against her throat again.

A helpless rage swept through her as she thought of what he had forced her to do. Her sharps, her tools of healing...She had taken a vow to use them well, and he had caused her to turn them into weapons.

Picardy ran her fingers over the cautery, staring at it as if she had never seen it before. Then, feeling very close to tears, she sheathed it and began to walk again.

The glucose the quartalist injected had given her a measure of strength, but the sudden flow of adrenalin sapped it. Now she was ravaged by a sick hunger.

The familiar building that was Field 18 lay just ahead. Skirting her office door she took the outside stair that led up to her room.

A pale glow from the two moons glimmered on the stone steps, then abruptly turned to black as the shadow of the next building sliced off the light.

A bath, she thought. Food, then a hot bath. Turning, she reached her door and felt for the lock.

Suddenly, with a knowledge as cold as the ice that crept in her bones, she knew she was not alone.

Chapter 12

As the little scoutship hovered in the wide bay of the Ram, Jacoby gave Kurt a quick grin. "I guess we're getting a little long in the cap for this sort of thing."

Kurt gave back a slow grin of his own. And you love it, he thought. You love the excitement of it. Jacoby—as his cap grew, so did his curiosity. He had never felt the crushing boredom that led the occasional immortal to suicide, but then not many had. Most rebounded with a change of cap and view or a structured retreat. But Jacoby.... Everything was a challenge to him.

Once he had said to Kurt, "We're not immortal, you know. Not really. An accident, and"—he snapped his fingers—"we're gone. And then there's the other death—the long, slow one. I've seen it suck out everything. There's a guy in bio—practically born this morning. He's young, Kurt—if his cap was any shorter, he'd be bald—but nothing interests him. Everything is routine. He's letting his brain die, and he doesn't even care." Jacoby had shuddered then. "That's what really scares me." He stared at nothing for a long time. Then, suddenly cheerful again, he grinned. "That's his trouble. He thinks he's going to live forever. But not me. Something out there will grab me someday, but I'm going to do it all before it can catch me."

Kurt looked at the man next to him and sensed his warmth. When long shadows threatened his soul, Jacoby had always been there with a quick grin or a new point of view. Often he wondered at the man's resilience, but he benefitted from it always.

The scout's drive came to life, and Jacoby quickly scanned his instruments. Before his eyes had time to focus, his cap, set for navigation, had read the peaks and hollows of his brain waves and sent a demand to the navpanel. In turn, the navpanel, activating neurons in the cochlear division of the eighth nerve, sent its stream of data directly into his brain where it was translated as sound. He glanced up at Kurt. "We're all right." But Kurt was staring through the port with eyes as dark as space.

No sign yet, Kurt thought, but the Ram was between them and the object. The object... There seemed to be a tacit agreement between them to call it that—not ship, not she, just the object. It was as if to call it anything else would be to make it so. His lip curled slightly, scorning the idea. Atavistic foolishness —give the Devil a name and you call him up. And yet he couldn't quite bring himself to call it Ram, or false Ram, or even ship. The implications were too much to think about just now. After all, he told himself, that's all it is, an object. Anything more was nothing but speculation. He formed the thought with care, emphasizing it in his mind as deliberately as he would speech, yet a part of him knew that his careful and objective choice of words came not from the logical part of his brain, but from somewhere more primitive.

He wondered if Ooberong knew. She had maintained an absolute and discreet silence since he and Jacoby left the ship. In a way he was grateful for her tact; perversely, he resented it. Her silence made it too easy for him to drop his guard, to forget that she was there, listening. He was not sure if she could read beyond crude and direct thoughts. The idea that she might catch the undertones of intensely private portions of himself was an invasion he did not want to accept.

Kurt looked at Jacoby. The man had volunteered for the interface with Ooberong. Why had he been so quick to say no? Why had he felt compelled to take on the responsibility himself when he knew how personally distasteful it would be? Feeling his mind creep toward dangerous ground, he banished the thought and substituted another: The object. They should spot it soon.

The scout followed the vast, curving body of the Ram so smoothly that it seemed almost motionless to Kurt. Then abruptly its pitted hull slid away and the black of space intervened.

"There," said Jacoby.

The distant face of the disk was silver and featureless as a jeweler's blank. It seemed not to move, but that was no more than illusion. It followed the same circling path as the Ram, always maintaining its distance, never gaining, never falling back.

Kurt felt the vibration as the scout's engines gained power. Just as the little ship engaged its drive, something moved in his mind.

Ooberong's voice came into his head without further warning: "Something ahead. A field of some sort. Point-two ramins from—" Abruptly, it was gone.

Jacoby's sudden expletive was drowned out by the squawk of the navpanel as its lights flared to an angry red. "Malfunction."

Jacoby's eyes were riveted to the panel; Kurt's were not. His brain blared a cacophony of disjointed thoughts as he stared through the port: Ooberong's broken, "...smear...object dissipat—...reading point zero two...transmission fault—" And his own, "My God...My God..."

Chapter 13

A sighing breath split the darkness.

Heart pounding, Picardy whirled toward the sound.

Then the voice: "You've come back."

"Dorian!"

"I waited so long. Help me!"

His hands clutched at her shoulders. She felt the tug of his weight as he fell against her. Fumbling at the door, she managed to get it open. As light streamed over them, Picardy's eyes widened in disbelief. He was streaked with mud. His quartals and the Polytext stripe he was so proud of were covered with drying sea floss, and his beautiful blue sleeves were bloodstained rags. "What happened to you?"

His pale eyes were dark with strain. "I nearly drowned."

"How? What happened?"

"I don't know." Dorian looked at her uncertainly, then with a half-turn, he collapsed onto her bed, soiling its pale blue cover with yellow-brown streaks of mud. As it took his weight, the whisper gave a welcoming sigh and began to murmur its sleep sounds of wind and sea. He raised his blood-streaked palms, staring at them as if he could read an explanation there. Their weight proved too much, and his hands fell weakly to his chest. "I was trying to record the petit anche. I heard a sound—something humming across the mud flats. I was—" His eyes sought hers, then slid away. "It was frightening."

Picardy studied his face. Just like the Baguette, she thought, shivering as she remembered how she had pushed through the canoners' lines without realizing it. "What happened then? How did you get hurt?"

He shook his head slowly as if to clear it. "I couldn't get away from it."

"From what?" She pushed up his ragged shirtsleeve. Abrasions crisscrossed his hands and forearms.

"From—" His voice stopped, and a strange, almost furtive look came into his eyes. "I don't know."

Picardy caught the look. He was lying. She was sure of it.

He shook his head again. "All of a sudden it was dark. The tide was coming in and waves were breaking over my head. I must have been swept up the inlet."

Picardy filled an old, chipped warmstone bowl with water and pulled out a soft brush from her medpack. She examined his scraped palm. "You've been on the rocks for sure."

Dorian winced as she plunged his hand into the bowl. "Stings," he said, pulling away.

She recaptured his hand and began to scrub. "You'll get infected if I don't." When the water took on a red-brown tinge, she threw it out and refilled the bowl, this time adding a small packet of clear green fluid. "Don't you remember anything else?"

Again the strange look. He turned away abruptly as if to hide it.

"Dorian?"

When his eyes reluctantly met hers again, he said in a low voice, "You'll think I'm crazy."

She looked at him evenly, "No, I won't."

He stared down at his hands as if he were unwilling to meet her gaze. "Something happened— an earthquake—something. I don't remember. And then I was in a place I'd never seen before. It was nearly dark. I could hear a stream running, but I couldn't see it. Then a moon came out—bigger than Allegro. And it was round. Perfectly round."

When he looked at her at last, his eyes were vague and his focus was unsure. "I wasn't here, Picardy. Not on Aulos. I wasn't here. But that wasn't the worst. Something was with me. Some *thing*." He shuddered. "It wasn't an animal—and it wasn't human."

Dozens of tourists packed the curving balconies of the Nocturne and watched the canoners vainly try to hold back the crowds at the fountain. At the sound of distant drums riding the night wind, they tore their fascinated gaze from the people below and stared expectantly down the dark stretch of the Baguette.

"They're coming," shouted a boy leaning over the rail. A young man wearing a saltlace neckpiece swung the long, yellow strands around his neck in imitation of the Tatterdancers and began to dance with a girl who wore a tumbled wreath of seaflowers that matched her pale green eyes. Lost in each other's gaze, oblivious to the press of bodies around them, they moved with jerking thrusts of hips and thighs to the throb of the drums.

A woman, intoxicated with tash, pulled off her thin white garment and tossed it from the balcony. It caught for a moment on a spike of railing and billowed in the wind like a pale flag until a sudden gust tore it loose and sent it plunging in a tangled, spiraling fall. She was naked now except for a flutter of crimson and purple ribbons around her neck. Spurred by the gleeful howls of the others, she began to weave in a drunken dance.

A thin man whose glittering eyes never left her body drew out a slim packet. Opening it with one hand, he blew a faint cloud of silvery dust in her face. She froze, staring at him, at his fixed, hard eyes, at his lips still pursed in a kiss that blew the scent of guilefly.

Nostrils flaring, she sucked deeply, head back,

small, high breasts riding the outward thrust of her ribs. Then, gaze locked on his, she began to stroke her thighs, sensuously kneading the flesh beneath her fingers.

With a low laugh, he caught a long red tatter fluttering at her throat and slowly pulled her toward him.

In the distance, yellow flames, moving like demon lights in fog, flickered behind the blind, glass eyes of the Ram. The giant beast's upper lip slid back, exposing fangs and a blood-red tongue as the night wind brayed and howled through a thousand reeds.

Suddenly the drums stopped. At the foot of the Fiata a hundred hands tugged at rigging. Valves slid shut, and the voice of the great wind organ ceased. "The Hexentanz," said the people in low voices to one another. "It's beginning." Then an expectant hush spread through the crowds pressed along the Baguette. Within a few moments there was no sound except the wind straining at the huge crimson sails.

While Clarin stood silent in the group of thirty girls, her heartbeat quickened as the rush of adrenalin overcame emotional fatigue. A pale girl standing next to her nervously shifted her weight, and the quick metallic ching of ankle bells shattered the unnatural quiet. Stricken with embarrassment, the girl sent a quick, sheepish look toward Clarin.

A giant stretchskin drum, rolling on wide, wrapped wheels, glided from beneath the Fiata. Hands pulled at rigging; oiled valves on the Fiata opened, and a single reed began to sing in a low, throbbing voice that rode the air like velvet. Sighing, another reed spoke. Hands tugged in synchrony and new voices joined and drifted toward the bay to mingle with the sound of tide swell tossing white foam in the glimmer of the moons.

The sails of the Fiata rippled, and a crimson sheath slid away. Clarin fixed her eyes on the narrow platform high above her. A figure dressed in white stepped out, from nowhere it seemed, into a circle of

light. Silken streamers, pale as the moons, fluttered
from the girl's outstretched arms. Her name was
Jota. She was barely seventeen, still a girl, and they
had practiced together for many measures, yet as
Clarin watched, the magic began to work as it always
had. She closed her eyes for a moment, and when
she looked again, the girl was transformed—not Jota
now, but the Fate. The Hexen.

Haunting, atonal notes came from the Fiata as
reeds opened and closed. Suddenly the Hexen leaped
outward. She hung motionless for a moment, a flying
creature, silken wings filling with the wind. Then she
plunged.

The crowd gasped. She plummeted straight down
until the thin wires that held her reached their limit
and stopped her fall within inches of the giant
drumskin.

With an almost imperceptible movement, she
shrugged off the thin silver harness that held her. As
her feet touched the drumskin, it began a deep-
pitched roll, counterpointed by the cry of the Fiata.

Tuners tugged at oiled levers, and the skin began to tighten, sliding upward in pitch to the increasing rhythm of the Hexen's feet. At Clarin's left,
a drummer began a scraping beat on a winged
nagareh strapped to his chest. The wings began to
vibrate, and the thirteen strings on each hummed to
life.

Clarin was taut with nervous energy. She stared
expectantly at the young man across from her as
Sheng, the scentsinger, pumped his windtrope. Holding the body of the instrument with one gnarled
hand, Sheng set it spinning. As its phosphors began
to glow with a green as soft as sunlight through
seawater, the windtrope gave a sighing note—her
cue. She counted, and on the twelfth, at the puff of
sea essence touched with human musk, she leaped
and thirty girls moved with her.

The street was alive with fluttering colors. Muscles straining, the tuners tightened, then loosened
the drumskin. Responding to the dance of the Fate,

it played an ancient, eerie tune that echoed the cry
of the Fiata. The scentsinger's magic filled the air
with the scent of holiday and promise. The Seduc-
tion had begun.

Whirling suddenly, the Hexen leaped, and two
golden bracelets gleamed in her hands. The assem-
bled dancers froze, then began to move with underwater slowness as they fixed their eyes on the glittering
promise.

The beat quickened the dancers' feet, and they
began to spin. Faster it came. Faster. Now, thought
Clarin. Her hands flew in a blur of tatters, and two
golden bracelets gleamed in her hands.

Each dancer held bracelets over heads thrown
back in triumph. A half-turn, and the bracelets slid
over wrists. A touch, and both joined with a sharp
click until the dancers' hands were bound together in
a figure-eight. Running now, head low, Clarin joined
the ensemble in a tight knot that rippled and bloomed
into a chain of people bound together with golden
links in an infinite circle.

Silence fell. Then with a single reedy note they
began to move again. Gradually the tempo quickened.
The linked circle turned—faster now to the beat of
nagareh and drumskin. Heads back, tatters flying,
the dancers spun in a frenzied wheel of color.

With shocking suddenness a thousand reeds
opened, and the great horned Ram began to bray.

Laughing, the Hexen leaped, and a black cloak
covered her pure white silken ribbons. Its hood
dropped in place, sliding glazed Ram's eyes over
hers, transmuting her mouth into a hideous grimace.

Betrayed! The wheel of dancers spun in confusion. The bracelets were not gifts, but curses. Bondage.

As the drumbeat pulsed, they spun, bodies
straining back, swooning with fatigue, but there was
no breaking free. They were bound to the bracelets
forever, condemned by the Hexen's treachery to
circle mindlessly until the end of time.

But there was a choice—a way to defeat the
Hexen. A girl, hair streaming in disarray, screamed

once, then broke free into the center of the ring. Her hands rose in triumph. The figure-eight was broken. She was free.

Dancing alone now in the center, she stretched her hands toward the others, calling, imploring. The clasp of Clarin's bracelet sprang open, and she leaped free of the circle. Metallic clicks, and a dozen others broke away.

Shrieking her rage, the defeated Hexen, failing to draw energy from the broken ring, swayed in confusion. Her power was gone; she was dying.

Retreating, the Hexen vanished.

Hands reached out quickly to conceal the girl from the spectators. Doubling her body, she disappeared into a narrow trapdoor beneath the drumskin, and the drum began to glide back to its berth below the Fiata.

Sweat dripped from Clarin's face as she joined the others in a deep bow that held for a count of three. Then beneath a fire-eyed Ram that howled in the night wind, the procession began to move again.

Dorian ate hungrily from Picardy's small store of thick sourbret and wedges of milkset. Though she felt weak, her fierce appetite had faded to almost nothing, and she did no more than pick at her food. Her muscles were beginning to stiffen.

She went to the bath and wearily stripped off her clothes. The jet of water hummed like a sharp. Like the cautery, she thought with a sudden shiver. She turned up the heat and let the hot water pour full-force over her body.

Hair damp and curling from her steaming bath, Picardy stepped out and covered herself in a thick, white muffle. In surprise, she realized that her appetite had come back. Something to eat, then bed, she thought, and wondered what to do about Dorian. He hadn't seemed able to go home before, but maybe now that he had eaten. . . . There just wasn't room for him here. Not unless he slept on the comfort by the window.

She padded barefoot into the room. There was nothing left of the meal she had brought except crumbs. And Dorian was asleep.

He lay on her bed as if it were his own, dirty feet sprawled carelessly over her neatly folded night clothes on the end of the whisper, hands clutching the cushions as if to claim them all. When she reached out to rouse him, he moaned and flung a hand up, palm outward, in a pathetic little gesture of defense.

She looked down at him and shook her head. What was the use? She could have done with a different day. Failing that, she could have used a little understanding. Picardy brushed away a rueful smile. Ask the gods for sympathy, and instead they give you Dorian.

With a faint sigh, she turned off the lights and crawled into the comfort by the window. Curving her body into it, she stretched out as far as its confines would allow. It was going to be impossible to sleep half-sitting up like this, she thought, but almost before she was settled an overwhelming drowsiness fell over her.

The faint, distant sound of drum and Fiata sent a montage of images through her mind: The old man hallucinating at the fountain; Clarin, turning before her, bright tatters slithering through outstretched fingers; the image of the dead woman's face as soft purple cloth covered it. Then she saw Shawm, lips moving, saying something—what was it?—something....

Presto's light dimmed and winked out as the little moon set. Only Allegro was left, shining through the window in a pale stream. Lazily, Picardy turned her face toward it. Just as sleep came and her eyes dragged shut, a half-formed thought traced through her mind: The sky. Something was wrong with the sky.

Chapter 14

Tatters fluttering in the night wind, Shawm attracted the attention of the pack of revelers near the bridge. As one of a group in bariolage, he was simply a part of Festival; alone, he was a curiosity.

It was very late, and the crowd near the Pontilargo was too drunk and too beguiled to be predictable. A girl of about twenty pointed unsteadily at him. Laughing, she began to dance in an obscene imitation of the Hexentanz. Shawm dodged to avoid her, but she caught his hand and thrust a bare leg against his. Eyes half-closed, she pressed her body to his and began to sway.

Without warning, a burly man grabbed the girl and sent her staggering with a hard slap. "Bitch!" His violence turned instantly toward Shawm. With a brutal shove, he threw the boy against the railing. His thick hand clamped Shawm's throat and pinioned him to the upright. Silence struck the crowd. A moment later a voice yelled, "The blue dance." Then another. "Till his eyes pop."

The man stood no taller than Shawm, but he outweighed him by half. His eyes glittered dangerously from narrowed lids. "Killer. Tatter scum." His grip tightened.

Air cut off, Shawm fought against a rising panic. Calm. He had to stay calm. His pulse pounded in his ears, nearly drowning out the girl's howls of pain and rage and the excited bleat of the crowd. He locked eyes with the man; it was his only chance. Don't show any fear.... Don't show it. Don't show anything.... Nothing....

A black veil rippled at the edge of his vision. With effort he kept his eyes on the man, but his sight blurred with the hideous overlay of memory. He had been only eight when he saw a man throttled—slowly—until his limbs writhed in a grotesque dance and the man was left for dead. But he didn't die. Not then. Not till after measures of half-brained idiocy.

Please... not that.... The ragged veil drew closer and fluttered over his eyes. Please....

The man's eyes stared, slid away, came back. "Killer scum." Chin thrust out, he let his grip loosen, then fall away. "Get out. Get out of here, or you'll be the dead one."

Don't run... don't run... they'll kill you if you run.... Shawm drew a long shuddering breath. Then another. With a final look at the man, he turned and forced his legs to carry him onto the bridge toward Tema District.

He did not dare look back. Ears straining for the sound of footsteps behind him, he forced himself to hold his pace. He heard nothing but the hollow echo of his own footsteps and his gasping struggle for air. Near the end of the bridge, he broke into a halting run.

The streets in this part of the Tema were deserted. He dodged down a narrow side street, not stopping till he was hidden by the shadow of a darkened building. Leaning against it, he sucked in deep, rasping breaths and tried to quiet the hammering of his heart.

Shawm's fingers explored his throat. Bruised, he told himself. All right... just bruised. The flesh was beginning to swell, causing a hard ache just below the angle of his jaw where the man's thumb had been.

A second floor light across the street winked out, turning its window to black. Allegro's pale light glimmered on the white building and cast shadows from the raised letters on its street door. Shawm stared at them: Medical Field 18. Why had he come this way? Of all the ways to go? But as the question rose, he knew the answer: He had chosen the long way because he didn't want to go home, didn't want to see his mother lying on the jig, didn't want to think of that now. Yet somewhere below awareness his thoughts were of nothing else and they had brought him here.

He should have gotten help sooner. If he had only defied the midwoman and stayed. Shawm squeezed his eyes shut against the memory. Too late. He had been too late. He had run first to one Senza med field, then another, only to find them locked. The third was closing, and the dour fielder who ran it gave him a flat refusal; on no account would he go to Tattersfield. Finally his frantic loping run had sent him clattering over the bridge to Tema, to this place.

Killer. The old epithet. He had heard it all his life. He had tried to ignore it and the hate that lay behind it. Now he felt the real pain of it. His people...the only ones who had shown him kindness....Because of them, because of what he was, everyone died. And now his mother....

Her call echoed in his head—his mother's I. Today, for the first time, he had let its familiar sound well up in his throat. And when it came, when finally it came in his own voice, he had sensed a movement in his chest and then an emptiness as if part of his soul had fluttered away with it. Now he would never hear it again, not in her voice, only its dimming echoes in his mind.

Somehow that was inconceivable. She couldn't be dead, not really—she was his mother....Then the wrenching pain inside him twisted again and Shawm felt the tears he had kept back boil up like acid. Sinking into the black shadows of the lonely Tema street, he curled his hands into futile fists and cried till he was dry.

*   *   *

Finally spent, Shawm rolled over and stared blankly at the late night sky. Somehow even the stars seemed wrong tonight. He thought briefly of the immortal girl—what was her name?—Alani. A grim smile twitched at the corner of his lips. What would they think if they knew what he knew? What would people do if they knew their devil Ram was up there, hiding, pretending to be one of the stars? But thought took too much effort now. Exhausted, he pulled himself up and began to walk.

Soon he began to see people, only one or two here and there, then more as the sounds and smells of the Am Steg came to him. Beyond the market, the dark lines of the Pontisenza stretched over the river. Not yet. Tired as he was, he could not go home just yet.

The Am Steg never closed. Anything could be had there: food, drugs, clothes. And for customers with the price, women or boys. From beneath a filthy cloak, a narrow-faced man brought out a yellow tartold and blew into it. Its nasal whine grew louder, and the tartold extended fire-red devil wings. The wings pulsed with the sound, flapping wide with the quick rush of air, dropping as the man took breath. When he had attracted a small crowd with the diversion, he flung open his cloak and displayed his rows of jewels caught in the lining. With a quick, appraising glance, the man flared his cloak across Shawm's path. "You dance good," he said in a crowing voice that rose an octave from first to last syllable. "Money tonight, eh?" He plucked a green stone from somewhere below his ribs. "You want to buy? A real chroma, that. Wear a chroma, all the girls look at you." The stone glittered with false lights as dirty fingers maneuvered it under Shawm's nose.

Shawm stepped around him.

"You fa-la-la?" persisted the vendor. "You crazy, maybe? You let the girls pass you by?"

Turning, walking away, Shawm heard the man's scornful, "Tat!" followed by a sound half hiss, half spit. Just ahead, a dingy tam-tam awning slammed shut, exposing painted eyes with closed lids as its owner prepared to nap. Across the way, another opened with the hollow throb of pulser and nagareh and the hope of drumming up a crowd.

Shawm drew out his challenge coin. In the flare of yellow light from a tash stall it glinted silver with touches of red. It was enough money to blind him with tash for two days, he thought. After all, wasn't that what was expected of him? Didn't they say: "Give a note to a Tat and he's tashed." Setting his jaw, he closed his fingers over the coin and walked away.

He wandered aimlessly through the Am Steg for a long time and finally stopped to watch a metalist at work over a small forge. Gnarled hands worked the redhot metal, drawing it, deftly hammering it into a round medallion of the type rich women wore, then plunging the piece into a vat of cold water that sent a cloud of steam around the old man's head. Fascinated, Shawm drew closer. Ignoring him, the old man bent over his work, bringing his leathery face close to a bracelet as he polished it. The buffer moved over the bracelet and brought up a dark golden sheen. Shawm stared, but not at the glimmer of the bracelet. Instead, he watched the old man's hands. They wore thick scars from a lifetime of working half-molten metal. One rose, ridged and silver-white, between his thumb and forefinger and extended nearly to his wrist as if the thumb had been soldered onto the rest.

Somehow Shawm could not take his eyes off the man's hands and the long silvery scar. It was as if the man wore his life there for everyone to see. A single splash of boiling metal years ago, a single day, and he carried the scar forever.

"What can you make with your metals?" he asked at last.

Without raising his head, the old man answered, "I'm an artist. I can make anything."

Shawm stood for a moment more without speaking. Then, possessed by a compulsion he did not completely understand, he reached out and touched the long, thin scar with the tip of his finger. "Can you make that?"

The old man looked up, then down at the scar on his hand, then back to Shawm. "I can make anything."

Shawm opened his hand. The challenge coin lay there, shining in the light. "From this?"

The metalist touched the raised quartals on the coin with a practiced finger. "Yes." His eyes met Shawm's. "What do you want of it? What use?"

"I want it here," he said evenly and touched his own cheek.

The old man's brow rose almost imperceptibly and then knitted in thought. "It will take prongs to hold it there. You'll have pain."

Shawm looked down at him, at the long silver mark that scarred his hand, "What of it?"

Nodding slowly, the old man took the coin and held it between thumb and forefinger. He gazed at the play of light over its face for a long moment before he dropped it with a clink into a thick gray crucible.

As Shawm stared into the crucible, his thoughts grew as shapeless as the melting coin. Nothing rose in his mind but immediate things: the heat from the forge; the rising sweat on the old man's brow; the smell of fluid metal as the quartals ran from the face of the coin—and the scar—gliding over bone and sinew, reflecting dead white in the light, then suddenly glinting silver.

Under the old man's hands the coin grew long and thin and ridged in the middle. Four pointed, inward-curving prongs, two at each end, sprouted at the back of it. With a sharp hiss, it plunged into the vat and sputtered angry steam that rose in curling, mist-white plumes.

When it cooled enough, the old man touched it with his buffer here and there, raising highlights. At last he said, "It's ready now." He did not add, "Are you?" but Shawm nodded as if he had.

"Pay me first."

Shawm reached into a deep pocket. When he opened his hand, it held an array of coins.

The metalist selected one, then another. "That's enough," he said and put them into an oiled pouch. He stood then, and Shawm saw that the old man was unable to straighten his back, as if years of bending over the metal had softened his spine to a new curve and then tempered it into rigidity.

"Now, then...." The man pinched Shawm's cheek between two fingers. With a quick thrust, he plunged the top-most prongs deep into flesh. When he pressed the metal sharply upward, the bottom two bit in and held. His hands came away blood-streaked.

A fierce pain sprang from near his eye and raced to the corner of his lip. Throbbing with each pulse, it spread through the left side of his face. Shawm touched the scar in wonder and felt its hardness under his fingers, its smooth, curving line indivisible now from the rest of him. There was only so much pain, he thought. Just so much a person could feel.... Swelling flesh pressed against silver, etching its pain in tempered metal, drawing from the deeper hurt that burrowed in his soul.

Turning, the old man reached for a rag of cloth to wipe away the blood, but when he turned again, Shawm was moving into the shadows toward the long, dark bridge.

In the deep blackness before dawn, the crippled girl Zoppa stirred at the cry of a baby. Lying still and drowsy in the darkness, she heard her mother's soft croon as she reached for the infant and put him to her breast.

Another sound then: footsteps and the faint rasp of a jig door opening. Was it Shawm? Had he come back?

Scrambling up, she stepped out through the tent flap. Yellow light from a lantern turned low blurred the shadows. When she saw Shawm bending over the jig, drawing something from inside, she slid her crippled foot behind her and hid it in the dark.

Holding a digging tool, he straightened and turned toward her.

She gave a little gasp when she saw his face. Forgetting her foot, she ran toward him. "You're hurt." Her fingers grazed his cheek. Shocked, Zoppa stared down at her fingertips, then back at Shawm's face.

The silver scar gleamed in the yellow light. Wordless, she took an awkward step backward.

His hand reached out toward hers and then drew back. Shouldering his digging tool, he turned and walked away.

Drawing her crippled foot beneath her, Zoppa stared after him, but there was nothing there but dark and shadows. A lump grew in her throat until the pain of it twisted her lips and stung her eyes with tears. "Yours didn't show," she whispered. "Yours didn't have to show...."

Chapter 15

It materialized from nowhere. One moment only the stars and the object's silver disk filled the scout's port; in the next, a thick white mist swirled just ahead.

Jacoby slammed a hand toward the controls. Before he could touch it, the navpanel reacted. The scout stalled, then abruptly reversed direction.

Kurt's eyes locked onto the port, "What is it?"

Jacoby's head tilted sharply as the navpanel spoke to his brain. "It isn't there. There's nothing there.

Wait—" At the raucous squawk of alarms, the scout stalled again then veered to starboard.

The little ship careened past the cloud, then maneuvered again. "What the flogging hell..." Jacoby spun toward the band-port and punched it on. Instantly the inside of the scout vanished as its circular walls became an electronic window. The effect was no ship at all; only the glowing navpanel suspended in the black of space and the two men, eyes fixed on the cloud.

Jacoby's astonished epithet echoed through the scout as the mist swirled and coalesced into a giant curving hull. "My God," he said, "there's two of them. There's two."

The giant object hung silently overhead. Then slowly, almost imperceptibly, something on its curving surface began to move.

A seam split open; a line of black dilated.

"It *is* the Ram," whispered Jacoby.

Kurt stared at the huge bays—impossible bays—leading into the ship. It's not the Ram, he thought. It couldn't be.

"Ooberong's 'eddy,'" said Jacoby. "...a whirlpool in time." He spun toward Kurt. "Don't you see? We're following the Ram's orbit in reverse. She was right there when the bays opened, when we left the ship."

The scout trembled in response to the navpanel and began to creep toward the phantom Ram.

Kurt's voice and the voice in his head spoke simultaneously: "Wait." He could feel Ooberong there again, moving in a corner of his mind. "I see it," she said, "I have it now."

Excitement edged Jacoby's voice. "It's a clone. A way into the past."

For a brief moment Kurt saw Ooberong's eyes, wide and gray, hanging in space, superimposed on the giant silver hull above them. Then they were gone. He searched his mind for a trace of her and found nothing.

The bays stretched wide. Inside, a beacon flared red against black. The airlock. The Ram's lock. Kurt's eyes strained in the darkness. It was familiar and somehow different all at once. "Illusion," he whispered.

"No," said Jacoby. "If that's illusion we almost collided with it."

"The instruments didn't read it."

"Not at first. Not till it came through. But it's real all right."

Illusion, persisted the thought. The instruments too.

"I'm sending out a tracer." Jacoby's hand sprang toward a hidden seam on the control panel. A drawer slid open. "We'll image on board."

The scoutship's voice came on:

RECONNAISANCE ACTIVATED. DESIGNATE RANGE, PLEASE

The scout's brain responded to Jacoby's quickly spoken code:

CALIBRATING

Jacoby leaned over the shallow image lens. Suddenly he recoiled as a fierce white light blasted his retinas.

Warning bells chimed.

FAILURE. FAILURE. PARTICLE DEFLECTION. ONBOARD CIRCUIT OVERLOAD

Jacoby's expletive split the air. Then he was leaning forward, staring through the ship's transparency, as if he could will himself toward the false Ram. "We have to go in there," he said in a low voice. "We have to find out."

"We don't know what it is."

"Look at it. Look at it, Kurt. It's the Ram."

Kurt stared at him for a long moment. Damn you, Jacoby, he thought. He always knew how to make native caution seem like cowardice. They had always struck an equilibrium before—a carefully balanced blend of audacity tempered with discretion, but now he felt the tug of the man's excitement. It was stupid. Foolhardy, he told himself, but at the same time he knew that he had never felt more alive than he did at this moment. "An approach, then," he said at last. "No more."

The scout responded instantly.

The giant bays of the ship yawned just ahead. Like a maw, thought Kurt. The scout's lights, aimed at the distant bulkheads of the ship, bled away to nothing.

"Steady," came Jacoby's low prompt to himself. "Steady."

The docking beacon flared red, winked out, flared again.

The little ship slid just inside the gaping bay, hovering there like a firefly in the night.

Kurt's belly lurched as he felt Ooberong's presence again, but this time it was faint and overlaid, unaccountably, with the vibrations of the Earth Song. He sensed her trying to speak, but he could make out no words, only her eyes, vague and gray as smoke. Suddenly they focused, and he looked through. . . .

He saw with something less than eyes, and more. He saw the familiar bulkheads of the Ram, the beacon's growing flash, the locks. And oozing from each seam and pore of it came the growing sense of something so alien—so utterly foreign—that as the thought moved in his mind it sucked the breath from his lungs.

His hand sprang to the scout's controls. Even as they touched, he knew that the wide bay doors were sliding shut behind them.

The scout shot free.

The bays of the false Ram closed with shocking suddenness.

"You knew." Jacoby stared as the object shrank in the port of the speeding scout. "How did you know?"

Kurt drew in a ragged breath and shook his head.

Suddenly, Ooberong plunged into his mind like a knife: "Kurt! It's coming. It's huge. . . ."

"Watch out!" he yelled.

The sky boiled dead-white.
"Out!" Jacoby yelled. "We're getting out!"
The scout leaped.
Ooberong's sharp distress erupted in Kurt's body; her words mimicked the beat of his heart. "Too late...too late...too late...."

Bodies tied together with swags of green and cobalt seaflowers stolen from the hotel's decorations, the young couple clung unsteadily to each other on the balcony of the Nocturne and swayed in half-time to the music. Below them in the predawn darkness, straggling tourists splashed with fountainlight danced the mezzo to the thrusting rhythms of a Porto Vielle ritmo band. Nothing but sunrise would banish them from the streets. Then they would sleep until the bray of the Fiata brought another night of Festival.

The tight line of canoners, grim in their riot gear, still ringed the Baguette's fountain, but now their numbers were reinforced by stun barriers guaranteed to keep out any and all who tried to breach them. Yet not even the disturbance had dimmed the couple's pleasure. Instead, it had been an event, something staged for their diversion.

Head on the man's shoulder, fingers twined through a lock of his hair, the girl looked up dreamily at the sky. Staring for a moment, blinking, she squealed in delight, "Oh, look. Fireworks."

Beyond the dark rush of the Largo and the sprawl of Tattersfield, near the place where plains met woods, a lone figure wielded a digging tool by the dim light of a lantern.

High in the west a splitting point of light made two. Shawm looked up as another point of silver touched the night sky. He caught his breath. One-by-one the stars were bleeding drops of light in a giant, shining arc across the sky.

Chapter 16

One by one, the ghost Rams appeared in the sky like a dazzling graphics display on a giant back stage.

"God! Look at them." Jacoby stared through the scout's transparency. "They're going to ring the whole jabbing planet."

Kurt found himself shaking from the jolt of adrenalin. Ooberong's? Or his? He dragged in a deep breath to ease the tension and searched his mind for a trace of her. He found none.

"And which is the real one?" Jacoby curled his lip and stabbed at his instruments. Leaning over them, again he scanned the growing ribbon of Rams, each an exact image of the next. Without a homing signal, it was impossible to tell the real Ram from the false.

The scout spoke:
RAMCORE MALFUNCTION

"Still cut off," said Jacoby, poking panel after panel more in antipathy than expectation. "I'd give my left bouncer for a mainbranch to the Ram." He narrowed his eyes at the growing arc. "I can't prove it without a live main, but I know it just the same. That thing's tracking back over the Ram's orbit."

"If you're right," said Kurt, "the question is: for how long?"

Jacoby frowned. "How long?"

"Just how long will it track? We're leaving a trail

of them—one for each degree of arc. Star drive is out; we're committed to this orbit."

Jacoby knitted his brow for a second. Then he whistled softly. "It's going to wrap that planet like a hunking ball of twine."

And then? thought Kurt. He stared through the port. Aulos hung low to starboard. As he watched, the bright crescent of day moved over the ocean and crept toward land. For how long? How long could the light of Cuivre fight through a smothering network of Rams?

He raised his eyes toward the growing arc of false stars. First contact, he thought, and his jaw tightened, swelling a lump of muscle. First contact with a force that doomed a little world.

Jacoby's eyes narrowed as he looked at the blue-green planet. "They're going to die down there. Aren't they? And so are we." He jabbed savagely at his instruments. "Where's Defense? Where the hell is Defense?"

"You think that's the answer. Blow it out of the sky? Blast it into mist and atoms?" Kurt's voice dropped low. "It's growing out of twistors."

He tried to imagine it, the enormity of it. Somehow the alien manipulated the very fabric of space, and in a way that made the Ram's sophisticated twistor drive look like a baby's toy. A twistor had no mass; it wasn't a particle at all. But a single twistor could produce a photon or a neutrino; two, an electron. How many would it take to make a Ram? How many more to make a thousand?

Kurt stared at the growing arc and knew he hated the thing that caused it. He hated it because it was unknowable and because it hid its blank face behind a mask of Rams. He hated it because he could not fight it, could not resist it, could not run from it.

"Twistors?" Jacoby stared helplessly at his instruments for a moment. Then he narrowed his eyes at the arc. "I don't care if it's making Rams out of

hunking tomatoes. We're going to do something."
He attacked the panel again.

RAMCORE MALFUNCTION

"If thy mainbranch offend thee," said Jacoby in
his best religion-researcher tone, "pluck it out." With
muttered commands and sundry overrides, he
extracted the offending branch and effected the dis-
connect. "Now we're *really* cut off," he said. "But,
what good was it?" Cheerful again after the frustration of impotent inactivity, he pressed Engage and
began to speak to the scout's limited brain.

"We're going SCAN-ALL," he said a few moments later. "It's not much, but maybe it'll tell us
something."

As the scout activated its emergency probes, a
red light flashed from the overhead:

RAMCORE DISABLED

Instantly, its voice changed to a soothing female
tone:

WE ARE NOW ON EMERGENCY STATUS.
DO NOT BE FRIGHTENED. ALL WILL BE WELL.
SCOUTSHIPS ARE NOT EQUIPPED FOR LAND-
ING; HOWEVER THIS VESSEL CARRIES A FULL
STORE OF EMERGENCY SUPPLIES...

The light changed to a soft purple designed to
calm panicky passengers.

...LIFE PROBE SHOWS BODY-MASS/ ME-
TABOLISM, TWO PASSENGERS. REMAINING
OXYGEN SUFFICIENT FOR 388 RAMINS. RE-
LAX NOW. ALL WILL BE WELL

"Not much more than six hours," said Jacoby.
As soft music, chosen for its soporific effect, began to
play, he rolled his eyes in exasperation. "We've got a
hunking alien out there playing God and what do we
do? *We* play hunking cornsugar."

ALL WILL BE WELL. I AM NOW SCAN-
NING ALL SIGNALS. ALL WILL BE WELL

A few moments later the scout spoke again:

I HAVE NOT FOUND A TRACTOR SIGNAL
YET, BUT I WILL CONTINUE LOOKING. RE-
LAX. ALL WILL BE WELL

The scout's display darkened:
TRACTOR NOT FOUND. DISPLAYING ALL
OTHER SIGNALS

The scout showed as a miniature three-dimensional blue "X" in the center. A tiny arc of Rams bloomed across the little stage. Suddenly, thin gold filaments shot from each star and converged on a single point in space.

"Look at that. What are they aimed at?" Jacoby leaned forward and looked down. The crystals on his cap swayed with the motion and brushed against the topmost curve of the little stage. "The probe that went out. Is it that?"

Kurt shook his head, "No. The probe's here." He indicated a faint spot of light that radiated a misty aura, the searchprobe's omnidirectional beam. "Alani. It has to be Alani. But, why?"

Almost before Kurt's question was spoken, Jacoby reached for Engage and spoke quickly to the brain of the scout.
AUGMENTING

The image blinked out, and for a moment the little stage was dark. Then it flared. This time a shaft of gold gleamed from a single ghostly Ram.
AUGMENTING TO YOUR RANGE

Kurt swung back as if he had been slapped. It began beyond hearing. It wrenched its way into his gut and spread to his heart. And it was so familiar, so poignantly familiar that it took away his breath.

He stared at Jacoby. The Earth Song. Dear God, it was sending the Earth Song.... Kurt felt a sudden helplessness grow inside him. Somehow he could accept the alien's disguise as long as it was metal and artifice. But this? To turn the very feel of Earth into a trick...To play cat and mouse with the core of him....

Why? And why Alani? Why turn a lost skimmer into a target? This time it was Kurt who reached for the scout's Engage.
TRACKING

The scout leaped to its new coordinates. And on

its tiny stage the blue three-dimensional "X" hung in the center of the false Ram's beam.

"What the hell are you doing?"

Ignoring Jacoby, Kurt spoke again to the scout. Before the echo of his words died away, a slender scanner slid from the overhead. In moments, it had read him.

SENDING

Kurt stared down at the little stage and saw his own face synthesized in the alien's beam. He touched Engage again, and over the scout's calling signal said again and again: "The Ram. Calling skimmer. The Ram. Calling Alani. The Ram..." While a tiny surrogate-Kurt moved its lips from within a stream of golden mist.

As the scout sped toward Alani's skimmer, Kurt looked up. "Still no answer."

But Jacoby was leaning forward, tensely looking through the transparency to starboard. "I see her. There."

Kurt followed his gaze. The skimmer's beacon flashed firefly green in the blackness.

Jacoby sprang from his seat and pulled a ring on the narrow panel behind them. "I'm going out there." The lifesuit puffed into his hands, and he began to pull it on. "Her oxygen...There might be a leak."

Kurt looked up at Jacoby and nodded sharply. Alani had been missing for over fifteen hours. The skimmer carried enough oxygen to last one person three times that, and food and water for as much. But why didn't she answer?

Jacoby ran a hand over the shoulder mobile as if to reassure himself of its soundness. Then, hand raised in a quick goodbye, he touched the lock and was gone.

The sudden hiss of the lock activated the scout's scanners:

LIFE PROBE SHOWS BODY-MASS/ METAB—OLISM, ONE PASSENGER. REMAINING OXYGEN

SUFFICIENT FOR 758 RAMINS. RELAX NOW.
ALL WILL BE WELL

Dazzling like tiny red suns in the blackness, twin
beacons flared from Jacoby's lifesuit. Then its minute drives came to life, and he streaked toward the
skimmer.

Catching his breath, Kurt watched. The beacons
dwindled to points of light and then grew again in
the reflection of the skimmer's distant hull. Then
there was nothing but the intermittent firefly light of
Alani's little ship.

Chapter 17

The morning sun beat through the window.
Picardy muttered in her sleep and threw a protesting
hand over her eyes to ward off the light. Then,
stirring, she tried a luxurious stretch. It stopped
short when the back of her head collided with the
top support of the comfort.

With a groan, she opened her eyes. Confused
for a moment, she looked around the room. Dorian
still sprawled on her bed, legs spraddled, arms
clutching a pillow to his chest. Unconscious as a
stone, she thought. Had he moved at all?

Her neck felt stiff. She ran tentative fingers over
it and turned her head first left, then right in a futile
attempt to work out the soreness. What else could
she expect after a night in the comfort? It wasn't so
aptly named, was it?

The left corner of Dorian's lips slid open and
expelled a hissing puff of air. With its passage, the

lips sealed shut again. Like a steam vent, she thought
and giggled at the sudden, idiotic notion of Dorian,
vent blocked, expanding like a child's bubble toy and
drifting away in the wind.

Her smile faded when she saw his hands. Last
night they had looked bad enough, but now the
abrasions wore wide, streaked scabs, and the flesh of
his forearms were red and swollen. What had he
seen out there? She tried to imagine Dorian gripped
in the ecstasy that victimized the people at the fountain last night. And was it over yet? Picardy leaned
over the bed and turned the whisper to its daytime
setting. When the voice of the communications practitioner blared through the whisper's speaker, Dorian
grimaced and blinked.

Picardy gave him a quick glance—half contrite,
half defensive. After all, wasn't it time to get up now?
Then, forgetting Dorian, she concentrated on the
comprac's words:

"...starry arc appeared just before dawn and
could be seen throughout the Plagal and much of
Anche.

"Experts at the Aulos Celestial in Baryton were
reluctant to speculate on the cause of the phenome-
non; however, the Monodist in Charge stated that
ionized gasses arising from the Great Coastal Swamp
may be responsible.

"Here in Porto Vielle, people are openly wondering whether there is a connection between the
predawn ring of stars and last night's mysterious
Brio beam, which caused the injury of dozens of
Festival goers.

"The beam is not visible to the unaided eye, yet
according to the Office of Canon, scanning devices
can at times detect faint objects inside it. Exactly
what the scanners were able to see, the Canon de-
clined to reveal...."

Beam, thought Picardy. No one had called it
that before.

Dorian glared at the whisper, rubbed his eyes,
and glared again—this time at Picardy.

"Your lips will fall off," she said cheerfully.

The half-somnolent glare deepened.

"That's what my mother always told me: 'Frown and your lips fall off.' She used to warn me that hungry lip-gobblers were lying in wait, listening for the sound of plopping lips."

Dorian stared at her blankly and then mumbled, "Got a pitch?"

"I don't think so."

At his groan, she rummaged through storage shelves and then the food cell in the vain hope that one might be found to improve his disposition. "They're all gone."

"I need a pitch," he complained. "I get headaches without my morning pitch."

"Sorry. There's nothing to eat, either. We'll have to get something at the Am Steg."

He pulled himself to a sitting position and looked down at his ragged clothes, "Like this?"

He had a point; not only were they filthy, but the drying sea floss had ripened in the night. Wrinkling her nose, she said, "Don't worry. There're several pairs of fieldovers downstairs. One of them will fit you."

"You expect me to wear fields?" he said with a snort. An incredulous little smile curled up one side of his lip.

Picardy's eyes widened, then quickly narrowed. "I don't care what you wear, or what you do. But I'm hungry and I'm going to the Steg." Whirling, she stalked off, muttering all the while under her breath about people who accepted other people's hospitality and then complained about it—and on her day off, too. She rummaged through her wardrobe and, pushing aside the little stack of red-trimmed gray uniforms, selected a bright yellow singleset and pulled it on, knotting the sash a shade too vigorously.

Without a word to Dorian, she snatched up a handful of coins and headed for the door.

Dorian followed her as she clattered down the

sun-blazed steps. Ignoring him, she turned left at the street.

"Uh, wait."

At Dorian's voice, she slowed, then stopped, but did not look around.

"I suppose . . . that, uh, fields would be all right."

Eyes flashing, she whirled toward him, "Lowerstave clothes? For you? Next thing and you'll be wanting to sleep in lowerstave beds."

Dorian blinked and a look of chagrin tracked over his reddening face.

Ashamed of her outburst, Picardy looked away, then turned and opened the door to Medical Field 18. After a quick glance to be sure that no patients were lurking around to follow her, she stepped inside. Her eyes met Dorian's, slid away, came back. "We'll both feel better when we get something to eat. All right?"

Nodding, he meekly followed her to the back where a narrow cabinet opened to a stack of folded shoe covers, a red sunbreak, and behind that a stack of light gray fieldovers with a red and gray Field Practitioner clef at each shoulder. Picardy eyed him for size and went through the stack. "I think this one—" and held it out to him.

He stood, holding the fieldovers, staring at her.

"Well," she said, "put them on."

Still he hesitated. Then reddening again, he turned his back to her and slowly began to strip off his clothes.

Of course, she thought in surprise. He was embarrassed. It was perfectly amazing how people from Anche thought their bodies were mysterious and somehow different from everyone else's. Now he was blushing to the roots of his hair.

Sighing, Picardy turned toward the waiting room, giving thanks as she went that her patients, no matter what else was wrong, weren't afflicted with modesty. If they were, how would she manage to treat them at all?

As she opened the door to step out, a faint answering sigh came from Dorian's direction.

The morning sun, still low in the hard blue sky, was already hot enough to scorch toes unwary enough to come in contact with the whitewashed pavement. Across the way, a portly grocer leaned in the shade of his doorway and thoughtfully sniffed at his morning pitch. Picardy raised a hand in greeting while Dorian looked wistfully at the pitchstick the man balanced so carelessly.

Few people were out so early on a Festival day, but those who were seemed to converge on the Am Steg. The market gave off morning smells that mingled with the salt air blowing in from the bay. When the cant of a pitchman rose, Dorian followed the sound. Pushing past the dingy sideflap of a bomba vendor, he turned up the next aisle and homed in on the yodeled, "Pe-e-e-ah, pe-ah, pe-ah, pitch-pitch...ah pitch-pitch here...."

The wandering pitchman pulled the thin cane from his quiver and held it out to Dorian. With one motion, he extracted the coin from Dorian's hand and deposited it into a waistpouch.

Dorian held the stick in the pitchman's flame until the brown pitch that oozed from the cane's joint turned a glistening amber. Holding it to his nose, he sniffed deeply. "Want one?" he asked Picardy.

"Just a touch." Picardy took the stick between thumb and forefinger, rolling it. "Smells wonderful." She sniffed once more, then handed it back. She could already feel the effects of it. Too bad she was so sensitive to pitch. More than two or three sniffs and she'd be jittery all day. As it was, the pitch gave an edge to her appetite. "Let's eat."

This time, it was Picardy who led the way, walking deliberately past vats of frying flamefins and rows of fleshy savoroot to the intersection of tamtams closest to the Pontisenza.

The aubade vendor stretched two lumps of dough and, with shrugging flips of her hefty arms, wound

the two into a long braid. The braid curved into a
squat figure eight with one large loop and a small.
Plopping it into a vat of smoking oil, she began to
prod the bobbing pastries with a thin cane clamp
while a dirty-faced child at her elbow hopped on one
foot, thumped a tambourine against his thigh, and
howled a sing-song, "Oh-oh...bades-aubades. Au-
bades here."

Pocketing their coins, the woman captured a
sizzling braid with her clamp, gave it a quick shake,
and poked it toward Picardy. Taking up a tossaway
from the stack, Picardy grasped the small loop and
held the aubade over the crystal jet. A press of her
foot on the worn pedal and the jet began its whirl-
wind. In moments, the aubade was studded with
sweet brown crystalset.

"I love these," she said to Dorian.

His answer was muffled by a mouthful of aubade.

As there was no place else to sit, they wandered
onto the bridge and perched on the railing. The
Larghetto was dotted with harvestmasters heading
toward the bay. On deck, their crews unfurled long
rolls of yellowed netting in anticipation of open
water and the sea harp shoals.

On the other side of the river, beyond the old
town, the crimson sails of the Fiata rose high above
Tattersfield.

"Why do you hate Porto Vielle?" Picardy asked
suddenly.

Dorian was startled by her question. He did not
meet her gaze. Instead, he found himself staring at
the curve of her neck where feathery wisps of dark
curls fluttered in the breeze. "Who said I hated it?"

"You did. Not out loud, but you did all the
same."

He looked away, upriver, where the dark Larghetto turned to silver in the sun. The dream came
back to him then: The rivers pulsing with warm
blood-red tides like arteries through flesh. Almost as
if it were alive—the whole Plagal alive. In the dream,
he heard its song—a song beyond hearing, yet it was

real. Then somehow he had known he was dreaming. He struggled to wake up, knowing that he had to, because if he did not, if he let himself listen. . . . He blinked in surprise. What then? He tried to remember, but nothing more came to him but the memory of waking—the smothering darkness, his heart pounding in his chest, and the sticky wetness spreading on his belly and thighs.

He licked his lips, "It's just different. That's all." He had come to the Plagal completely unprepared for it. He had spent all his life in Baryton, and his existence had been as ordered there as the sculptured hedge of the Capitol's labyrinth or the shaped stones in its symmetrical buildings. The people were mostly of his stave, homogeneous, compatible, predictable. Only in Porto Vielle's Brio had he felt anything of home, and now that Festival had begun, not even there. He thought of the faces of the tourists who filled the streets. Familiar, yet disturbing, as if what he had believed them to be was a mask, as if every note of the Fiata had crazed the familiar molds and now they had begun to crumble away.

Far below the bridge, the Larghetto lapped against its banks, slowly, irresistibly, eroding the rock that confined it. Dorian stared down at it as if he were hypnotized. Only one thought was in his mind then, one unanswerable question. His room was in the Brio. He knew people there of his own stave: the chief medical quartalist; his neighbor, a monodist of spirit who had known his father in Baryton; the assistant to the Conductus of Porto Vielle. Yet, last night he had crouched, half-drowned, on a deserted stair and waited for a lowerstave girl to come home. Why? She was no more like him than this baked land was like Baryton. She was what she would always be: "Set in stave, set in stone,"—a saying as old as Anche and as incontrovertible. And yet, last night there had been no choice, nowhere else to go, nothing else to do but wait for her.

When she finally came, he had had to fight off

the terrible urge to cry like a baby. He would not let go, he had told himself. He would *not*. He had not cried since he was five years old.

The memory came back as if through a glass stained with faint yellow. The sun had been a fat orange ball that day, like the one in his toy box at home. It was warm and pleasant on his skin.

He stood in a close, ordered crowd that towered over him—a thousand voices mingling with a thousand different smells. His mouth was dry, and he tugged at his father's hand and whined for a drink.

Suddenly the crowd fell silent, until only his treble voice broke the void.

"Quiet." It was a whisper that bore the weight of stone. Then his father's big hands were grasping him, lifting him to wide shoulders so he could see.

The sun dazzled his eyes and he squinted against it. Row upon row of people stood facing a platform. Two men were silhouetted there. As his eyes slowly adjusted, he saw that they wore the scarlet clef of Canon.

He heard a sound like thunder and turned his face toward the sky, but it blazed clear with a sun that had burned off the clouds. The thunder roll grew and he saw that it came from a silver drumhead flashing in the sunlight at each stroke of the mallet. Suddenly a murmur went through the crowd. "What is it?" he asked.

"The Conductus," said his father sharply. "Be quiet."

He stared at the man who strode to the center of the platform. He was tall, taller even than his father. The man was holding something in his hands, a bright shield flanked with two blades that glittered in the sun. "The law." The thin girl ahead of him stood on her toes to watch. "He holds the law."

Three men marched to the platform next, the two flanking a third. Then the two stepped down and he saw that the man in the middle was bound with thin wires that held his arms to his sides. Sunlight washed his pale hair; his eyes were dark blanks.

The Conductus began to speak. His words held
no meaning to Dorian, but the timbre of the man's
voice broke on his ears like a dark wash of music.
What happened next was to remain disconnected in
his mind, like glittering shards of broken glass: The
shield, the law, held out in the sun. The two men
reaching out, scarlet clefs of Canon gliding over the
thick muscles in their arms. Two swords drawn from
the upheld shield of law, blades flashing fire in the
sun.

The bound man raised his face to the men as
they struck. He raised his face to them, and it
seemed to the boy that the dark blank eyes stared
into his and widened in surprise.

He caught his breath at the quick bright gouts
of blood, and when his breath came back, it came in
short coughing sobs that shook his body as he pressed
it against his father.

"Stop it."

But he could not. The tears clogged his mouth
and his nose in rivers thick as blood.

"I said stop it."

Something in his father's voice caused him to
catch his breath again in shuddering little gasps.

"You think you've seen a horror. You can't imagine the horror when Canon fails." His father's voice
was low, but resolute. "Look at him."

He shook his head; he burrowed his face against
a broad shoulder.

"Look at him, I said." And then his chin was
caught in a broad hand that gently, but inexorably,
turned his face toward what had been a man.

"He breached the law and now he's dead. Canon
was upheld today, but it wasn't always so. You must
learn this, and you must learn this well: it is our
responsibility, each of us, to see the law upheld. We
failed it once. Because we did, each of us will die."

He shook his head again and stabbed at his eyes
with small, knotted fists.

"Listen to me. God gave us eternal life and we
threw it away. Thieves came and took it from us and

we let them. We let them break the law of Canon, and now we all have to pay. Do you understand?"

His voice was small and muffled against his father's shoulder. "Did God say?"

The dark look in his father's eyes lightened. His fingers stroked the boy's pale hair, "Perhaps he did, son. Perhaps he did."

The sun dazzling on the Larghetto caused Dorian to narrow his eyes. He felt a tug on his arm. "What?"

"I asked you twice," said Picardy. "What's wrong?"

He shook his head, "Nothing."

"You were thinking about last night, weren't you? You were thinking about the beam."

"Just remembering something."

Picardy's eyes missed his. "Funny. I've been trying to remember something too, but I'm not sure what." Her gaze was fixed as if she looked through him toward some distant point. A beam. . . . The thought nagged in her mind. Something about a beam. Squinting against the bright sunlight, she tried to remember. Then shrugging, she said, "I guess the wind blew it away." Suddenly her eyes widened slightly, "Shawm."

She could almost hear his voice: *I stood in a beam I couldn't see and I heard...*

"Dorian, what's the Earth Song?"

He looked at her blankly. Then suddenly, "Oh. They told us about it in school. It's supposed to be a piece of music from the old land thousands of years ago. Something from the Ram."

It was Picardy's turn to look blank. The Ram? She had heard the story of the great ship all her life, but she had never given it much thought. "We don't know that there really was a Ram. It can't be proved."

"Yes, it can. A few of the records are left. I've seen them."

Her eyes were skeptical.

"I *have*," he said defensively. "There was a quake nearly eighteen hundred years ago. It leveled Baryton. It took out a beacon that was supposed to communicate with the Ram. There wasn't much left afterward. Just a few records. Nothing else."

"And the Earth Song?"

He shook his head, "Gone. But it was mentioned. I couldn't read the records, but I saw translations. The Earth Song was supposed to be a part of the Ram somehow."

A part of it? Picardy frowned and stared across the river. The Fiata's sails fluttered like a red flag in the wind. She remembered the look on Shawm's face; she remembered his voice:

I heard the Earth Song and it's driven me a little mad.

A beam that drove people mad, and then this morning a ring of stars that nobody could explain.... Still staring across the river, Picardy slid down from her perch on the railing. "Come on."

"Where?"

"To Tattersfield."

A startled look crossed his face. "Why?"

"The Ram," she said. "Maybe it's come back."

Tattersfield was as confusing in the daytime as it was at night. Picardy stared at the thicket of tents and jigs and tried to remember which way to turn. Using the towering Fiata as a guide, she said, "This way, I think." The path was narrow and strewn with debris. Dorian followed, holding himself stiffly, meeting suspicious stares with one of his own.

The sound of singing came from just ahead, and they found themselves in a clearing where a dozen girls, bodies bent backward, practiced the dance under the stern gaze of an old woman. The woman turned her dour glare toward Picardy and Dorian, who stopped in confusion.

The girls giggled, and Dorian shifted from one foot to the other. Picardy turned abruptly, and they found themselves in a dead end of tents.

A narrow-faced child stared at them, but when Picardy spoke to him he disappeared into a tent and pulled the flap shut. In a few moments a head poked out. An older boy of about ten eyed them suspiciously.

"I'm looking for Shawm. And Clarin," she added.
His eyes narrowed.

"I'm a fielder," she said. "I was here last night.
When the new baby came."

Surprisingly, he whistled a short phrase. It seemed
familiar to her, but she could not place it. Then
suddenly it came to her: it was a corruption of the
phrase Shawm had sung when he held his new
brother. The baby's I. She nodded. "Yes."

The boy gave a quick jerk of his head toward a
jig pressed close to a tent wall, and then, with a quick
jerk of the tent flap, disappeared. When Picardy
looked, she saw a narrow, scuffed path leading toward another cluster of tents.

It took her a moment to recognize Shawm's
tent; it seemed smaller in the bright light of day, and
dingier. The jig that had been just outside was gone.

When her call went unanswered, Picardy hesitated a moment and then reached for the tent flap. It
was stiff and heavy. She lifted it and poked her head
inside. When her eyes adjusted to the gloom, she saw
that no one was there. When she looked up again,
eyes squinting against the glare of the sun, she found
herself staring at the club-footed girl, Zoppa.

The girl laughed. "You buying a tent? I can get
you one cheap."

Picardy grinned self-consciously. "I'm looking
for Shawm," then, "Dorian and I are. This is Dorian
and—" She stopped in confusion. What was the girl's
real name? She couldn't remember. All she could
remember was the awful name "Zoppa"—cripple.
But the girl laughed again and said to Dorian, "They
call me Zoppa. I can dance the one-foot like nobody
you ever saw."

An uncertain smile flitted across his face and
vanished.

Then to Picardy, "If you can make Shawm out of
an empty tent, you have a talent. But, me? I don't
have your gift." She pointed toward the south. "I'd
have to find him over there."

Picardy squinted against the glare. Beyond the

tents a dusty plain stretched toward the foothills. She could just make out a small group of people, tiny in the distance.

Zoppa cupped her hand around her mouth and began to sing a deep, wordless call. A pause, then a short higher-pitched phrase. A longer pause, then the call repeated. No answer came back, but she nodded. "He knows you're coming now."

Picardy stared at her, not knowing what to do.

The girl met her eyes with a frank stare of her own. "Go on." Then a rich laugh. "Do you need a cripple for a guide when you have eyes? Go on. This zoppa can't walk so far."

A small face peered around the tent followed by another, and Picardy recognized Shawm's little sisters. Zoppa waggled her finger at them and said in mock severity, "Shame, pocos. Shame. You're bad to leave your baby. He'll cry with loneliness. Go back now and we'll have a game of sand and pebble." The little faces disappeared behind the tent, and Zoppa followed in a halting gait.

It took them a while to cross the plain. The little knot of people stood near a jig. They were nearly on top of the group before Picardy knew what they were doing. She caught her breath in dismay. The burial. They had intruded on this private time without realizing it.

A half-dozen people looked up. Clarin stood at the edge of her mother's grave. Her eyes widened when she saw Picardy, but she said nothing. Shawm and another man paused, digging tools in hand. Picardy blinked when the sun glittered on something on Shawm's face, and she saw that it was a scar made of metal that stretched from near his eye toward his jaw. Acutely ill-at-ease, Picardy glanced at Dorian. He was staring at the silver scar as if he had seen something completely alien and not a little fascinating. "Self-mutilation," he whispered to himself.

Embarrassed, Picardy gave Dorian a quick, low *"Pss-sss"* to silence him.

Without a word, Shawm returned to his work.

No one spoke. There was no sound except the sough of the sea wind and the rasp of dry sand on metal followed with a plop as another shovel load landed on the grave.

Picardy fixed her gaze on the ground. Stupid, she thought. How could she have been so thoughtless— blundering into a burial unasked. Even her clothes must be an insult to these people. It seemed to her that the bright yellow she wore screamed its color over the whisper of their faded duncloth. Was it possible that these were the same people who danced their way through Festival in a whirl of brilliant colors?

Finally, it was over. With scarcely a backward look at the grave, a tall man caught the shafts of the jig. The rest followed the creaking little cart. Clarin hesitated for a moment, then turned and followed the jig. Now only Shawm was left by the grave.

Nothing more? thought Picardy. Not a word said over their mother. Not a song. And then she realized that she had seen the real funeral last night. The actual burial was no more than a task. "I'm sorry," she began. "We shouldn't be here."

Shawm listened intently while Picardy told him why they had come. A strange look came into his eyes, and he turned to Dorian, "You heard it too?" Shawm's eyes were fixed on Dorian's.

Dorian nodded. His gaze flicked for a moment toward the silver scar that glinted in the sun. He made himself look away. Don't stare, he thought, but he felt his eyes drag back to the metal that lanced the boy's cheek. It's not so strange, he told himself. After all, didn't some of the backstaves press bloodthorns through their ears? Shawm tilted his head just then, and Dorian saw a fleck of dried blood clinging to the lower point of the metal. Recent, then. He winced.

Shawm stared at him in silence for a moment. Then he said, "The song...?" And then a question that was not a question: "It's not the world song, is it?"

The world song? Dorian's brow knitted in confusion. Then suddenly it struck him, and his eyes widened. The dream came back to him: The bloodpulse of the rivers...the night smell of the Plagal—impossibly earth and warm flesh all in one...and the faint insistent song that lay beneath it almost below consciousness. He searched Shawm's eyes. Somehow he knew—beyond doubt, beyond understanding—that this offstave boy had felt it, too.

The world song. Had it sung at home? In the ordered streets of Baryton? He blinked at the thought, and as he did he sensed the music of Anche, the undercurrents, the rhythms that were so familiar he had never noticed them at all.

He stood staring at Shawm for a long time, all the while remembering the humming beam that had captured him in its unfathomable snare. Finally, he said in a low voice, "No. It wasn't the world song."

Shawm looked at Picardy, then Dorian. "I'll take you there. Where I heard it." He turned abruptly and said over his shoulder, "We'd better go now. It's a long walk."

Chapter 18

The sun streamed through the hand-carved clefs in the Canon Office wall and played over the broad face of Becken the Augment. The man stared down at the transcription for a moment more, then his fingers tightened over the thin sheets and they crumpled in his hands.

He looked up, lips set thinly, black eyes glittering

with a light hotter than the early morning Porto Vielle sun. Too far, he thought. This time Stretto had pushed too far. Yet, even as the thought took form, the slender knife-edge of fear cut into his belly.

Swallowing, Becken took a deep breath, then another. His eyes darted from side to side as if he followed an argument between two combatants. Why had he let it come to this? How? It had begun two years ago with nothing more than a token—a gift so negligible that he had scarcely thought of it at all. He was merely helping one of his own, he had told himself. After all, there was the integrity of the Canon to think of. And Stretto had seemed so sincere: It was only a lapse...a single temptation, he said...a regrettable one-time occurrence. If only the Honorable Augment would give him another chance....

It had been simple for Becken to destroy the record, to discredit the single witness who was scarcely competent to begin with. It made him feel almost noble. After all, no one had been hurt. And hadn't he saved the Canon from scandal? Who could separate the Office of Canon from the law itself? Who would be served by smearing the Canon with filth? As for Stretto, he had seemed so humble, so circumspect, that Becken had been sure he had done the right thing.

He gave little thought to the other gifts that began to arrive with increasing frequency. Stretto had seemed so genuinely grateful, so indebted, that it was natural to accept the little tokens that found their way to his office. It would have been rude to refuse them.

The muscle in Becken's jaw tightened, relaxed, tightened again. Fool. Self-deluding fool. For a year he had taken Stretto's largesse. First small things; later, cases of the finest Anche wines, clothing suitable for a Conductus, a blondstone ring that he suspected—and denied to himself—was worth more than he made in a year.

Then the "accident."

Becken cringed as he remembered the tone his own voice had taken. "I am truly shocked," he had said. "Your conduct is reprehensible...criminal ...monstrous...." And all the while, Stretto had smiled his despicable smile, curling his thin lips at one corner, stretching them broadly when he heard Becken say, "This time you stand alone. I wash my hands of you."

"I don't think so."

Becken closed his eyes. His nails cut crescents in his palms as he remembered the litany of Stretto's carefully compiled evidence: The sound of his own voice accepting Stretto's bribes: the pictures; the ring—the damning ring—with his name scrawled below Stretto's on the certificate of transfer.

"And so you see," said Stretto with no trace of his former obsequiousness, "we're associates. Partners. Duet, if you like. Wash your hands of me if you choose, but be aware you wash them in your own dust."

He should have killed him. He should have killed him while he had the chance. Yet was there a chance, even then? Stretto had laid his net of evidence carefully, sequestering it God knew where. It was insurance, guaranteed to give him a powerful ally in Canon if he needed it. But when the need of it came, it was not over the many shadowy businesses that Stretto conducted in the Senza. The Augment could have lived with that. Instead, the accident had insured not only Becken's silence, but his active complicity.

He stared down at the crumpled sheets of the transcription. They weren't dealing with an offstave this time, or a befuddled drug user who scarcely knew whether it was day or night. This one's testimony would be believed.

Abruptly, Becken slid open the flat panel on his desk and touched a plectrum to the silver strings. In answer, the voice of his errander came back: "What service?"

"Get me Stretto," he said. Again the cold blade of fear slid in his belly. "Get him here now."

The man on the Baguette raised his head from his instruments and stared, puzzled, at the fountain.

There was nothing there, of course. Nothing but the tight lines of canoners, riot gear at the ready, who flanked their hastily erected barricades.

The second assistant to the Monodist of Science blinked and again stared into his instruments. The tiny analyzer screen showed a different scene indeed: The lines of the fountain and the arched entrance to the Nocturne beyond faded to shadows of pale gray on black. The beam was superimposed. Its nebulous outline danced on his screen like a cloud of goldendarts in mist.

He stared at the screen. Nothing met his eye now but the empty beam itself. The man frowned. Nothing there at all.

Screen fatigue, he said to himself. Small wonder. His eyes had been fixed on that luminous little oval since before dawn. How like an eye it was. He squinted and decided that he had seen a reflection. The sunguard was narrow, not wide enough to shade him or the screen until the sun was higher. By then, Cuivre would have him broiled and rendered.

Sighing, he thought fondly of the cool laboratory and vowed never again to leave it. For at least the fifth time since sunrise, he asked himself why he had been so quick to volunteer when the call came in from the Office of Canon, yet he knew the answer. He knew that he would have taken nothing for the moment when he began to see the images: Mountains at first—strange, impossible mountaintops covered with what looked like white seamilk, then the clusters of thickboled green plants and a strange tawny creature prowling among them—a sight straight from a guile dream.

At first it was disorienting even though his instruments stood between him and the real beam. It hung invisibly over the Baguette, but in his lens, the beam whirled like a seaspout—a golden, misty seaspout that was somehow able to suck out the reason from anyone who stepped into its path.

Before dawn, under the great arc of stars that flamed from nowhere into the sky, the images had come thick and fast. Then at sunrise they began to fade. For a time he half believed they had never been there at all, yet he had captured them, tucked them away into whirling little memory spheres and sent them on to the Office of Canon, with copies duly dispatched to the squat, cool fortress that housed the Monody of Science.

He had seen nothing more until now. Eyes fixed on the little oval, he stared. The reflection again. He interposed his body between the screen and the sun's bright fire and leaned toward his instruments. Cupping his hands into tents of shade, he looked through them and caught his breath.

Through a golden, whirling shaft of light the face of a man stared back at him. He was young with deep, dark eyes, and he wore a cap set with tendrils fine as hair that hung almost to his shoulders and glittered like a million stars. And though the cap was richer and stranger than anything the second assistant to the Monodist of Science had ever seen, it was the mouth that he looked at now with eyes wide with wonder. The mouth had moved, had spoken silently: It said, "...the Ram..."

A thrill went through the assistant's body. Involuntarily, he tore his eyes away from the screen and looked up into the hard blue sky as if he thought to see the man's face looking down from the magic starship of a child's fable. Impossible. And yet when he looked through his cupped hands again, the face stared back from the screen.

Fingers fumbling with unaccustomed clumsiness, the assistant reached inside the casing and pressed a switch. A moment later, he held two memory spheres in the palm of his hand. He gave a whistle to the boy dozing in the overhang of the Nocturne's balcony. With a start, the boy sat up.

"Presto," cried the assistant. He reached into a pouch, pulled out a carved imperative, and tossed it to the young courier.

The boy caught the ornate wand with one hand. For a moment, he stared at it stupidly as if he had never seen one before. Then, as comprehension dawned, he sprinted toward the assistant and caught up the two spheres the man held out.

The assistant watched for a time as the boy darted away on long, thin legs toward the Office of Canon. Then leaning forward once more, he cupped his hands and stared into his screen.

While he waited for Stretto, Becken tried to put his mind to the business of Augment. A row of memory spheres sat in their shallow tray on his worktop. Selecting one, he dropped it into the scan. Pulling the scancord to its length, he released it. The sphere began to whirl in a spiral of silver. Becken drummed his fingers impatiently while it wound. In a few moments it began to play its pictures against the concave surface of the scanplate, and for the second time that morning, he stared at the arc of stars that stretched like glittering blondstones across the dark sky.

Frowning, Becken watched as the stars faded with the coming of dawn. There had to be a connection. It was expecting too much of coincidence to believe that the Baguette disturbance and the arc were unrelated.

His fingers strayed toward his plectrum. He could question the Monodist of Science again. But, no. Let him come to Canon. He would soon enough—grudgingly to be sure—but he would come.

He had seen the resentment in the monidist's eyes when he told him the matter was not in the domain of Science, but was a matter for Canon. For a few moments Becken was afraid the man would rebel and put the matter before the Conductus. With a tone of authority that he had carefully cultivated over the years, the Augment spoke confidently of precedence: Law and order—certainly order—were at stake here. While he would request—no, insist on—the Honorable Monodist's assistance, the concerns of Science were clearly secondary to Canon.

With satisfaction, he read the defeat in the monodist's eyes. He had won. And with Canon in control . . . well, could he help it if the Conductus were to duly note how expertly the Augment handled the crisis?

The bank of silver strings vibrated, and the voice of the errander said, "The Assistant to the Augment is here."

The door slid open, and Stretto walked into the room.

Again Becken felt the edge of fear, sharpened by the certain knowledge that Stretto felt none. He had never felt it. Of that, Becken was certain. Only those interested in self-preservation were capable of fear. Stretto, like a man impervious to consequence, felt none, felt no qualms of conscience, no guilt whatsoever, and it was this that was so frightening. It gave him license. It gave him the incontrovertible right to do as he pleased, exploit whom he pleased, without the mitigating twist of ice in his gut and cold sweat on his palms.

With fascinated revulsion, he stared at the man. Even the "accident" of a year ago had failed to curb Stretto's aura of invulnerability. Instead, he wore the scars with arrogance. He did this now, smiling his thin smile, turning his knife-cold gaze toward Becken.

Stretto's single eye fixed his. The eye was malevolent in its blankness. It was a shield of gray metal that reflected nothing back, an eye that revealed no more than its blind mate caught in its twisting net of thin silver scars.

Becken dropped his gaze. When he raised his eyes once more, he stared at a point on the wall just above and beyond the man. "Last night," he began. Then feeling the need to clear his throat, he said again, "Last night you made a serious mistake."

Without waiting for the acknowledgement he

knew would not come, Becken waved a hand toward
the array of memory spheres. "The girl said she
wounded you."

Stretto shrugged, then smiled faintly. "Your concern is touching, but it's not necessary. A touch of
guile, and the pain was gone."

"You don't deny it, then?"

Again the shrug, followed by a low laugh.

God damn the man. Becken's gaze dropped to
his polished worktop. The distorted reflection of his
own eyes stared back. He caught one hand in the
other; his thumb worked its way across his palm. He
opened his mouth to speak, then closed it as the
string bank chimed and the errander's voice came:
"With respect, an interruption. A courier—"

"Not now."

"Again, respect. The courier comes with an
imperative."

"All right, then."

When the door slid open, a thin boy with a
badge of Science on his shoulder stepped in. He
paused for a moment on the threshold, as if awed by
a chamber he had never seen before. Then he stepped
toward Becken and, reaching into a pouch, handed
over a memory sphere. "From the Baguette," he
said.

Becken took it, "You can go now."

The boy shook his head. "Respect for the Augment, but I can't. I'm under imperative. I go to the
Monody next with your directive."

Becken looked at the boy for a moment, then
nodded. He placed the sphere in the scan. As it
began its spin, he stared at it as if he were hypnotized.

At first, nothing but the now familiar beam of
gold dust appeared. Then suddenly a pair of eyes
stared back. Becken caught his breath in surprise.
The image of a man's face was forming in a cloud of
stars. Slowly the stars regrouped, and he saw that
they were crystals flowing from a sort of headdress.
Becken turned to the courier. "Did you see this man?
At the Baguette?"

Eyes widening, the boy stared at the scan. "No." He shook his head. "Just the canoners and the second assistant. Nobody else."

An image then, like the others, thought Becken. But this time it was a man and therefore a focus. A man could be dealt with; a mountain could not.

"It's speaking," said the boy in astonishment.

Becken stared as the silent lips moved.

"Ram," came Stretto's low voice. "He's saying, 'the Ram.'"

When the courier left, Stretto fixed a pale gray eye on Becken. The flicker of a smile played at the corner of his lips.

Becken caught the look. How cool he was, how very cool, how very much above the law. He tried to imagine the other Stretto, the one who crawled below Canon law with as little regard for it as this one. Becken had not quite believed the first evidence. How could he take seriously what was nothing more than flimsy evidence at best? Not till later. Till too much later.

Even now, he had trouble imagining it—not Stretto the "businessman." No, not that. But the other thing....And in a man with so little human emotion in him. Yet why not? he thought. Perhaps it took just such a stimulus to stir any feeling in him at all.

There was no hard proof now, he thought, and this time he had to admit to himself that he was the cause of that. Since the accident he had been hopelessly caught in Stretto's corruption. The corner of Becken's lip curled in the slightest motion as he looked at the man. How like an insect's opaque eye his was—a gray crawling thing's eye. How must it have looked to the girl last night? Was that part of it, part of the sense of power when he saw that look of revulsion in a woman's eyes.

Officially, the victim's body was never found. Becken felt his stomach turn as it always did when he thought of her face. She had been a small girl—an offstave Tatterdancer who played her stringtam in the market for small coins or a bit of food, who now and then earned more from the men who came at night to the Am Steg.

An accident, of course—and here Stretto's lips had stretched in a parody of a smile made worse by the thick swelling that crept from below his ruined and bandaged eye. They had never intended for her to die. It was all meant as an object lesson. After all, there are things a girl should never dabble in unless she has a protector.

The little Tatter still wore the stringtam picks on her fingers—picks brown with clotting blood and bits of flesh caught in the sharp curves of metal. And Stretto? A hero. His eye was never lost to a tiny girl whose body swelled in the depths of the bay. No. Instead, he had lost it in the line of duty while coming to the rescue of the visiting Conductus of Punta D'Arco, who, of course, could be forgiven if he was too drunk to remember just who it was who fought with his attackers, just who it was who held his head while he emptied his stomach of too much tash and too many drugs. The Conductus of Punta D'Arco was an important man—important enough to merit a promotion for his rescuer.

Becken looked up at the Assistant to the Augment and said, "The girl you attacked last night...did you know she was a fielder?"

Stretto shrugged.

"A fielder, I said. A credible witness. Do you believe that a field practitioner, a person trained in the skills of observation, couldn't pick *you* out of a crowd?"

Again the slow, mocking smile. "But you've thought of something, haven't you?"

Becken turned to a cabinet, pulled out a small package, and slid it toward Stretto. "I can't do anything more than this. It's up to you to do something now."

Stretto opened the wrappings. When a small sphere rolled into his palm, he chuckled softly.

A taste of bile rose in the Becken's throat. The

canoner's Witness, he thought to himself. How innocent it seemed. Nothing more than a little ball of
silver wire. It bore the face, the startled eyes, the
voice of the girl; it carried her name and the place
where she lived. A little silver ball, that's all, he
thought through the buzz that filled his head. A little
silver ball... A death note.

Chapter 19

In the light from Cuivre, the scout hung like a
glittering live thing caught in a widening net of stars.
Kurt stared out at the growing points of light. A
shell game, he thought. Find the real Ram. Win a
prize.

Within the darkened scout, Kurt seemed to hang
in space. The glow from the instrument panel reflected
in his eyes as he looked through the little ship's
transparency. The distress beacon pulsed from Alani's
distant skimmer, its firefly-green light dying on his
retinas in ghostly phosphors, then flaring again.

No word yet. Gone at least an hour, and no
word yet. Breath hushed, he listened for the familiar
voice of Jacoby, for Alani, but he heard nothing
more than the faint hum of the scout's machinery.

Then something came, something so faint he
could barely distinguish it from the sound of blood
rushing in his ears. He strained to hear, staring
down at his instruments, touching them into response. And when nothing came back, it was then
that he began to listen inwardly.

Ooberong. Ooberong, moving on catpads in his

mind, moving so silently, so . . . haltingly, that he had
not known her approach.

Unaccountably, he felt suddenly weak, as if a
debilitating chill had passed over him. It was gone in
a moment, leaving its trace in a cold numbness that
touched the left side of his body and dragged at the
corner of his lips. He saw her eyes then. When he
did, he knew that his body had felt a reflection of
hers.

"You're ill." He felt her cringe against his words,
and with faint surprise he realized that she was as
private in her way as he was. And now he was the
intruder.

"It's only worry. It's passing." Her voice was no
more than a rustle in his mind.

"No one knows you're sick, do they." It was a
statement, an accusation, not a question. He sensed
her barriers then—thin, strong walls holding him
off. At what cost to her? He moved away; he felt
them ease.

Her voice came stronger then. "We can't contact
it, Kurt. We've tried. We can't." Then a pause, as if
she drew breath. "We have to. It's our only hope."

"It's going to strangle Aulos, isn't it?"

In answer, an inexpressible emotion came to
him, a feeling overlaid with the knife of grief and
laced with a foreboding so dark that a sudden coldness
grew in the pit of his stomach. What else? What else?

"It's unstable, Kurt."

And then there were no more words. Instead, a
montage of images etched his brain:

*The arc of Rams growing into a sine-wave—a shell . . . a
shell of electrons shimmering in a blazing dance around a
blue-green nucleus . . . a terrible Shiva locked in writhing
embrace with a Shakti of flame. . . .*

*A single electron splitting off . . . a sun . . . a shell of
suns . . . Cuivre growing red as blood . . . an enormous glowing, blood-red blotch of light . . .*

*The strong, thin fabric of space tearing into curling rags
. . . casting a universe of stars, of planets, into chaos . . . a Shiva-
dance destroying . . . dissolving . . . gone . . . gone . . . gone. . . .*

The images stopped abruptly. Kurt sat immobile, stunned by their terrible afterglow. The universe? Gone? All of it? At first he could not speak. Then the thought formed: When? How long?

The tenuous thread between their minds trembled with her effort. "... not clear ... not sure ... not long ..." Then she was gone.

Dorian looked up from the flat rock where he sat by the shallows of the river. "How much further?" His question was tinged with pique. His heels had sprouted such fiery blisters that even the upland Largo failed to cool them. Withdrawing his painful feet from the water, he examined them with a critical eye.

"You'd better dunk them again," said Picardy. "If only I had my medpack ... But, I'll fix your feet for you when we get back."

Dorian, not overly anxious to crawl uphill again, plunged his feet back in the water and stretched out on the shaded rock.

"Don't get too comfortable," said Shawm dryly, "or we'll never get there."

At Dorian's groan, Picardy grinned and said, "He's teasing."

Dorian glanced up in surprise at the tall boy who balanced easily on the knife-edge of a jagged rock that stretched to midstream. The sun glinted silver on the scar that stretched across his brown cheek. Teasing? It would never have occurred to him that Shawm had humor enough to tease. Yet somehow his mood had lightened with each stride away from Porto Vielle. *He doesn't like it there either,* came the startling thought.

"He told me it was just over that rise." With a wave of her hand Picardy pointed toward a copse of greenlace edged with tall slenderboles. "Besides, we won't have to walk back. We can ride the river home."

With innocent raised eyebrows and a shrug, Shawm looked back at Dorian, who was sure he caught another gleam, this one in Shawm's eyes.

"He's mean," said Picardy laughing, "mean as a hairy-bellied tweak."

Sighing, Dorian leaned back again, plastering his body against the cool stone, feeling his feet bob pleasantly in the water rushing through the shallows.

Plumes of white sprayed the cliffs on the far side of the river. Growing in a crevice of layered rock, a clump of delicate webset hung in a confusion of hair-thin shoots that reached nearly to the ground. The rock stretched dark upward-angling strata toward the sky. Inside its charcoal layers an area of bleached stone pointed like a finger as if to say, "This way."

Dorian stared at the pale finger frozen in the rock. Sure that he had seen that shape before, he narrowed his eyes and struggled up on his elbows to take a closer look. Yes. In Baryton . . . "Look there," he said pointing at it. "It's part of a spine." Excitement tinged his voice. "The spine of a tri-tail."

"A fossil?" Picardy followed his gaze.

He nodded. "I've seen them before. In a museum at home. They were sea creatures," he said to Shawm. "Huge. They've been extinct for a million years or more."

Shawm looked first at the pale finger of bone, then back at Dorian. "A sea creature," he said solemnly, yet a smile twitched at the corner of his lips. "Here?"

"Yes," said Dorian defensively. "A million years ago these rocks were layers of mud under the sea."

Shawm raised an eyebrow.

"It's true. The seas were deeper then. When they receded, you could have almost walked from Porto Vielle to Punta D'Arco across the flats except for a channel. There wasn't any Brio Bay, then. The cliffs were inland."

"They taught you this—in your school?"

"Yes. And a lot more besides."

"Oh," said Shawm thoughtfully. "Then they must have taught you that *my* people tamed the tri-tails. They rode them, you know. Like this." With a quick step along the edge of rock, Shawm leaped. He landed astride Dorian, and in a movement too quick to follow, pinned him, helpless, to the flat stone.

"Of course," said Shawm with an innocent smile, "my people were much larger then than they are now. Swelled as they were from all that water."

And as Dorian stared up in complete confusion at the grinning boy, Picardy's giggle echoed the chuckle of the stream.

The scout's display pulsed once. Then it darkened, and Jacoby's face appeared on its stage. "Finally," he said.

The face wavered, then flickered out. The pause was punctuated by a sharp clicking sound followed by a muffled expletive. Abruptly, Jacoby's face was back wearing an expression of supreme exasperation. "Can you guess what a lancinating pain in the stainer it was to patch this through?"

"Alani?"

"I'm here, Kurt." Alani's face appeared next to Jacoby's. "I'm all right now. You can't imagine how glad I was to see this man." She glanced at Jacoby with a smile, but her eyes shadowed to cobalt as she looked back at Kurt. "I've been trying to understand."

She turned away then, and he imagined her staring through the skimmer's port. Her voice when it came again was subdued. "It's my fault. I know it is. I just don't know why."

"Nothing's your fault. How could it be?"

"The Earth Song, Kurt. I caught its signal from the Ram and everything got worse. I couldn't break loose."

He leaned over the little stage and listened intently as she told him what had happened.

"Those people. All those people. If you could have seen the way it affected them. I tried to tell them to stay away, but I made it worse. I couldn't really talk to any of them, except one."

"None of this is your fault," he said again, thinking: If she's going to die, if we're all going to die, then let's do it without guilt.

"Don't lie to me," she said quietly. "Jacoby told

me about the signals." She waved a hand toward the port, toward the net of false Rams. "The Earth Song from each one of them. And they all were pointing at me." She dropped her eyes. The thumb of one hand stroked the palm of the other, pressing, smoothing, as if she tried to erase the lines written there. "It's the infrasound, Kurt. I know it is."

The infrasound. The whispered sound of Earth that spoke to the hidden part of him, the part that had never left it for the stars. He could feel its echoes now, as if its sound patterned the very bones and sinews of his body.

Ooberong's images of destruction melded into one, and in his mind he saw a blue sapphire against black-velvet night. It was a memory he had held for centuries, an image of Earth as she swelled in the port of a little ship that carried a boy to L-Five. And with it came the most awful desolation he had ever known.

He knew then that he could accept his own death and the death of the Ram. He could accept the winking out of every life he knew and every star, if only that one bright jewel were left. But with its death, any meaning was stolen, trampled, trivialized, until there was no meaning left at all.

He raised his eyes to the two faces on the little stage. They needed to know, he thought. It was their right. And yet he could not bring himself to tell them what he knew, just then.

He caught a look from Jacoby; the look in his eyes carried a penetrating curiosity, and perhaps an accusation. "Has there been more? From Ooberong?"

How well he knows me, thought Kurt. "A little," he said aloud.

A silence hung between them.

Finally, Jacoby said quietly, "I'm going to stay here with Alani. You might want to join us. Later on."

And Kurt took his meaning: Jacoby meant that he had taken careful measure of the oxygen that remained. Kurt was to stay there until his was exhausted, until there was no choice left. Then the three of them would share the rest, would wait together for what was to come.

Kurt looked around the little scout and beyond to the shining net of Rams. So this is where it ends, he thought. So this is how.

Then knowing he would never leave the scout again, he turned to Jacoby and slowly nodded.

Chapter 20

The trailing fingers from a clump of catchweed snared Picardy's clothes and clung tight as she picked her way between a rock outcrop and the riverbank. Dorian, nursing his damaged heels, lagged behind.

Shawm had stopped ahead at the bend of the river. When Picardy caught up to him, his raised thumb passed across his lips and warned her to be silent. "Listen," he whispered.

At first she heard nothing but the river drumming on the rocks and the wind sighing through a stand of bitterboles. Then she caught the faint humming. Cocking her head, she looked toward the sound, then back to Shawm.

He nodded.

She stepped closer. The hum came no louder, but she could feel it now, quivering in her bones like a plucked string. A shiver chattered down her spine. Silly, she told herself sternly. Without realizing that she did, she took another step toward the sound. She shook her head; it felt light. Suddenly she was quite dizzy.

Squinting, she stared ahead. Strange. It wasn't invisible—not invisible at all, but she could see right through it. It hovered over a bank of sweetset, washing it with a dark glow as if the sunlight there had turned to bronze.

She blinked. The beam moved closer. The shaft of amber light hung motionless before it glided toward her again.

She gave a little gasp as the humming in her head deepened to a throb and blazed in liquid notes of fire....

Alani's voice rang in Kurt's ear. "Oh, no. Another one." She was staring at the shallow lens of the skimmer's imager.

Kurt spoke quickly to the scout's brain. Responding, it sought the skimmer's signal and his own imager came to life.

REPLICATING

The scout's imager swam in clouds of milk. Then suddenly it cleared and he saw the girl.

She stood in a wooded glen by a river. The sun streamed down on her upturned face. Her hands were held out, fingers curled, as if she sought to catch the beams of light.

Alani reached for a switch and tapped it on. "Back! Go back." Then, in dismay, "She walked right into it." Her voice rose in pitch. "Get out of the beam. Get out!"

"Wait." Kurt narrowed his eyes. The girl was in a sort of ecstasy, but there was something more ...something about the look in her eyes. Something crept in the back of his mind just beyond his grasp.

The girl sank to her knees. Her eyes darted back and forth as if the shadow show that prowled her mind had crawled into reality.

Alien, he thought, as the faint vibrations of the Earth Song pulsed in his chest. She was Aulosian. The sounds of Earth were completely alien to her— as awesome as the shifting net of Rams was to him.

Yet, the moment the thought came, it rang false.

How would the Earth Song seem to him, feel to him, if he had never experienced it before? It was impossible to answer. But the children of the Ram accepted it without thought. They were born among the stars, yet they had come from the sun; they were made of the sun. The Earth Song told them that and every cell remembered.

The look in her eyes? What was it? He shook his head as if to dislodge the reluctant image. What was it that impaled a girl on a beam of infrasound from a thousand Rams? Why?

The echo of Ooberong's last words came to him then: *"We have to contact it, Kurt. It's our only hope."*

He blinked in surprise at the sudden thought that came to him. The infrasound. It had been a pathway once, an empathic bond that found its focus in the brains of damaged children. It was an ancient bridge between minds, one so old, so long ago, that he could scarcely remember it now. They had supplanted it with the ship's brain and with the caps—devices that were so much more reliable, so much more controllable, that a method that used a piece of music and a single retarded child seemed laughable, almost pitiable, now. And though the Earth Song remained, no child like that had been born on the Ram for thousands of years.

He stared at the imager. Hands reached out now, pulling the girl away from the thrall of the beam. Could he find one down there? One retarded child? Just one?

Foolish, he thought. Hopeless. He stared through the transparency as the widening web of ghost Rams cast its snare. Like a spider's web, he thought. What was the use? And yet, flimsy as it was, what other plan did he have? What other course?

Even as the thought came, he reached for the scout's console, touched on a switch, then shut it off abruptly. No. He couldn't contact them that way—a voice from nowhere thundering down like God's. No wonder Alani's had made it worse for those people. He scanned the console.

As if he read his mind, Jacoby's voice came low in his ear. "Kurt. Maybe we can use infrasound to reach that thing."

He nodded quickly.

"The tracer. Try the tracer again. Open the Reconn drawer."

Kurt stared at the unfamiliar console. "Where?"

"Eyes front," said Jacoby, "now track right to the red pressure sensor—that's the square one next to the white—and up ten degrees."

The Reconn drawer was no more than a faint seam on the console. The door sprang open at Kurt's touch.

The scout spoke:

RECONNAISSANCE ACTIVATED. DESIGNATE RANGE, PLEASE

"Tell it to circumscribe—eye range, ground level," Jacoby prompted. "Otherwise you'll get distortion on one to one."

When Kurt did, the scout spoke again:

CALIBRATING

A series of clicks, then an amber light flashed on. Kurt felt a slight tingle in his scalp as the ship's brain sent minute adjustments to his cap. In a few moments, the light changed to green.

As it did, a tiny burst of light sped from the scout and followed the beam to the planet's surface.

There was a sharp beep in his ear, and the lens became a dilating window.

With part of his mind, Kurt knew that his body remained in the scout. Another part looked out with his eyes through a window into alien woodlands and a river rushing over worn stones.

"Do you have it?" came Jacoby's voice, but distant now like an overtone in his head.

"Yes."

"Damn." And his single word spoke pages: It spoke of wanting to be there too, of wanting activity— any activity. It spoke resentment that he was trapped in an ineffectual skimmer with no tracer, with nothing but limited imaging, with no way to land, with no way any of them could find their Ram. It spoke with the hollow knowledge that he had nothing meaningful left to do, nothing but useless waiting, until even that ran out.

The dilating window of the lens became a door, and Kurt stepped through.

Shawm stared at Picardy. She was walking directly into the beam, hands outstretched as if she reached for something. Out of the corner of his eye he saw Dorian give a start and then leap backward until his body was pressed against a ragged outcrop of rock.

Without moving, Shawm watched the two. Why had he brought them here? He had been curious from the start about Dorian. He wore fielder's clothes like a lowerstave, yet he spoke with a reedy intonation that Shawm associated with the upper classes. And then there was the school he seemed so proud of, as if the notions he had picked up there made any sense at all. Anche—it must be a land of fools.

But why had he done it? Why had he brought them here? nagged the thought. He came up with a rationale at once: They were curious. It was what they wanted, wasn't it?

He knew it was a lie. It had made him feel powerful—important—to know something they didn't know, to be able to show them so. He blinked at the thought and pushed it away.

A splinter of conscience stabbed when he saw the wide-eyed shock on Picardy's face. He could sense the pull of the beam, the feel of it in the flat bones of his chest.

He could pull her out. He could pull her out any time he wanted, he told himself. Suddenly he began to tremble. Could he? Could he really? Could he keep away from it himself?

He heard the voice then; the woman who called herself Alani.

His darting gaze scanned the glen. Where was she? He narrowed his eyes, searching first the area

of the beam, then the riverbank where he had seen
her last.

But had he? Had he seen her at all? Had he
really heard her voice just now?

Each time he had thought about it, it seemed
less real, less believable. He had wanted to tell Clarin,
to tell Zoppa. But he could never have brought them
here; he would never have risked it.

At Picardy's low moan, his teeth began to chatter, and in one crystal moment, he saw his motive
with terrible clarity: He had brought them here as a
sacrifice—a sacrifice to his overwhelming fear that
the shifting thing in the woods had triggered something in his mind he could not control. They were
his validation, his proof that he was not mad. *And if
they were harmed, they were not his own kind.*

Whimpering, Picardy sank to her knees. The
image flashed in his brain, and he saw her that way,
kneeling beside his mother. Frozen with dismay, he
stared. Then he was leaping, reaching out, pulling
her away.

He felt her struggle against him. Clutching her
against his chest, he half-pulled, half-pushed her
from the angry insect-hum of the thing. And all the
while he was saying, "I'm sorry, I'm sorry, I'm sorry."

Driving her fingernails deep, Picardy struggled
against the restraints. They rippled and knotted
under her hands. Surprised, she let go and looked
down. Red crescents welled and spilled over into
dribbling streaks of blood. She dabbed at them and
shook her head to rid it of the thousand alien voices
that congregated there.

Gradually, she saw the restraints as a pair of
arms holding her tight, keeping her away from something. The voices thinned until there was only one,
Shawm's, saying something she couldn't make out.
Then at once, another sound: the sharp intake of
breath.

She looked up, blinking stupidly at the man who
appeared in the glen. He was tall, with eyes like

storm clouds; his hair was a cascade of stars that
glittered darkly in the amber light of the beam.
Then suddenly she couldn't see the beam at all.
There was only the man now, standing motionless,
watching her with a steady, searching look.

Again the sound of a breath, this time escaping
with a thin, drawn-out hiss. Her eyes darted toward
the sound. Dorian, back pressed against a rock outcrop, clutched the stone that held him, his hands
pressing, curling into claws.

The man spoke. "Don't be afraid."

Shawm's arms wrapped tighter around her. The
pulse in his throat beat against her ear.

"Don't be afraid."

A shiver rippled through her body, then another, and she was trembling violently. Echoes from
a thousand voices gibbered in her head. Words detached themselves, swam together, joined again: "Ram.
I come from the Ram."

Ram. The sound beat in her head, but not the
sense of it. Ram. Ra-aam-m-mm.

"There's no time."

No time, notime, notime.

Gradually, the voices dissolved again. Gradually,
dribbles of meaning came to her. The Ram. It was
the Ram. Come back. She stared at the man and
tried to make sense of him.

Shawm's voice came low in her ear, "It's an
image. He's not really there." Then louder, "What
do you want?"

The man's voice blurred again in her mind. She
struggled as if she were crawling out of a nightmare.
No wonder, came the detached thought. No wonder
sedation didn't work at the fountain. It would push
everybody back down—into this.

Then Shawm was speaking again. His words
buzzed from his throat against his ear and, buzzing,
entered her brain. Sound. Nothing but sound. She
felt dizzy. So dizzy . . . The sounds merged to a drone,
a humming drone that echoed like the beam. . . .

She started as a single voice broke loose from

the others and lodged in her head. It was thin, but
clear; it was Dorian's: "We'll try. We can try."

Hands pulled her then—it wasn't clear where.
She felt herself sink down, and her eyes dragged
shut. A bobbing motion began that added to her
dizziness, and she heard the rush of water. When a
cool spray touched her face, she blinked and squinted
against the dazzle of the red-glazed sun hanging low
in the sky.

The pair of oilnut fronds that held them slapped
the water and skipped through the rapids. Hands
closed over her, holding her tightly as the current
tossed them like children's toys. Only the figure of
the man just above her hung motionless against the
river's assault.

Squinting at the improbable sight, Picardy blinked
and closed her eyes again.

They were halfway to Porto Vielle before she
came to herself and began to ask questions.

Chapter 21

Cuivre was setting now. Shawm's face glowed
with the light from her dimming rays and gave back
glints of red from the silver scar.

Under his knees the oilnut raft, bobbing with
each thrust of his makeshift oar, dipped and rose
again. The Largo was wider here and lower. As it
slid along its canyon to the sea, one high bank was
washed pink with evening; the other wore the growing shadows of night.

The last of the day wind brushed Shawm's face

and tossed a lock of his hair. He caught a scent of the bay. They were close to Tattersfield now.

His rising gaze met the steady image of the man from the Ram and then moved beyond to the graying sky overhead. He narrowed his eyes and tried to see the net of stars hiding behind the last light of the sun, but nothing was there except a cloud touched with purple and edged with gold. A shadow fell across his face as he turned again to the man who called himself Kurt Kraus.

What was it like? he thought. What was it like to live forever and play with the minds of people as if they were toys? He had kept his silence while Dorian, and later Picardy, had asked their dozens of questions. He had listened until they lapsed into silence and only the wind and the lap of water moved in his ears.

Shawm thrust his oar savagely into the dark water. The little raft skimmed downstream into the narrowing strip of light. He stared at the man. The cap he wore reflected the setting sun with a thousand lights; his eyes met his with a steady, dark gaze.

The thought flowed in like a storm tide, and Shawm set his jaw. How like a god you think you are. A cheap god with magic tricks and images. A god who plays the crowds with guile.

He was a little god who talked of Rams and nets of stars and chaos, yet—and the thought touched coldly in his mind—he had a power. He had come here on a beam of illusion so awesome that the God Shawm knew from childhood had shriveled to nothing in its light.

"Prove it then," he said aloud. "Prove what you say you are." The dying light from the sun was cold fire in his eyes. "Give us your immortality."

Kurt recoiled at the boy's words as if he had been struck. For a split second he felt a sudden loss of balance, a disorientation of time and place. It was a fragmented instant more before he realized that he had momentarily raised his eyes from the scoutship's windowing lens.

He blinked and stared at the dilating scene. Once again he saw the river and the three people huddled on the little raft.

The boy's words echoed in his brain. Had they lost it? Lost the process? How? Why? He stared at first one, then another. Not immortal? Not one? He scanned their faces and tried to see a sign, a touch of the stigmata that marked so early the faces of those doomed to age and die, but nothing was there.

So they were very young yet. Children. He stared at Shawm. Red lights glittered from the silver scar and echoed darkly from his eyes. A boy? This one? How could a mortal boy seem to carry the pain of centuries in his eyes?

But then the ancient thoughts moved again in his mind, and Kurt remembered....

He was fifteen years old again—and newly immortal. The world was a wonderful, incomprehensible place, and it was his. It belonged to him and the children of the world, and it was his forever.

Abruptly a floodtide of memories washed over him, and he staggered against the sudden freshening of an ancient pain: He was fifteen years old and hunted like an animal by a pack of mortal men not quite sane with rage. He had celebrated a birthday wrapped in blood and the cries of dying children. In a world of ash and chaos, he sought the safest refuge....

Once again, he looked into the face of his dying father, and millennia fell away. He looked into that face in a frantic search for love and guidance and hope. What he found was the cold metal of hate.

I wanted very much to kill you, Kurt....

His answer to his father had been fluid then. Words. Just words. Centuries laid upon centuries had crushed them, crystalized them, turned them to •immutable stone: *I'm going to live...I'm going to live and watch you die.* They rose to his lips now like silent monoliths as he looked down at the face of a boy on

an alien river in an alien world. And when he met
Shawm's eyes, he saw his own.

No, he thought. Not again. He could not loose
those demons on this little world. They had lost the
process. Should he give it back so they could lose
their souls?

But what did it matter now? What did it matter
when time was sliding away to nothing for all of
them?

The waters of the Largo turned to ink under
the graying sky. Night crept silently after the sinking
sun and stained the clouds with purple. Picardy
raised her eyes and gave a faint gasp. Dim points of
light began to pierce the growing night—points of
light that snared the clouds in a net that grew
brighter and denser with each passing moment. Her
vocie was low, "It's really true, then." She sought
Kurt's eyes as if she expected him to deny it, to say it
was not so.

When the answer came in his silence, in his look,
she fixed her eyes again on the darkening sky, but
her hand crept out toward Shawm and Dorian, toward the comforting touch of another human.

Rough stone steps brushed the raft. Shawm dug
his oar into a niche of rock. The raft steadied against
the current. With one motion, he rose and stepped
off. "Tattersfield," he said with a thrust of his head
toward the dark stairs that led upward from the
water.

"I'll help you get off," said Dorian reaching out
to Picardy.

"No," she said, pulling away. Ahead, the lights of
the Pontibrio burned yellow against the graying sky.
The streets of the Senza would be dark now—darker
than the bridge.

Dorian gave her an uncomprehending stare.

"We can get off further down, near the Pontilargo."
But not here, she thought. Not here. Not in the
dark. Silly, she told herself, you're not alone. There
won't be anyone waiting. Not tonight.

"The records," said Kurt. "There isn't much time."

She tried to remember what he had said to her. She still felt odd since her encounter with the beam. Drugged almost. But he had been so insistent when he learned she was a medical fielder. Something about a way to communicate with the thing that spun its lights around the world. Something about the slow ones—the poco tardos—and the records she had of all the patients.

"The records," Kurt said again.

She gave a quick look toward the shore. Shadowy steps crawled toward night. Anyone could be up there . . . waiting.

"The Pontilargo," said Picardy. "It's closer."

"Do what you like," Shawm said. "I have to dance." With a quick outward thrust of his chin he leveled his gaze at the man who stood so motionless at the head of the little raft. "I have no choice." He fixed first one, then another with a look Picardy could not read. "Till dawn," he said, ". . . or the end of the world." He gave an elaborate bow. Then he was running up the high stone steps toward Tattersfield until he was no more than a shadow in the darkness.

The raft glided downstream past anchored harvestmasters. Their drying nets, ripe with the scent of salt and sea harp, hung like giant raggwing webs in the shadows.

Picardy's eyes dilated in the creeping darkness as she stared at the motionless figure of the immortal. Blinking, she wondered at it. He seemed slightly luminous now, as if the last rays of the vanished sun still shone on him. She saw that his hair was not hair at all, but instead a million iridescent crystals touched with pale light. His eyes were dark and brooding; they seemed to span gulfs she could not fathom.

The lights of the Pontilargo stretched yellow beads across the river. She looked at the man, and suddenly she wanted to laugh. It was all a silly dream. She was going to walk through the streets of Porto

Vielle with the image of a man who didn't quite touch the ground, who wore crystals instead of hair, who looked for a little poco tardo to save the world. Even in the half-madness of Fesival it was a strain to credulity.

She wanted to laugh, but the impulse died in her throat when she looked at the net of stars that filled the sky. Suddenly she felt like prey, like a hapless sea harp caught for someone's dinner. A dream, she told herself, and blinked. As if to validate herself she trailed a hand in the dark river. Blood-warm water lapped against her skin. She raised a finger to her lips and tasted the faint tang of salt.

The lights of the Pontilargo ahead were yellow eyes. Ram's eyes, she thought with a slight shiver. Devil Ram ... Ram ... None of it was making sense. She still felt so queer. She shivered again, more violently, when she thought of the strange amber beam. She had stepped inside to a world as strange as a guiledream, to music like she had never heard before. To overtones, undertones, of thoughts so alien they made her shudder.

She was drowning in it again. Fluid ... swirling fluid and the wash of faint voices in her mind. Then she was spinning violently in a bright whirlpool so alien, so incomprehensibly foreign, that it flooded her brain and nothing else existed. . . .

She felt her mind surface again. The dark lines of the river stretched toward the bridge; the taste of salt on her tongue was an anchor. The man was saying something. What?

"—going to kill the image."

Then quite suddenly he was not there. Not there at all.

The raft was dark. And where he had stood, nothing remained but shadows pierced by an infinitesimal point of light.

Dorian groped for the stone steps. He swayed awkwardly for a moment, one foot on the raft, the other on the rough stair that led upward to the Brio shore. Balancing, he caught at a niche with one hand and reached out toward Picardy with the other.

She felt the raft slide away under her foot. With a little leap, she found the landing and fell against Dorian. The leathery raft bobbed in the bridge lights for a moment, then glided into the shadows underneath.

The point of light that was the immortal hung like a tiny lost star for a moment before it traced their steps upward along the stony river bank.

At the top, Picardy paused for breath. A knot of people pressed around the tam-tams and tash stalls at the neck of the bridge. A girl dressed in flutters of white stood head back, dark hair flowing, and stared at the sky. The man next to her, touching her, stared, too. Then he looked abruptly down at the cone of tash he held and downed it in one gulp.

Suddenly weak with hunger, Picardy moved toward a stall, but Dorian was there first, buying hot wedges of pastry stuffed with spindigs fresh from the bay and pale, crisp sea-curls.

"What is it?" said a boy staring at the sky. "No one knows," answered a man who held a fistful of coins toward the tashstall. "What is it?" whispered a woman to the tashman twirling his cones on a flat tray. He shrugged and, pocketing the man's coins, slid the tray toward him and reached for another.

"It's part of it," said a fat woman wearing strips of purple in startling contrast to her pale flesh. "It's part of Festival, isn't it?" She clutched at Picardy's arm, and the pierce of anxiety entered her voice. "Isn't it?"

A low laugh: "It's planned." The man pressed his body to Picardy's. Guile glittered in his eyes like a thousand cold stars. "Everything's planned."

Frantically, she pushed him away and turned in confusion. Dorian's hand took hers. He pulled her toward the bridge and thrust the pastry at her. She took it with a murmur of thanks.

As the two crossed the great bridge, no one watched. Although the bridge was crowded, no one

noticed the tiny point of light that traced the steps of
the boy and girl. Every pair of eyes—some steady,
some with the glitter of drugs, some bright with
fear—was fixed on the sky.

The flare from the grocer's sign across the way
sent a shaft of light into Picardy's darkened room. A
shadow on the floor shuddered and lengthened.

The man moved silently, gliding from dark to
shadow, avoiding the streak of light that glazed the
center of the room with dingy yellow.

He moved slowly, deliberately, learning the room,
learning every crevice, every turn of it. Now and
again his thumblight flashed. It did now, its gleam
hidden from the street by a cock of his hand. The
light slid along the seams of the door, paused, went
out.

He moved toward her wardrobe and opened it.
The light flared on again and darted over the neat
stacks of gray uniforms, over the rainbow of singlesets
and sashes. It came to rest on a pair of shoes, then
glided away, stopping at last on a little pile of filmy
cloth. He reached out and the light gleamed on the
dark sheath snugged against his arm and glittered
on the hilt of the knife sequestered there.

The thin undergarment slithered in his fingers.
His hand slid into it. The thumblight caught on an
edge and lifted it, lighting the pale blue cloth, outlining
the black lines of the fingers inside.

A fold of the garment moved between his thumb
and forefinger, slowly at first, sensually. Then as the
film of blue stretched tight over the flat plane of his
nails, stretched and moved under the brutal thrust
of thumb and fingers, the faint sound of tearing
cloth gave way to the leathery whisper of flesh against
flesh.

Chapter 22

The lock to Medfield 18 clicked, and Picardy pushed open the door. A tiny point of light blazed on the threshold for a moment, then moved silently inside. Dorian followed.

The lights in the examination room were dim. She turned them up. "Take off your shoes," she said to Dorian. With a quick movement she tossed a handful of blue-gray crystals in a small tub at the floor and filled it with water.

Suddenly she looked up, eyes darting toward the ceiling and the faint scratching sound that came from it. "Did you hear that?"

"What?" asked Dorian.

She scanned the ceiling again, then shrugged. "Nothing, I guess. You can soak your heels while I check the records." She looked around the room for a sign of Kurt and said in a voice not quite steady, "I'm not really sure what you want."

Then she blinked. Where was he? The spark had disappeared with the brightening of the lights. "Where?"

When Kurt's voice sounded in her ear, she jumped. The feeling of unreality flooded her again. Childhood memories of ghost stories and demons came back with a rush; stories that always ended with a flapping of hands and a loud, breathy "oo-oo-ooh" in small ears pricked with delicious anticipation. She wanted to laugh. She wanted desperately to laugh, but she did not dare, because to laugh might loose the ragged edges of hysteria. She took a slow breath. "Please ... can we see you?"

Almost at once the image of the immortal formed. Kurt spoke again. "I've frightened you. I'm sorry."

She forced herself to look into his eyes. Just eyes. That's all. Like anybody else's. Not so different; not so strange. She felt like the little girl in the fable—Vesper, riding the nightwind to Magnificat, trying to hide from the blazing eyes of God. But there was no dark, safe cloak to hide in here. Not in Medfield 18.

The ridiculousness of it all struck her, and a smile crept across her lips. Maybe this wasn't really a dream, but it was best to treat it that way.

The smile faded and her gaze darted toward the ceiling again, toward the sound that might have been a puff of wind or a faint sigh. When she dropped her eyes, they met Dorian's frankly curious stare. "What's wrong?" he asked.

"Nothing. Just hearing things again."

In the shadows of Picardy's room above Medfield 18, the man lay motionless and stared down at the little group in the examination room below. Quiet. He had to be quiet.

Stretto lay with his face close to the ventilation duct. He had worked the cover loose with barely a sound, but still she had noticed. He had made no other until his sharp gasp of surprise when the man appeared from nowhere.

A thrill of excitement ran through him. The man from the beam. He closed his eyes for a moment and pictured the scene in Becken's office: The face forming in a cloud of stars that flowed into a headdress, the lips moving silently, forming again and again the word "Ram."

One of the immortals—gone for nearly two thousand years, gone so long that no one was really sure they had ever existed.

Why was he here? Why did he appear to a lowerstave girl in a tiny Medfield?

Why this girl?

Stretto narrowed his single eye and stared through the duct. It made no sense, none at all. A fielder for the Tema's poor. A girl who wandered through the Am Steg at night and stole into Tattersfield like a common whore.

Why?

Tattersfield!

The thought, when it came, was stunning. It stole his breath with its clarity, its cohesion. Tattersfield. Of course. The thieves—the killers. It was said they had it still, had the process that gave immortality. He sucked in a slow breath that was sweet in his lungs. So it was true. And that one, that small girl standing below so close he could almost touch her—she was the key.

Clever, he thought. Who would have suspected? A poor girl who could wander freely among the offstaves...a girl trained in medicine, in the secrets of the body...a girl who spoke intimately with an image from the Ram.

So it's you, he said silently, intimately, to Picardy. You have it. She was the one who carried the knowledge a hundred thousand would kill for. He stared down at her and a wet glaze spread in his pale eye. How slender her neck was, how easy it would be to snap, how like the sound of a dry reed bundle breaking it would be. He smiled to himself. Not yet. Not till he had her secret. And she *would* give it to him, that was sure.

He felt for the little silver ball tucked inside his shirt. He felt its curves through the cloth and his fingers caressed it. The Witness. A dry laugh rose in his throat, a silent paroxysm of a laugh that curled his lips and narrowed his eye until it was a silver scar in a coiling nest of thickened tissue. Yes. The Witness. Becken had handed him more than he knew.

"The children," Kurt began, "the ones you call the poco tardos—not all of them were empaths. Only a few. They all seemed alike, but they weren't. Only the ones with the inherited form could read the infrasound. The others had an extra chromosome, but these children didn't."

Picardy stared at him. "Chromosome? What's that?"

Kurt looked at the girl in dismay. The fact that they could speak to each other, understand each other, had made him forget the enormous gulf between them. The great quake had cut them off from the Ram, from their own kind, for nearly two thousand years. It had taken them till now to rebuild their technology to a primitive level. Yet, the girl was trained in medicine. Was it possible she knew nothing about a human cell?

He tried to explain, drawing on the crystals of memory, painting a word picture of the inner workings of a cell and its tiny core of genetic material.

"Oh," she said at last, "I see." With a quick laugh, she turned to Dorian, who soaked his heels in the soothing bath. "He means the dark bodies."

Kurt felt a smile of relief creep over his lips. "One of the chromosomes—the dark bodies—is large."

Picardy frowned for a moment and then turned abruptly toward a small cabinet. She opened it and selected a small silver ball from a rack. She dropped it into a battered old scan and pulled the scancord. After a balky start, the sphere began to wind with a high-pitched hum.

As Kurt stared at the scanplate, a code number appeared and then the imprint of a tiny hand marked by a single crease across its palm. The simian crease, he thought. The words came to his lips, but not the translation. How could she understand that this child was marked with a palm similar to the great apes of Earth when no Aulosian had ever seen such an animal?

"Each baby has a signature done,", she said. "That is, most babies. We try to do them all, but some of the nomadics won't bring their children in, and we can't do these in the field."

As Kurt watched, the projection changed and a series of pictures that he took to be blood samples came on followed by more code. Then it changed again to a pattern of wavery X's.

"The dark bodies," said Picardy. She pointed to a shadowy chromosome much larger than its mate. "Is that what you mean?"

Kurt stared as the memory switched in. "Yes," he said. "That's it."

"Poco tardos with this pattern are rare. Only three percent of the population carries the dark bodies that cause it."

"Less on Anche," said Dorian sloshing his feet out of the basin and padding wetly toward the projection. "Barely two percent on Anche."

A loud squawk startled them all. Then Picardy groaned and answered the call box with a quick, "Eighteen here."

The voice of the comfielder was pleasant: "You're due on now."

"But I'm supposed to be off tonight," Picardy protested.

"Quartalist in charge says you're on. He says he let you off last night. He had to call in Twenty-two to replace you, so you take over for Twenty-two tonight."

Picardy stared at the call box with a look of chagrin. "Right," she said with a slow, rueful smile.

"Have a good night."

The comfielder clicked off and Picardy looked first at Kurt, then Dorian. "I have to go up to change and get my sharps." She headed for the door. "I'll be back in a few minutes."

The dying bay breeze caressed Picardy's face as she stepped out of Medfield 18. It was growing darker, and soon the calm would come before the wind turned.

She looked up uneasily at the web of stars that snared the sky. They seemed thicker now, as if somehow they had multiplied in the darkness. She felt a sudden vertigo and dropped her gaze to the moonwashed steps that led up to her room.

The lock gave way. Stepping inside, she fumbled for the lights. The bed lay as rumpled as when Dorian left it; dried mud streaked the pale blue cover. She sighed faintly at the mess and turned toward the wardrobe.

Strange. She didn't remember leaving the door open. Unknotting her sash she folded it twice and tucked it away. Her yellow singleset, loose now, slipped from her shoulders and slithered to the floor. She stepped out of it and was reaching down to pick it up when something made her pause.

A shiver touched the nape of her neck. Hand poised over the singleset, she froze. Something... something not quite scent, nor yet sound....

Idiot, she thought. She was nervous as a skitterwind, and about as smart. That's just *fine,* she scolded herself. Go a little jitty in the head. Solves everything, doesn't it?

She scooped up the singleset and deposited it in the reed basket at her feet. Again, a shiver crept up her neck. Shrugging it off, she reached for a uniform, gave it a shake, and stepped in.

Pulling her sash snug around her waist, she scanned the room. Now where had she put her sharps? For a moment she did not see them. Then she spotted the end of the quiver half hidden under the comfort where she had slid it off last night.

Leaning over, she reached for the quiver and slung it on in one easy motion. She was reaching for her treatment belt, hoping its portable communicator would be silent tonight, when the lights went out.

Startled, she blinked at the sudden darkness.

The sound came from behind—the quick intake of a breath. She whirled, hand darting for the cautery. She spun off balance.

Hands closed around her wrists.

She pulled one free, clawing at the man, clutching.

She grasped only cloth. She felt it give way, heard it tear.

A light shot in her eyes. Bright white. She gasped and clawed at nothing. Pupils constricting, heart beating in hard little spurts, she saw the glitter of his knife and felt its sharp point prick against her throat.

Too late. The words were a whimper in her mind.

Too late, too late, too late. . . .

Chapter 23

Not much time, thought Kurt uneasily, not much time. Where was the girl?

Dorian stirred uneasily and stared at the clock. "She should have been back a long time ago."

"We'll go on without her then. You'll have to help me find this child." With a nod Kurt indicated the silver ball still lodged in the scan.

Dorian looked at it, then slid his eyes away. "Maybe we'd better wait."

"We can't."

Dorian hesitated. "It's in code. They're all in code." He dropped his gaze for a moment as if he were ashamed, then he looked up at Kurt and said, "I, uh, don't know the system. I can't even read the names."

Before Kurt could answer, a voice, shocking as it was sudden, rang in his ears. He recoiled at the sound.

The scoutship spoke:

REMAINING OXYGEN SUFFICIENT FOR 88 RAMINS. RELAX NOW. ALL WILL BE WELL

Blinking, Kurt stared around the little ship as if he had never seen it before. His concentration—his involvement—had been total; it was Aulos that was the reality, the place where he *was*. It took a moment more before he heard Jacoby's call and answered.

Jacoby's voice was sharper than it needed to be. "I've been calling for the last ten. You wouldn't answer." Then a pause, a lowering of his voice. "I didn't know what to expect."

Without waiting for Kurt's answer, he went on, "You've been hours. Any luck? It hit me that we can't get through to the alien without a transmitter. I'm going to try to rig the skimmer. Then we can get ground to you and relay via the beam."

"We're close," said Kurt in a low voice. "A possibility. The child may be empathic."

"Anything more from Ooberong?"

"Nothing," he said, but he wondered uneasily if she had tried to reach him and failed to break through his single-minded concentration on Aulos.

Then Jacoby was gone, and Kurt turned his eyes toward the dilating lens once more and moved through. . . .

Dorian was staring at him with a mingled look of curiosity and dismay "What? What did you say?"

"I was talking to someone else."

Dorian's eyes widened, and Kurt thought he saw the sparkle of fear in them. "I may do that from time to time," he said. "Don't be frightened."

"I'm not," he said, too carefully. Then with another glance at the time, "We'd better check on Picardy. We'd better go up and check."

The door to Picardy's room was unlocked. Dorian reached for the lights. He looked around the empty room for a moment before he called to her.

There was no answer.

At first the room and its adjacent bath yielded no sign. It was only after a second careful look that he found the shred of black cloth on the floor. When he leaned over to pick it up, he saw the little silver

ball. It had rolled partway across the room and
lodged in the tangle of Picardy's communication
belt.

He turned it over in his hand. Surprise tracked
over his face. He stared at the sphere a moment
more before he said to Kurt, "This doesn't belong to
the Medfield. Look."

The emblem on the silver ball was scribed in
fine red lines: a curving triangle flanked with two
pointed blades. "Canon," said Dorian. "It's a canoner's
Witness."

Dorian dropped the Witness in the scan and
pulled the scanchord. As it wound, the high-pitched
sound whined in counterpoint to his quick breathing.

Just a little winded, he told himself, and yet he
knew it was the uneasy feeling about Picardy that
quickened his breath more than the run back down
to the examination room.

He thrust his hands into deep pockets and
hunched over the scanplate, frowning impatiently as
the old machine hummed its almost interminable
whine. At last it stopped.

The image flickered and he looked into Picardy's
eyes.

He listened in shocked silence, unable to speak,
scarcely able to think. Last night. It happened last
night. Why hadn't she told him?

He tried to reconstruct what she said, what she
did. Not a word. Not one word. In chagrin he
realized that he was the reason. He had been so
wrapped in his own problems, he had never once
thought of anything else.

"...the Senza..." she was saying.

That was why. She didn't want to get off the raft
near Tattersfield because of last night. Not in the
dark. It was near the bridge where it happened.

She gave a street name. In vain, he tried to
picture where it was. Nothing came to him but a
shadowy maze of abandoned government buildings
from the old town.

Dorian raised stricken eyes to Kurt, "She heard something upstairs. Maybe it was him." He waved a hand toward the scan. "It could have been him." He stared at the strip of black cloth he clutched as if it could speak. "We've got to find her."

Kurt stared in dismay, first at the scanplate, then Dorian. Find her! He wanted to laugh. The universe was about to crumble to nothing and this boy expected him to look for a missing girl. "There's no time. Not now."

Dorian narrowed his eyes at Kurt. "There is. There is if you want to know who that is." He flung an arm toward the silver sphere that held the tiny handprint. "They're Picardy's records. I told you I can't read them."

A faint thought moved in Kurt's mind. Ooberong? What? What was it? The image came to him of Picardy, standing in the little glen by the river, hands outspread, eyes raised. Something...Something so faint, so dim, he could not say what it was, or why it mattered. But it did. Somehow it did. The conviction grew that somehow it was of the utmost importance that he find the girl—and soon. "All right," he said.

Dorian tugged at the narrow strip of black cloth as if it were a spring that could propel him into action, "Shawm. Find Shawm. He knows the Senza." Then he scooped up the Witness, turned, and headed for the door. "I'm going for help," he said. "I'm going to the Augment."

An infinitesimal point of light hung over the river, hovered for a moment, and began to move. No one noticed as it sped upstream toward the bridge that led to Tattersefield. Though many stared above the darkened sails of the Fiata toward a field of stars gone mad, not one among the nervous throng that packed the Pontibrio noticed.

Pausing as if it searched for something, the dot of light moved again and vanished among the glittering reflections of bridge lights skittering toward the shore.

It skimmed above the empty sails of the Fiata, causing a young boy who hung in the rigging to rub absently at his eyes as if a speck of dust lodged there. Dipping, it hid in the flaring light of a torch and scanned the gathering knots of people before it darted off to dance in the sparks of a dying campfire.

Where? How could he find him?

A dozen people moved by, swirls of bariolage darkly brilliant in the flicker of firelight.

Where? They were alike...all alike. Where?

The thought came bright as the spark of light: *The scar*...

Far above the plains of Tattersfield, a man in a small scoutship turned and spoke to the brain of his ship.

ADJUSTING

Then, leaning forward once more, he looked through a darkened lens.

He looked into a world of grays and whites set with angry flaring jewels. The metal spokes of a jig wheel glittered with feverish red lights. A tent stake glinted orange. Over a fire of white flame, a cookpot blazed bronzed green.

He skimmed over a whitewashed landscape peopled with flat gray moving shapes. Scanning each one, he moved like a will-o-the-wisp over the pallid, dusty land.

A gray girl clutched a shadowed harp with star-blue strings. Her ash-gray fingers wore rings of flame. Her ankles rang with glistening umber bells.

The Fiata's slackened sails hung dead white. A nimbus of yellow ringed the dead eyes of the Ramshead; glowing purple struck with blue lights flickered from the great horns.

The silent hexen drum at the foot of the Fiata glimmered white in a circle of fire. Ghostly tatters streamed from bone-pale bodies. Ash-hands plucked at instruments of flame.

The tiny spark moved in widening circles, searched a hundred faces washed with gray, paused, then skimmed away again.

Each tent of Tattersfield was a mushroom topped with a glittering orange jewel. Shadow figures moved on tangles of white paths.

There? But it was only the glimmering shank of a string-tam caressing a waxen cheek.

And then he saw it: The scar burned from a face as pale as death. Its lights, now red as blood, now restless scarlet, shimmered with an inner heat like a tongue of lava creeping over ash.

The point of light moved close and spoke.

Startled, Shawm whirled in the direction of the voice.

Kurt tried to read the expression in his face, then gave it up. There was no time.

The boy stood clutching a nagareh, hands touching the sparkling yellow circles of its metal-banded drumskins, colorless fingers curved over glittering hoops. He cocked his head as Kurt told him why he had come. He listened in silence, then raised his eyes to the point of light. "When we were on the river, I asked you for something," he said. "You didn't give me an answer."

The process again. Kurt felt suddenly, profoundly weary. No, he thought. No. He looked at Shawm without seeing him, without wanting to see him. He was grateful for the distortion of sight that turned the boy into an abstract of white planes on bone. It was easy not to care whether an abstraction lived forever or if it died.

He could not care, he told himself. He could not afford to. What did it matter if this boy, this planet, took on immortality and all its attendant problems? He did not really care—as long as it was not his responsibility. He could not, would not, take this on again. It was too much.

Wasn't the alien enough? Wasn't it enough to know that he—he alone—was responsible? He had taken a dead boy's song of Earth and sent it out to the stars. It had made him feel noble, this quest for something beyond himself, this sure feeling that he would find it.

Magical thinking. The three year old's dream of power: wish and make it happen. How very godlike of the three year old.

He had meddled enough. He had played with life and death and destiny for long enough. It had taken him ten thousand years to realize that he was a fool, a god of tin and brass, a three year old. Now the last notes were dying, and the piper's hand was out.

He stared at the boy, at shadowy eyes in a pale, still face. I'm sorry, he thought. I'm sorry for you, but I can't take the responsibility anymore.

As if he read Kurt's silence, Shawm looked away, then back. "Come with me." Turning quickly, he strode back toward the pallid mushroom tents of Tattersfield.

Kurt followed.

Shawm touched a flap of tent, and they entered. A sand-pale girl dressed in flutters of moonlight stood near the glistening center pole of the tent. A shadow girl with a twisted foot attended her. On the packed-dirt floor three shadow children huddled, two girls and a baby boy. Shawm's chin went up, "They call us killers." Catching the hand of the smallest girl, he pulled her up and thrust her toward the tiny spark of light. "Who has she killed?" He crouched beside the infant. Scooping him up, he held him out like a sacrifice. "Who has he killed?"

"I can't," said Kurt.

"Shawm! What—" The girl's hand fluttered toward her mouth.

They didn't know, Kurt thought. They couldn't see him. He spoke rapidly to the scoutship's brain. Instantly, the point of light flared and became the image of a man. The lens dilated, and the yellow wash of a lantern gleamed on the brilliant colors of the girl's bariolage.

She stared wide-eyed for a moment then fell to her knees.

"Get up, Clarin," cried Shawm. "He's not God. He's a man." The look in his eyes was anguished. "Just a man."

Trembling, the girl got to her feet. "A trick then?" she said uncertainly.

"A trick," he said. "A man."

"From the Ram," said Kurt and told them who he was.

"Picardy." Clarin gave a helpless little shrug and turned toward Shawm, then Zoppa. "We've got to help her."

"She spoke of a man with one eye." Kurt looked first at one, then another. "Do you know this man?"

Clarin raised questioning eyes to Zoppa, "Koleda?"

Zoppa nodded slowly, "Maybe." Then to Kurt, "Koleda was one of ours. She played the stringtam in the market. The girls there warned her about a man named Stretto. 'He rules the "scope," they'd say, but she just laughed." Zoppa's eyes darkened, "She laughed, but then one night a year ago she disappeared. And that night Stretto became a one-eye."

"She's dead," said Clarin. "They say he killed her. The guileman saw it. But who would believe a Tatter?"

"The guileman?"

"He deals with Stretto," said Zoppa. "He sells him the guile we don't need. Then he gives us our share. It isn't much, but it's food."

"Where? Where does he do this?"

"In the 'scope," said Zoppa. Then, as the baby began to howl, she scooped him up with a murmured, "Hush. You'll call the hexen."

"The Kaleidoscope," said Shawm, "here in the Senza."

"It's the old Conductus building," said Zoppa with another murmur to the baby. "It makes one-eye feel powerful, I think."

"Show me where it is," said Kurt. "I need your help."

A look he could not read traced its way across Shawm's face. "Like we need yours?"

"Do it, Shawm." Clarin reached out and touched his shoulder. "For Picardy."

Shawm stared at her for a moment. "For Picardy then." He reached in the cookpot and drew out a ladle. Turning it in his hand, he said, "I'll draw you a map." The ladle handle was scratching a design in the hard-packed floor when the tent flap moved and a breeze scurried through fluttering the tatters they wore. "The wind's turned," said Shawm. "It's time for Festival."

Chapter 24

The mosso clicked past the Baguette's fountain and its ring of canoners. Just ahead, Dorian could see the lights of the Composition Complex. As the vehicle slowed, he stepped forward gingerly. The blisters on his heels had given way to raw, throbbing sores. Should have bandaged them, he muttered to himself, and swung off when the mosso came to its abbreviated stop.

The buff Canon Office was washed in alternating stripes of blood-red lights and white: the body of law and the spirit. One of the symbolic white lights had failed and a shadowy strip took its place.

Dorian stared anxiously at the building. It was late. Was anyone still there? With relief he saw a yellow glow puncturing the hand-carved clefs at the side of the building.

The canoner's clerk looked up. "What service?"

"I want to see the Augment."

"What for?"

"I want to report a person missing."

"Tell the Witness." The clerk pushed a lens toward his face and clicked it on. "Look at the red dot," he said, "and talk clearly."

Dorian fixed his eyes on the small glowing dot and cleared his throat. When he came to the part about the canoner's Witness he had found, he paused and stared at the bored, pouch-lidded clerk. No, he thought. He'd save that for the Augment.

When he finished, the clerk shut off the Witness and turned back to a task that seemed to involve the interminable shuffling of stacks of blue sheets with yellow and white, interspersed with an occasional stab of a finger on a scarred counter.

"Well," said Dorian.

"Well what?"

"I told you. I want to see the Augment."

"Why do you think the Augment wants to see you?"

"This is important."

The clerk snorted. "Important, is it? Do you live in a cave? At the bottom of the sea, maybe? We've got a beam that makes people crazy in the streets. We've got a sky that looks like a speckle-belly. And if we need it, we've got Festival and a thousand weeping weavers dunked on tash." He gave a short laugh, "And you're going to make excitement for us—with a girl who stepped out of the office."

"She didn't just step out," he began.

"Is that right?"

Dorian thrust out his jaw at the man's condescending tone.

"She's not a child. People come. People go. You said yourself she's not been gone long." The clerk narrowed his eyes shrewdly. "Chances are she'll forget the lovers' quarrel and come back to you by tomorrow." He patted his fingers together and grinned as if he was immensely pleased with himself. "Duet again, eh, fielder?"

"We didn't quarrel," Dorian raged. "And I'm not a fielder, either."

The clerk shook his head and grinned again.

"I want to see the Augment."

With a faint sigh, the clerk shrugged and pointed toward a chamber to his right.

The assistant errander shuffled his tray of reports, rolling sphere after sphere into a pattern that would make sense only to another errander. He looked up at Dorian and then pointedly at the time. "After hours."

"It's an emergency."

"I said 'after hours,' fielder. Come back tomorrow."

Dorian drew himself up, "I'm not a fielder. I want to see the Augment."

"And I'm not an errander," said the errander with an aggrieved sniff. "I do this for entertainment. I love it so much, I don't even stop to eat. As for the Augment, forget it."

"I told you, I'm not a fielder. I'm an Artisan candidate from the Polytext."

A thin smile quirked at the errander's lips. "An AM? Of course you are." The smile grew thinner. "And *I'm* the Augment. What do you want?"

Dorian's eyes narrowed. "I want to speak to your superior." And when he did, he was going to suggest that the Office of Canon harbored insufferable lowerstave fools.

The errander's glued-on smile slid away. "Now you listen to me, fielder. I've been here for thirteen hours. Thirteen hours. I'm busy. The Augment's busy. We're all busy. Come back tomorrow." His hand swatted the table by way of emphasis, causing the curving rows of spheres to jitter on their tray. Then he turned his back on Dorian and began to deposit his reports in a series of cylindrical filers.

Dorian stared at him for a moment. Then impulsively he headed around the table and stepped on a pedal near the errander's feet. The accordions gave a faint whoosh as they slid open. He pushed past the open-mouthed errander and ran into the passage that led to the inner heart of the building.

Before the errander had the presence of mind to hit the alarm, he was halfway up a curving flight of stairs.

The man's shouted, "Stop!" came muffled through the rapidly closing accordions. By the time they slid open again, Dorian was inside the atrium marked AUGMENT.

Another errander, this one a thin-faced woman, looked up in surprise. "How did you get in here?"

The room was a curving triangle. Six unmarked doors led off from it. "The Augment? Where is he?"

A quick dart of her eyes told him. As he strode toward the door, she jumped up. "What are you doing?"

"He's sick," came the quick lie. "The Augment's sick. He sent for me."

Shock tracked over her face, then disbelief, "He's not. I'd know it."

An alarm chimed from the wall. It rose in pitch, wavered, rose again.

Dorian darted through the door.

Becken the Augment looked up in annoyance. Pique turned to surprise when he saw that the intruder was not the familiar figure of his errander, but a boy. A fielder. "Who are you?"

"I'm Dorian. Dorian Rynn. I have to talk to you. It's important."

A frown flashed across Becken's broad face. It was replaced almost at once by a carefully neutral expression made second-nature by years of diplomacy.

"It's about a fielder. She's missing." Dorian glanced nervously over his shoulder toward the door. "We went looking for her." He pulled out the canoner's Witness, "We found this."

Becken's black eyes narrowed almost imperceptibly for a moment. He held out a hand and examined the little sphere that Dorian placed there. "It might be one of ours," he said carefully.

"It is. She reported an attack—by a one-eyed

man with a knife. He may have her now. We have to
find her."

Becken's voice took on a soothing tone. "Of
course, we do. And we will."

Dorian hunched forward and lowered his voice,
"There's something else."

The door burst open and two grim-faced canoners
strode in, followed by a nervous errander.

In one move, the first canoner pinioned Dorian's
arms to his sides. "Come along, fielder."

"I'm not a fielder," he protested. His feet scrabbled futilely for a purchase as they dragged him
toward the door. "Please. You've got to listen."

"Wait," said Becken.

The canoner who held Dorian stopped short
and looked in surprise at the Augment.

"Let him go. I'll hear him." With a wave of his
hand and a quick, "Wait outside," he dismissed the
canoners. The errander stared at him expectantly
for a moment. Then, at his raised eyebrow, she left
the room and closed the door a little too noisily
behind her.

"I'm not a fielder," Dorian began. "I'm not
lowerstave at all. . . ."

Becken's face was a mask. He knew it seemed
kindly to the boy, and interested. He wore the expression partly because of long habit, partly to conceal the emotions writhing inside him.

Stretto was a fool. How could he be so incredibly
stupid? He raised black, fathomless eyes to Dorian.
This boy had seen the Witness. Who else? "You
weren't alone," he said evenly. "You said 'we.' "

Dorian nodded and began to speak.

Inside, behind the mask, Becken felt his heart
quicken as the boy told him about the immortal. The
beam, he thought. Was it the man from the beam?
"Describe him."

As Dorian talked, the Augment's mind spun
feverishly. The boy wasn't lying then. He'd seen him

too. The immortal—and he was looking for a fielder
girl. "Why?" he said aloud. "Why does he need her?"

The boy was talking gibberish now—something
about an alien, a poco tardo. And something else:
The net of stars that circled Aulos.

So they *were* connected, the beam and the arc of
stars. They had to be distress signals, and from a
ship he had barely believed existed. A frown flitted
across his face, then smoothed away. Almost at once
a hint of a smile moved on his lips. Even immortals
needed help, it seemed. This one from a fielder girl.
How badly? he wondered. How much would he give
for her?

Immortality. Was she worth that to him?

The thought took away his breath. An exchange—
the girl for the process.

Immortality—controlled by the Augment of Porto
Vielle. He almost laughed out loud. Controlled not
by a secondary official of a second-rate city, but by
the richest, most powerful man on the face of Aulos.

But it was necessary, he told himself. What if it
fell into the wrong hands? The Tatters? Or Stretto?
Or some misguided group that believed immortality
was for everyone, even offstaves and misfits. He had
no choice. Not really. It was a chance for Canon to
give immortality back to the world.

His eyes were neutral when he looked at the boy.
Careful. He had to be careful. Find the girl first.
But what if he was too late? The sudden image came
to him of the stringtam player: The girl lying so still
on the table. The shafts of colored lights moving
over her body, flickering in the glazed, staring eyes.

Becken's gaze slid restlessly around the room.
He had to be quick. He could deal with Stretto later,
but now he had to move before anyone knew.

But someone did.

He stared at Dorian for a long moment. Then
rising, he said, "Don't you worry. We'll find her."
Sliding a small door on his desk open, he touched a
plectrum to silver strings. At the quick, "What service?"
he answered, "The Assistant Augment. I need him."

The errander's voice came back a few minutes later. "With respect, no answer. No one is at home."

Becken smiled to himself. He hadn't expected an answer; it was a confirmation. There was only one place Stretto could be.

He extended a paternal arm around Dorian's shoulder. "We'll find her." Then, as if the thought had just occurred to him, he said, "Perhaps you'd better come along. We might need your help."

Dorian looked up with a grateful sigh and nodded. On the way out of the Augment chambers he looked steadily at the errander and said, "The lowerstaves here are incredibly rude, aren't they?"

Becken gave a faint practiced smile toward the errander and shrugged. Then in a low voice to Dorian, "You know how they are." He gave the boy's shoulder a reassuring pat. "Not to be trusted. Not to be trusted at all."

Chapter 25

Like the rest of the abandoned government buildings of the old town, the Conductus was buff sandplaster reinforced with underlying metal. And like the rest, its salt sand, culled from the Brio's beach, had eroded the life from its metal skeleton.

It was an inward-turning structure that looked to the street only through narrow, curving, f-shaped windows set high in its walls. Its two entrances were guarded by heavy metal-clad doors.

Stripped of its art and statuary, crumbling from years of neglect, the Conductus was a magnificent ruin. Ornate tile topped with the Shield of Quartal climbed a third of the way up its inner walls and ambled through the arched alcoves that flanked its domed atrium. More tile traced the angles where wall met ceiling. Here the downward pointing blade of the Trigon of Monody stabbed at walls stained with streaks of corrosion that in the somber light reminded Picardy of blood.

She struggled once more against the bonds that held her to an alcove pillar. The strap-bands of reed drew her hands tightly against her back; their thin edges cut into her wrists, and her fingers felt numb. Swelling, she thought.

The man with one eye sat at a table in the center of the atrium. Blue-white light, intensified by the shifting colors surrounding it, streamed down and bled the color from his skin. She stared at his profile, at the blind eye in its nest of dead-white scars. Two men stood facing him, now washed blue in the moving lights, now green. Another man stood some distance away near the heavy doors that opened to the street.

The man with one eye had not bothered to speak to her. He had brought her here and had her tied like an animal. Then he had busied himself with other things, other people. Now, he turned to look at her, a half-smile twisting his lips.

Picardy thrust her chin away. She would not look back. She would never look at him no matter what he did. Instead, she leaned back with her head against the pillar and her legs tucked under her and stared in despair at the dome.

The giant kaleidoscope turned slowly. White light blazed from its center; its surrounds, glistening with jeweled patterns, cast shifting rays of color onto the pale stone floor. Over the rise and fall of the men's voices she could hear the rasp of its mechanism and the faint clink of its hidden shards of colored glass as they slid past one another on their bed of oil. Her

eyes dragged past it toward a featureless patch of
ceiling a hand's-breadth from its curving edge. Though
the night was warm, she felt a shiver begin.

She stared at the kaleidoscope again, willing its
patterns into her mind instead of thought. She felt
numb now and chilled. The first violent rushes of
adrenalin had drained away her strength. Although
her hands still worked against their bonds, it was as
if they were alien things. The chilliness spread. She
felt the cold tremble through her legs.

The kaleidoscope turned, casting its central white
light on the table below, flooding the atrium with
evanescent jewels. She huddled just under the alcove
arch, her face in shadow, the floor near her feet
washed in color. Deep purple glided into green, then
red, staining her quiver of sharps where they lay.

He had tossed them down contemptuously—
artfully—near her. Near enough that she could almost touch them with an extended foot; far enough
away that they intensified her helplessness.

He had done it on purpose. She was sure of
that. Although he had not spoken, he fixed her with
a look as if to say, "There they are. Help yourself."
And there was something else that came into his pale
eye when he looked down at the quiver and at the
cautery that had wounded him. When he fixed her
again with a stare, faint smile twitching at the corner
of his lips, she was stricken with a sick terror.

He was going to kill her. She knew it as surely as
she had ever known anything. He was going to kill
her at his leisure, at his own pace. She could feel him
savoring it as he looked at her.

The kaleidoscope turned, and a patch of yellow
danced near her feet. Yellow like the sun. She tried
to draw warmth from its impersonal light. Her hands
throbbed and a growing pressure in her bladder
tormented her. She was going to die without relief
from either of these, and it wasn't fair. Not fair. She
prayed again to the God of her childhood, lifting her
face toward the shifting colors as if she hoped to see

Him there, drawing up her knees until her body curled like a child's in sleep.

She prayed for release. She prayed for it all to be a dream. She cajoled in half-formed pleas; she bargained. And finally, there was nothing left but the faint litany of "Please...oh please...oh please..."

She drew on her own scorn then. Stop it, she told herself. You're not a child. The image came of her own death: everything she was, everything she knew, streaming away in puddles as red as the moving light at her feet. Stop it, she said.

The words of the immortal came to her again. She had heard what he said, had seen his face when he spoke, and yet she had not completely believed him. He had talked of the end of everything, and she had denied it, tucking it away in her mind, going about her business as if tomorrow were on schedule. His words had had no more meaning than the colored patterns playing over the stones.

She tried to think of his meaning now, but it eluded her. It was too vast; it was not personal.

Leaning back against the pillar, she turned her face toward the kaleidoscope again and tried to fill her mind with color and the play of pattern on pattern. Red bled into jet. Glowing green blazed with yellow like the sun. The yellow spread and changed to a white so dazzling that she blinked, and in that instant a tiny spark detached itself from the blaze of light and shot toward her.

It glinted on the pillar over her head. Then it darted behind.

A voice whispered in her ear.

Picardy cast startled eyes toward the sound. The immortal? She strained to see, to hear.

"Don't speak," he said, "just listen. I'm going for Shawm. For help."

Hurry, she thought. "Hurry," she could not help whispering, but the dot of light was gone.

It glimmered near a window slot, then sped through into the dark streets like a truant speck of moonlight. Rising, it moved toward Tattersfield to look again for the boy with the scar.

From the other direction the private mosso came to a stop. The Augment gazed thoughtfully at the dark Conductus building in the distance. "We'll walk from here," he said to Dorian. "We'll be meeting my assistant."

The night was bright. Two moons hung over Aulos, throwing black shadows from the buildings, fading the net of stars to blurring points of light. As he followed Becken through the lonely streets, a dozen lurid stories about the Senza popped into his mind. Dorian's gaze darted nervously toward the inky puddles that spilled from every structure. Foolish, he told himself. Wasn't he with the Augment? His heart quickened when he saw a flicker of light from a black doorway. A moment later a wail split the night. The sobbing low-pitched cry grew to a shriek that made the hairs on the back of his neck stand up.

Becken gave a low laugh. "The Fiata."

Dorian felt his heart start again. He echoed Becken's laugh with a shaky one of his own. "I didn't know we were so close to it." He stared in the direction of the sound, but he could see only the outline of black rooftops against the charcoal sky.

He moved on, but when the night wind shivered down his neck he glanced toward the rooftops again and gasped. Giant eyes stared down at him. A mouth splayed open; a scarlet tongue flicked over fangs. Twin curving horns stretched toward the moons.

This time Dorian's laugh was steadier. Only the Fiata. Only the face of the Ram peering over the buildings. He had been foolish long enough. Wasn't he with the Augment? The highest authority of law in Porto Vielle? What could be safer?

By the time they reached the wide doors of the Conductus, Dorian felt quite calm.

The point of light moved in the flicker of torches. Then it paused.

Over the bray of a thousand reeds, Shawm heard a voice. He stared beyond the sparkle of light, his eyes darkening as he listened. Then he nodded abruptly. "I'll have to tell the Master."

Turning, he began to run and the dot of light followed.

Tatters flying, he weaved through a group of dancers bending in muscle-warming exercises. Dodging a maze of rigging, he made his way toward the giant tuned-drum that lay at the foot of the Fiata.

He pushed past the old scentsinger, reached up, and swung easily onto the stretchskin.

The Fiata Master stood in the center. He was tall and reed-thin. The night wind rippled through his crimson tatters and whipped the white mane of his hair beneath a curving ram's horn headdress.

Shawm's feet sounded on the drumskin.

The Master turned in surprise and narrowed his eyes at the boy.

Involuntarily, Shawm dropped his gaze. Then he looked up again, awed by the man and his authority. In Festival the Master was law; to approach like this was an offense.

A quick apology, and then his words came out in a tumble. He told him of Picardy and his mother; he told him of the man named Stretto who held her—the man who had killed one of theirs a year ago.

The Fiata Master listened in silence. "Where?" he said at last.

"The Kaleidoscope. We can break in—"

"There?" Then, "Impossible. It's a Conductus."

"There are hundreds of us. We can do it."

"No. We can't. Not since the Taking."

The Taking? What did the ancient theft of the process have to do with this?

"The doors are fortified. The windows are nothing more than slots in walls thicker than your body."

Shawm looked blankly at the Master.

"Don't you know anything, boy?" he said. "Since the Taking, every Conductus has been built that way.

It's a fortress. They all are. It's meant to keep us out."

No way? No way at all?

The Fiata Master stared away for a long moment. When he looked at Shawm again, his eyes were dark. "If she can get out. If she can get through the doors. Then we can help her."

With a wave of a hand, the Fiata Master dismissed Shawm, who turned and with two leaps left the stretchskin. With another he signaled to the dozen tuners manning their levers on the periphery of the giant drum.

The tuners strained as the stretchskin tightened.

The Master tested the pitch with a quick stamp of his foot. Another signal, and the reeds of the Fiata closed. At the sudden hush, the group of startled dancers looked up from their exercises. The boys tending the Fiata's flickering lights left off their chatter abruptly. High in the folds of the billowing crimson sails, Jota the Hexen looked down.

When the only sound was the wind snapping billowing sails, the Fiata Master began to dance. The stretchskin responded to the thrust of his feet, the tuners to his hands. The giant drum spoke to the people, and they understood.

Chapter 26

The moonlight playing on the wide doors of the building outlined the ghostly Shield of Composition emblazoned there. Dorian felt his heart quicken as it always did when he entered a Conductus. One day, any of them could be his. The thought had always made the ordeal of his training bearable.

Even though this one was abandoned, it was somehow still sanctified in his mind. The call to Authority was a high one; the Conductus, highest of all.

Becken touched the summon bell once, then twice more. Its sound was lost below the rising wail of the Fiata. Abruptly, there was a silence so sudden, so complete, that Dorian cast a startled gaze over his shoulder.

Ram's eyes blazed above the buildings, eerie in the unnatural quiet. A moment later a drumsong began, modulating into a throbbing rhythm that sent a prickle up the nape of Dorian's neck. He raised questioning eyes to Becken, but the man was staring at the doors.

There was an almost imperceptible movement on the shield as an inner lens turned, then stopped.

Several minutes passed, and then as the wail of the Fiata began again, the great doors began to slide open.

A man was waiting as they entered the vestibule. A flicker of curiosity touched his eyes when he looked at them.

The outer doors slid shut with a clang. Inner ones over a hand's-breadth thick glided together. The man pressed a lever, then another. A heavy bar rolled into place.

Ahead, the atrium was washed in a swirl of color. White light drenched a table and an empty chair.

A sudden gasp came from a darkened alcove. His eyes darted toward it. "Picardy!"

Becken's hand touched his shoulder; its press was firm. When Dorian whirled to face him, he saw the group of men.

One of them stepped forward into the light: a man with one cold eye in a tangled net of scars.

"The Assistant to the Augment," said Becken.

Horror glazed Dorian's eyes. For an instant he was paralyzed. Then he leaped toward the doors.

"Take him."

He was clawing for the lever when the first man reached him. As the bar began to slide, a hand clamped his wrist. It twisted, and the stab of pain broke his grip.

The force of the next man's body threw him to the floor. Panting, he scrabbled away. A sudden kick. His breath rushed out; hot agony spread through his ribs.

A knee pinned him to the floor. A new pain cut into his injured wrist as tight reed straps bound his hands behind his back.

The men dragged Dorian to the alcove and tied him to the column next to Picardy.

From his chair in the center of the atrium, Stretto watched cooly as they did this. The boy from the Medfield, he thought. It was part of the pattern. There was always the pattern. He had known this all his life. He had traced its intricate turnings and knew that he controlled it as surely as a raggwing spun its lair.

At times he could see all of it at once. He could see it stretching its tendrils into every mind, see it coiling, growing. When these times came, he felt himself caught up in its majesty. Sometimes, unexpectedly, he saw it in the eyes of a vendor or a casual tourist. The secret knowledge then was sweet. They never knew. They were blind—always too blind to see it.

He turned to Becken. He could see the pattern now in the man's careful look.

The Augment slid into a chair on the opposite side of the table. "Can we speak privately?" He glanced toward the other men.

"Of course." At a sign from Stretto, the three men moved toward the vestibule.

When they had gone, Becken leaned forward. "You've been seen with the girl. I've had reports. It isn't safe now." The side of a thumbnail glided across his lower lip as he glanced toward Picardy. "I'd better take her with me."

"And the boy?" Stretto felt a flicker of amusement. The boy had surely gone to Becken. How much had he told him?

"No one knows he's here."

"You're suggesting a trade?"

A startled look came into the Augment's eyes. It was replaced almost at once by a practiced look that almost hid what lay behind it. "Of course not." He glanced at the girl again. "I told you—you've been seen with her. She has to come with me."

"You're thinking of my safety."

"And mine." The answer came too quickly, too facilely.

A smile twitched at the corner of Stretto's mouth. "I see." The shifting lights of the kaleidoscope played over the Augment, staining his face, his tightened lips, with purple. So the boy had told him everything. Stretto almost laughed at the transparency of the man's ruse. There was just one question now: Who else knew? The answer came to him at once. No one. Becken would keep it to himself. He could be sure of that.

Stretto's casual glance searched for weapons. It was only a precaution. It wasn't the Augment's style to come armed with more than arrogance. He rose and moved around the table toward Becken.

The Augment was half out of his chair when Stretto's knife came out.

"The girl? Was she worth it?" Stretto's laugh was low. "How do you like the immortality she gave you?"

Becken stared at the knife. He shook his head and raised his eyes.

A smile flickered across Stretto's lips.

"You can't..." Becken's words were a whisper. The look in the single, pale eye chilled him.

The light shifted; the knife blade turned to

blood. He shook his head again as it darted toward him. He felt it enter, felt its upward thrust bite deep.

A startled look came into Becken's eyes. His hands fumbled toward his belly. He looked down in disbelief at the glistening stain spreading over them.

His legs gave way, and he sank to the floor. Blinking, he stared up at the face, the malevolent eye, hanging above him. There was nothing else in the world but that face haloed in a blaze of color.

Monster.

In surprise, he knew that Stretto had always been so. He had been so from the moment of his birth—with no choice but to be what he was.

And in that instant it came to Becken that he had had a choice.

No. No choice. Not really.

He peered at the face above him. He peered quizzically at first, then with a whimper, as he recognized the face of his mother staring down with terrible eyes at a very small boy.

He tried to speak. He tried to say, "Not bad. Not bad, Mommy," but when he did, the words drowned in a gurgling red rush and there was no sound but a final, ebbing sigh.

Dorian's breath came in a hard gasp that stabbed his injured ribs with fire. Unbelieving, he stared at the widening pool of blood. Then, dizzy from pain and the turmoil in his mind, he turned away, sickened.

He had been betrayed. He had been given over to a murderer, yet he knew that wasn't the worst. Becken was dead, but it was Canon that had fallen and a part of his own soul died with it.

And how was it possible? How was it possible to feel the throb of a dying belief as if it were flesh? How was it possible to see the core, the center of himself, die and fall away to dust?

Dorian turned his face to the wall and stared blankly at the scarred and broken tiles that marched across it. For a time they hid their pattern from him. When they gave it up, he saw the faint blaze of their design—the clef of Canon flanked with the twin swords of Science and Ethics.

It seemed to him then that he had built his beliefs of sand. He had built them of sand and called them rock and lived within them, complacent. Now they had crumbled and left him naked in the ruins.

Picardy gave a faint little sigh that clutched at his heart. For a moment his eyes met hers, but the look in them was so poignant, so unbearably private, that Dorian could not watch. He stared up at the shifting pattern of light, but the image of her stayed with him. And in that moment, he knew he loved her.

He loved her, yet again and again he had shown a blind contempt for what she was. Shame wrenched him, a shame so overwhelming that it left him numb and unutterably empty.

He stared blankly at the kaleidoscope and then at the ceiling a hand's breadth from its rim. Slowly, a rising sound penetrated his consciousness. Through the high, narrow windows of the Conductus he heard the Fiata and the faint rumble of its wheels. The sound grew louder. Dorian looked toward it. When he did, he failed to see the point of light that detached itself from the kaleidoscope and darted toward him.

Picardy was saying something in a low voice.

He turned his face toward her and strained to hear.

A fierce hope burned in her eyes. "They're coming for us. I know it."

With a wary eye toward Stretto, he shook his head. They could never break into a Conductus.

"My sharps." Her glance darted toward the quiver on the floor near his feet. "Can you reach them?"

He stared at them, then at Stretto. The man was back at his table now. The others had returned. Two of them leaned over the body. Grasping arms and legs, they carried it toward the wide archway that led to the vestibule. The third listened to Stretto for a moment, then followed.

Now Stretto was alone, his blind side toward the alcove.

Slowly, Dorian stretched a foot toward the quiver. Too far. He slid forward, straining at his bonds until the pain in his wrists and his tortured arms was agony. Panting, he shook his head.

The three men reentered the atrium. Stretto was waiting. He turned then, moving his upper body so that his single eye was fixed on Picardy. "I think it's time we had a talk."

He said something in a low voice. The three men wheeled and came toward her.

She shot a desperate glance to Dorian.

With a slash of a knife, one of the men cut the bonds that held her to the pillar. The other two dragged her to her feet. She went limp in their grasp. Suddenly she screamed. Flailing bound hands at one man, she kicked the other and dodged to her right.

As the third man seized her, Picardy's foot went out. With a quick backward kick it struck the quiver of sharps.

The quiver stopped within a foot of Dorian's hands. He stared for an instant, then swung his body to the left to conceal it. His eyes darted toward the men. They hadn't seen.

They dragged Picardy toward the table.

Dorian's hands crept blindly toward the quiver. He felt nothing but smooth stone.

As the sound of the approaching Fiata mounted, a voice spoke low in his ear: "Left . . . to the left."

Shock glittered in his eyes. The immortal!

"Left."

His fingers grazed the quiver. Straining against his bonds, Dorian panted. Pain stabbed his wrists. His fingers scrabbled for a purchase and closed over the quiver's strap. He dragged it close and stared at Stretto.

The man was saying something to Picardy. The Fiata's wail drowned his voice.

Dorian fumbled with the quiver. The cautery, where was it?

He felt its blunt end. He drew it out, turning it in his hands. Now the tip pointed toward his bound wrists. Set it low, came the desperate thought. On high it would blaze right through him.

The dial turned in his hands. He felt for the switch and threw it. The cautery's hum was lost in the blare of the Fiata.

Fire blazed on Dorian's wrist. His gasp stabbed his ribs.

"Lower," came the voice.

The tip of the cautery dropped. Again hot pain, and then he felt himself break loose from the column. He tugged, but the wrist bonds still held.

The spark flashed behind him. "Once more."

Cold sweat beaded. Trembling, he aimed the cautery again.

"Down . . . Now."

Fire struck his wrists, and he was free.

The cautery's dial twirled to maximum. He stared at the group of men clustered near the table. Too many. Too many. They all had knives.

"Overhead. The kaleidoscope."

Dorian's glance darted upward. The kaleidoscope's giant disk turned slowly just above the table. "Picardy?" came his urgent whisper.

"I'll tell her."

Dorian drew back in the shadows. A quick glance toward Stretto. The blind side. The other men were watching Picardy.

The tip of the cautery swung upward toward the center of the white light. As it did, the point of light sped toward the girl. He saw her blink and her gaze darted upward for a second.

Now, he thought. But as his finger touched the switch, it paused, and the cautery's tip glided to a point in the ceiling less than a hand's breadth from the edge of the kaleidoscope.

His finger closed over the switch.

The cautery's beam leaped. Red light glowed from a point on the ceiling.

A moment passed. Two.

A man shouted.

From the corner of his eye, Dorian saw movement. It was Stretto; Stretto rising with a half-turn, head raised, staring at the ceiling.

Then a leap, and Picardy was running.

The stone floor echoed a scurrying sound that came from overhead. With a sharp crack, the ceiling opened.

Dorian jumped to his feet.

The giant kaleidoscope seemed to hang in mid-air. Then it was falling—twirling down in maddeningly slow motion.

Dorian ran toward the archway after Picardy, grabbing for her.

She screamed, and the sound was echoed by the shatter of glass.

Another scream, and a man clutched at a dagger of red glass that impaled his chest. Clawing, he spun in a slow, bizarre dance while gouts of blood spiraled onto the pale stone floor.

Picardy screamed again as if she could not stop.

"It's me!" Dorian yelled. Spinning her around, holding her with one hand, he cut her bonds with a stroke of the cautery.

He pushed her toward the doors and fumbled with the bar.

The mechanism creaked. The bar rolled away.

The thick inner door slid open. Then with a creak, the outer doors began to move.

He leaped through, then turned.

Frozen, Picardy stared toward the atrium. He followed her gaze with congealing horror.

From the shards a figure rose, splattering blood from a dozen wounds. With a scream of inhuman rage, it plunged after them, consummate madness blazing from its single eye.

Chapter 27

The Fiata shrieked a wild cry born of mountain winds. Its torches blazed on the opening doors of the Conductus. Two figures darted from it.

Dorian plunged toward the knot of people clustered at the foot of the great drum just ahead.

Picardy stopped short. She stared at them and shook her head. A man streaming with tatters advanced. Another.

Terror flickered in her eyes, "No. No more!" Then she was leaping, dodging away. Whirling in blind panic, she ran toward the yawning doors.

"Picardy!" Dorian leaped toward her, but a dozen hands held him back. Half-fainting with pain, he struggled. A low door opened at the base of the drum, and he was thrust inside.

Again he fought, weaker now.

The arms that held him were strangely soft and at the same time unyielding. "Be still. Don't fight me." And in the dimness he looked into the face of the girl, Zoppa.

The blood-streaked figure leaped from the Conductus.

In horror, Picardy wheeled and dodged away.

Shawm stared in dismay as she headed away from help toward the scaffolding of the Fiata.

The man plunged after her. Light flickered on the blood-stained knife at his wrist. He reached out.

She leaped, grabbing at handholds. Then she was climbing.

Shawm gave a piercing whistle—the signal that she was safe. It was echoed at once by the Fiata Master far ahead, and the procession began to move.

For a moment Stretto stared at his escaping quarry. Then with a single-minded howl of rage, he sprang, and scrabbled for a hold. For a moment he hung by one hand. The other found a purchase, and he swung up onto the scaffolding.

Grabbing a trailing valve rope, Shawm swung toward him. A dozen others did the same. Valves opened with their weight. The Fiata brayed in response and rumbled back on course toward the Pontibrio.

Shawm reached toward the handholds, overshot, swung back.

Above, Picardy stared down, gasped, and climbed again.

A lantern tender, a boy no more than nine, ran on a crosspiece toward Stretto. Clinging to the rigging with one hand, he flailed out at the man with the other.

Stretto's hand swung brutally, and the boy fell back, dazed, as the Fiata began its swaying trip across the bridge.

Shawm's hands closed on the thin grips. Staring upward, he began to climb. Overhead, he saw Stretto reach up, his hand no more than a body length from Picardy's foot.

Next to Shawm, a spark blazed, a tiny, dazzling point of light that sped upward toward the girl until both were lost in a billow of crimson sail.

Helpless, Kurt stared as Stretto gained ground relentlessly. Picardy's breath came in ragged gasps as she climbed.

At the head of the procession, The Master wheeled to watch the Fiata's progress as it negotiated the sweeping turn beyond the bridge. He held up his hands to signal first stop.

Forward movement ceased, and a dozen male dancers leaped to their positions. Nagarehs and tams began to drum. Eyes widening, the Master stared past them at the two figures on the scaffolding emerging from behind the central sail. A sudden movement of raised hands called for silence.

A thousand reeds clicked shut. The Fiata gave no sound but the rasp of Picardy's breath and the whip of the wind on the great sails.

The dancers stared in confusion. Below the Fiata, tuners acted on the early cue. The giant stretchskin rolled out on muffled wheels.

"Is it the Hexentanz?" came a faint voice from far below.

"Hexentanz," answered another.

Hexen…hexen…hexen…, said the dying echoes.

Picardy looked down, staring blankly at the faceless mass of expectant tourists who lined the distant street like flotsam. She froze, hands clutching the narrow holds, body swaying as the Fiata's masts leaned against the wind.

Kurt caught his breath. Don't stop. Don't stop. He wanted to cry out, spur her on. But if he did, he knew she would fall.

Her gaze darted toward Stretto. Terror glazed her eyes. She clung for a moment more, then frantically clutching at handholds, climbed again.

In horror he saw her scramble onto a shaky platform that led nowhere. She dodged behind a fluttering red sail. Kurt sped after her.

Jota, the Hexen, stood there, shivering. Wind whipped her white tatters. Bright fear danced in her eyes. She clutched her trailing harness with one hand; the other clung to the smooth central shaft of the Fiata. Overhead, the great Ram's mouth splayed open in a silent howl.

The platform trembled at Stretto's approach.

Kurt stared down at the men climbing toward

them. Too far. Too far. Shawm was three body lengths behind. The rest clustered beneath.

Far below, the great stretchskin drum rolled out silently.

A single reed sang its throbbing note. Another answered.

Crimson cloth slithered through a blood-stained hand. Stretto's thin smile twisted his lips. Yellow light glittered on the knife that sprang into his hand.

Eyes fixed on Stretto, Picardy crept back. Her heels found the platform's edge.

In despair Kurt stared below. One chance. Only one chance. His urgent voice spoke to the brain of the scoutship—and it responded.

A tiny spark flew into Stretto's eye and blazed into a raging ball of fire.

With a gasp, Picardy fell.

"Catch her," yelled Kurt. "Catch her!"

Shawm wrapped a leg around the shaft and leaned out. Her body grazed his outstretched arms. He clung for a moment, then she slowly slid out of his grip.

Below another reached out...and another.

With a howl, Stretto spun away. Blinded by the light, he staggered toward the terrified Hexen.

Her hand drew back and she flung the harness at him with all of her strength.

It struck him full in the throat. Clawing at it, he staggered, and spun again.

Below, caught tight in the arms of a stranger, Picardy stared up blankly.

Stretto teetered at the edge of the platform for a long moment, body swaying, hands clutching the tangle of harness wires that circled his neck.

As he fell, his hands dropped away and flailed at nothing. He plunged straight down until the thin wires reached their limit.

The shocked crowd gasped.

Then there was no sound but the great tuned drum throbbing beneath the slow swing of his feet, pulsing, beating like a dying heart until even that grew still.

Kurt stared down at the chain of men helping Picardy to the ground. Safe, he thought. At once the grim irony of it struck him. For what?

How much time was left for any of them?

He searched his mind for a trace of Ooberong. No answer. He called out to her, softly at first, then urgently. Still nothing.

With sudden apprehension, he raised his head from the lens.

Beyond the lights of the scout's panel the black of space was studded with a thousand Rams.

"Ooberong!" he said aloud.

The scoutship answered:

REMAINING OXYGEN SUFFICIENT FOR 42 RAMINS. RELAX NOW. ALL WILL BE WELL

Kurt stared back through the windowing tracer lens. Far below, the knot of people gathered on the ground. The girl? Where was she?

A faint pulsing began in his head. In moments it grew to a fierce pain that took away his breath. Disoriented, he felt himself begin to fall.

The pain retreated a little, leaving a cold sweat in its path. Somewhere within it he sensed a pattern.

A faint image formed in his mind: a shadowy pair of eyes. Ooberong. . . .

The image shimmered in a mist of pain. Eyes. Gray eyes. Pupils dark as space, pupils that were not alike, not equal. Stroke. She had had a stroke.

The knowledge came in a flood, and he knew what she had done: She had never known illness and she refused to meet it now. She had ignored the pain at first. Then when it grew, she rose and, telling no one, locked the door and took her place before her instruments again with single-minded control.

Another image came—the net of stars deforming, warping into thin corded bands, vanishing into a well so deep, so vast, that it defied imagination. Kurt knew he looked into her mind at a simile—a meta-

phor for a dissolution that was beyond his understanding. He heard her voice then, distant in his
mind: "Not long...not long...."

"You can't go on. You're too sick."

"I...will."

"No."

Nothing. Then a faint laugh. "We're alike, you
and I." A pause. "We both have to fly." A faint breath
of a sigh, and she was gone.

Picardy huddled in Clarin's arms at the bank of
the river. Near exhaustion, Dorian sprawled full
length on the ground near Zoppa.

Clarin looked up and spoke to her brother, but
Shawm seemed not to hear. He stood facing away
from her and stared at the slowly retreating Fiata.

Just above them, a dot of light sped close, flickered,
and grew into the image of the immortal.

Dorian stared up at Kurt. "No. Enough."

Kurt fixed his eyes on the girl. "There's no time
left."

Scrambling to his feet, Dorian cried, "Leave her
alone."

Picardy blinked, then struggled up. "I'm all right."

"The record you showed me. Whose is it?"

Her eyes widened as she looked at his; her
hands flew out in a little shrug. "It's mine."

Kurt stared at Picardy in disbelief.

"It's mine," she said, bewildered at his look.
"From when I was a baby."

Kurt blinked in surprise at Picardy's words.
"Yours?" he said. "Those records showed a large
chromosome—a large dark body," he amended. "You
said yourself that only two or three percent of your
people carry it."

"I didn't say that." Picardy was openly puzzled.
"You asked to see a dark body pattern that showed
one larger than the rest. I showed you mine. Why
would I say that only a few carry it?"

"I asked you about retarded children with a
large chromosome. You said they were rare."

"They are," said Picardy. "Only the people with paired dark bodies have children like that."

"Paired?" He looked at her in astonishment. "What do you mean 'paired'?"

Picardy's face echoed his, "Why, forty-six pairs. Some of their children are retarded forty-sixers. Others have the same number, but they aren't affected." Then she said, "Some of their children are normal."

Kurt looked at her for a long moment before he said, "How many dark bodies do you think are normal, Picardy?"

Her hands flew out in a little shrug. "Forty-five, of course."

She stood before him, hands outstretched. In his mind, he saw her again in the beam by the river. Hands... outstretched hands...

Hands frozen in sunshine; pale hands washed in the yellow glow of the Pontibrio's lights. And each palm was crossed with a single, simian crease.

Chapter 28

"Let me see your hands."

They glanced at one another, then self-consciously extended their hands toward Kurt.

A solitary crease bisected every palm.

Carriers? All of them? He searched a dozen crystalline memories; he got back only scraps of answers. If they were carriers, why did they have that palm? Except for a single outsized chromosome, there was nothing about a carrier that looked abnormal.

And then he knew: They *were* carriers, but not of a defective chromosome. They—each of them—carried the distillation of millennia of genetic change.

It had to be, he thought. That's why they reacted to the beam. Kurt turned suddenly to Dorian. "You aimed the cautery at the ceiling, not the kaleidoscope. Why?"

"Why, I—" Dorian blinked. "I'm not sure. It was just the place to aim at," he finished uncertainly.

"It was a weak point," Picardy added. "At least, I think it was."

A weak point. A point where the stresses of metal straining against metal gave off vibrations pitched so low they could only be sensed subliminally, not heard. Infrasound.

He searched each face, one after the other, with a growing sense of amazement. He had been looking for a retarded child to be his empath. Yet children like that were no more than a way-station through eons of genetic trial and error.

These were his empaths, he thought. Empaths, all of them. And they didn't even know.

He looked at the little group. "You can read the alien's signals. Maybe we can stop it. Together."

And then he told them what they were.

The Fiata echoed faintly from the shore. The tide was coming in, lapping in protest against the hull of their stolen boat, but the wind was with them. Its breath bellied the sail of the little sea flyer and sent it skimming toward the dark mouth of the river.

Kurt's image rode the bow, an image as frozen in its expression as any icon, as over and over again the questions turned in his mind:

Why? Why were they different? And why here on Aulos? They had all sprung from a tiny gene pool. They had been irradiated by a G-2 star nearly as close as the sun to Venus, but it had to be more than that. The change had to be a survival trait.

And why would a sensitivity to infrasound be

that? Unless it had always been there in some rudimentary form.

He thought then of the birds of Earth that oriented their flyways to the subtle movements of tectonic plates. But birds were never the only migrating animal, never the only nomads who sought a tiny oasis. He thought of the teeming cities he had once known and the people who lived there—people acutely, exquisitely aware of boundaries and territories, people who knew that straying from them meant war and death.

And what of the people who carved out homes from the naked rock of asteroids? Were these the early signs of it? A way of tuning a life to the dimly sensed pulse of an alien world?

Changed, he thought, all of them. Human still, yet not. Something more. With a sudden restless envy, he searched for the trait within himself and found only stasis.

And the mortals on the Ram? Under his leadership they had bred for millennia with the illusion of freedom—a freedom tempered by the steady control of genetic counseling; coerced by "choice" and "good judgment" and the "common good" into a stasis as binding as his own.

He was a dinosaur. He was the leader of a ship plunging mindlessly through space with a cargo of fossils culled from an ancient world.

The night wind blew the rags of a cloud from the moons. Pale light gleamed on a silver scar. Shawm was watching him. The look on his face filled Kurt with sadness. They each had something that the other wanted, and the taste of it was ash.

Gray strips of tattered clouds fluttered over the moons. The dark mouth of the river gaped open to the bay. The wind fought with the rising tide, chopping its surf to peaks.

The water boiled with a billion phosphorescent creatures, tiny as insects. Hissing, the sea ran toward the stands of petit anche and filled old channels.

The reed beds were islands now, moaning and twisting in the wind, nearly drowning the humming of the beam.

Shawm threw a lever, and the sea flyer's twin anchors shot out. The flyer bobbed between the lines. They stepped onto a half-drowned island of reeds sobbing in the wind. Water rushed over their feet and stung their ankles with particles of swirling sand.

Though it was quite dark, the image of the immortal standing just above the water seemed to give off a light of its own.

They were close to the beam. Kurt could hear its faint humming, its overtones of the Earth Song. Suddenly, he remembered the gaping bays of the false Ram. Once more he saw them stream with a dead-white mist. A shiver rippled down his neck.

He remembered what Jacoby had said: "You knew. How?"

And how had he known? He searched his memory and found no clues. He tried again, and this time resurrected the image of Zeni Ooberong. Her eyes. *He had looked through her eyes* ...

Ooberong? Was it beginning in her too?

And then he knew that even the mortals of the Ram were changing. They were changing inexorably and all the genetic regulations put together could do no more than slow the process. The shadow dance of their genes would go on until one day they would be as altered as the people of Aulos.

Kurt looked up at the dark Aulosian sky. He stared as if he could see into the heart of the Ram and the minds of the people there. The wind whipped clouds across the moons, dark clouds that moved like flying creatures.

"We both have to fly," Ooberong had said. He wondered what her meaning was. In his mind he could see her in her dark red flying suit, slowing, banking, controlling her flight with subtle movements. Control and balance. "Control," she had said.

He shut his eyes for a moment, and when he

opened them, he felt strangely off balance. His gaze
met Shawm's. Empath, thought Kurt. He was riding
a new wave of humanity, but he wanted the anchor
of immortality. He shook his head. It was wrong.
Wrong to meddle with people's destinies and turn
their stable world upside down, wrong to keep them
from becoming what they should be.

Moonlight glimmered on the silver scar and
shadowed the young-old eyes that reminded Kurt so
much of his own.

"You had a choice," said Shawm. It was an
accusation.

A choice? Kurt looked away, not trusting his eyes
to meet the boy's. The question he had never been
asked rang in his head: *How do you choose, Kurt Kraus?*

What would he have answered? How would he
have chosen?

Then without quite knowing why, Kurt said, "If
we come through this. If we do, I'll see that Aulos
gets the process. You can have your immortality."

In the face of the fierce glaze of joy that sprang
into Shawm's eyes, Kurt turned away and tried to
quell a jumble of uneasy thoughts. He looked up at
the sky again, at the fluttering rags of cloud shrouding
the net of stars, while the children of Aulos stepped
into the alien beam.

Hands clinging together, the little group stood
on the dark reed island. Water swirled halfway to
their knees, black water sparkling with tiny luminous
creatures, echoing the star-net overhead.

The beam transfixed them. Fear and ecstasy
glittered in their eyes. Kurt strained to catch their
words.

Picardy grasped Shawm's hand and flung her
head back. Wind whipped her hair. "Fistula," she
cried. "It's a fistula."

Shawm began to sway in an odd, bobbing rhythm.
"It dances."

In dismay, Kurt tried to glean their meaning. He
stared at the upturned faces. Each one held its own

vision—personal, private. Their words made no sense
to him at all.

Frustration knotted the muscles of his jaw.
Empaths—all of them—linked to the false Ram's
beam now. They had the answer, but he could not
read it. It was there, so close, yet it was locked in the
personal metaphor of each mind.

He strained again to hear. *Fistula;* it was that to
Picardy. Somehow it wore the guise of medicine to
her. He stared at Shawm, at the rhythmic movements of his head and upper body. To Shawn it was
something else, something that spoke in the lan-
guage of dance.

Frantic, Kurt looked from one to another. Different. Each experience different—and unreadable.

Ooberong... He could look through her eyes.
She could tell him what it meant. She had to. He
framed a single cry in his brain.

He felt her touch his mind—distantly—as if she
held herself away from him. And with her touch
came the throb of agony.

He saw the pain mapped in her brain; he saw
the source of it: the area of cell death, and the
deadly swelling that was slowly choking off each vital
function.

She held herself away, and he knew it was not
only to shield him from her pain, but to shield
herself. She was going to die, and it was a private
thing. She wanted to do it alone without an invasion
from another mind.

"Ooberong..." His cry was a lament.

A pause. A beat. And then she let him in.

The pain came with teasing little stabs at first.
He felt it gathering, massing in a storm surge, and
then it was on him, boiling in from a dark sea in
yellow-green phosphors, engulfing him in cold flames
that flickered from bone to sinew and back to bone—
an electric pain born of Saint Elmo's fire, a cold pain
chilled by the night waters of Aulos.

He stood in the center of a conflagration of ice.
Flames fed on his bones, his flesh. A dagger of cold

fire pierced his eye and entered the socket to burrow beneath his skull. A pale spark leaped from wrist to fingers and smoldered in the small bones of his hand. A dozen more leaped over his body, touching, searing.

Pain crackled in his neck and hissed through the nerves of his arm. Faintly, over the rush of his blood he heard her voice: "...critical...critical now..."

He raised tormented eyes to the sky; he saw the star net through a haze of agony. The star points pulsed to the rhythm of the pain.

He saw her eyes, gray, gray as rain. He looked through.

The image stood on the angry waters, a spectre glowing in the night. It crackled with luminous energy and the black phosphorescent sea and the sky became one.

Pain drummed in his head. Through the link he heard Picardy's voice: "Fistula."

He stood inside the smooth walls of a giant gray vein. Blood-warm currents washed over him. Ahead, gray walls pulsed, and the current swept him toward them. On the wall, a tiny spot grew to a gaping slit...

The artery's tidal wave crashed through the breach. It surged against the current. He was caught in a whirlpool. Helpless. Swirling.

He heard Shawm's voice—and the whirlpool was a swirling devil dance of red and purple tatters, green and gold....

Kurt spun in confusion. Each image was too personal, too alien to his experience to make sense. "What?"

Ooberong's gray eyes anchored him. Ooberong, link to his own culture and understanding. The whirling tatters spun into two opposing dancers, spinning, dissolving into two undulating shapes, two amoebas, two dark universes—opposing, thrusting, touching.

The fistula opened.

A whirlpool of tatters...a whirlpool of dark genes mating...a whirlpool of energy swirling in a vortex of time.

Crimson and purple tatters twirled, green and gold.

He heard Dorian speak; he saw a cone. Golden liquid tash swirled inside it. The cone began to move.

Ooberong's eyes again. The cone became a top. A child's top spinning. Kurt knew it. It was red and its yellow stripe was worn from a small boy's fingers; it was his. She had found it in the recesses of his mind, and it was his.

He saw the point of a flashing knife, the tip of a cone of tash, the vortex of a red top with a worn yellow stripe.

The top skimmed backward in time, bored its way backward in time. Suddenly it paused, skipped forward, back, forward again, and he saw that its tip traced an infinity of points—an infinity of *nows*.

Earth's song swelled. Kurt saw her sapphire blue, her white on velvet black. Abruptly, blue-green Aulos swirled into the sky. The two planets hung in blackness, then merged into one.

Why, why, why, why...

The top hesitated. He heard Earth's song again; he saw the blue-green world of Aulos. He heard Earth's song, and it was magnified by a thousand empaths, fed back by a thousand empaths.

Paradox.

Why, why, why, why...

The top spun, teetered, slowed. The top bulged; twistor space warped.

Here, here...not here

And from its tip, its infinitesimal tip—its *now*—a point of light grew into an emerging Ram.

Another emerged...mist and milk.

Another. And he saw that there was only one of them—one Ram—created new each time. One Ram, both ghost and real. How?

The top teetered, expanded, bulged, turned inside out. The top was an hour-glass running out.

Chapter 29

The throbbing in Kurt's head gave way to a cold numbness that dragged at the corner of his lips and crept heavily into his arm, his leg. Latent images swam thickly in his brain.

The alien universe was a dark and mirrored twin to his own—a part of some unimaginably greater whole. It had been separate. It had been as separate as the passive flow of blood in the body's veins was separate from the warm rush of blood through its arteries: adjacent, intricately linked, but separate.

Then the touch had come: the minute fistula between two universes, the surge of an alien tide spurting into the quiet stream of this one.

Turbulence. Whirlpool. And the whirlpool was time, running backward against the current, dancing on tachyon waves that were faster than light.

He heard Ooberong's voice. "Paradox."

Earth, he thought. It was looking for Earth.

Like the tiny swell of a tidal wave in open water, the alien tide had run backward through time—under time—harmlessly, until it came to the shallows of paradox. It had sensed a song that began ten thousand years ago, and more, and it had answered. Following the curving path of a billion future Rams backward in time, it listened, searching for one small world that circled a tiny sun. Instead, it had found Aulos. It had found a world caught in the overtones and undertones of the Ram's song: Earth's song

205

reflected by a thousand bewildered empaths who sensed not only Earth, but a frightening alien intelligence.

The alien was on a cyclic path, a boomerang in space-time, searching for Earth, for a terminus. When it found it, the boomerang would curve back on itself, back to a future time so distant it was beyond imagining. Instead, it had encountered a paradox, a place that seemed to be Earth, but was not Earth. It had surfaced in Kurt's time; and somehow it had used his actual ship as a template for its ghostly twins; using the swirling twistors of space it had made them real by the creation of matter.

"Paradox," she said again. He felt her desperate effort to concentrate against the growing numbness, and he knew that she was dying now. She was beginning to die, and he felt the weight of it in his body and the cold reflection of it in his soul.

"Bottleneck," said Ooberong. "Break out. Break away."

She sent an image to him then: clouds of squat, transparent cylinders pinched in the middle with fat, curling rope—fields of undulating twistors locked in a static dance—the star drive fields of a thousand alien Rams.

The clouds began to bulge, warp, turn inside out.

"The ships are linked," she said, "like a single organism."

The molten center of a star blazed in his mind: Star drive. She meant the star drive.

A shudder...a paroxysm...a ship dying in convulsive agony...twisting, plunging into a sea of time.

Then the clouds of twistors abruptly vanished, and Kurt knew what he had to do.

Shawm thrust back his head and gasped like a beached sea creature. He shook his head and tried to sort the montage of images that thronged in his brain. He stared at the sky and felt the pull of the beam again, the invisible, searching pull of alien stars. His lungs emptied, his throat closed.

Stop it! Please...stop it...

Dizzy and sick, he sucked at the night air again. The scent of the dark bay water filled his nostrils.

Don't think of it. Don't think of it now.

The immortal was gone. Only a faint glowing trace of him was left glimmering on Shawm's retinas, then fading to night. He stared at the thick-starred sky. Gone.

Would he keep his promise? If he could? Would he? But he knew the answer: If tomorrow came, it would bring back immortality to the world.

The first fierce thrill of it was gone now, stripped away in the beam. He looked across at Picardy. She was clinging to Clarin, and both of them were watching the sky.

He looked from one to the other. He knew them all now. He knew things about them that he never could have guessed, never would have bothered to guess. He saw the quick sidelong look Dorian gave to Picardy. He loves her, he thought. She's pretending not to know. And he knows that; but he can't speak yet, not yet. Not until he believes he's earned the right.

He knew them. He knew that Dorian refused to look at the sky, refused to think about the alien. Instead, he had anchored his belief in a tomorrow that would have to come.

As if in answer, Dorian's eyes met Shawm's. "He made you a promise. But you may be too old. Too old for the process. They taught us about it. It doesn't work for everybody."

Shawm had never considered immortality as more than an abstract. He considered it now. He thought of a world of immortals; he put himself in that world and grew older in it, while everyone around him stayed the same. It doesn't matter, he thought. He looked at his sister. It would work for Clarin, for the little ones. And he was responsible. It was an offering, an expiation to a world of mortals, and he was responsible. "It doesn't matter," he said. "It doesn't really matter."

"It's going to matter to all of us. It's going to change things, change the way we look at things." Dorian raised troubled eyes to Shawm. "We aren't ever going to be able to be complacent again about what we believed." Then with a quick glance toward the star net piercing the clouds: "Or even be sure what we believe in."

Picardy gave Shawm a half-smile, tentative, trembling, and then looked again toward the sky. He saw an image of the tri-tail fossil, locked in stone. She's afraid, he thought. She's afraid that tomorrow won't come; and she's afraid that it will. She sees herself growing old too, in a world that wouldn't need her or her singing needles anymore.

Shawm's eyes met Zoppa's. Hers paused, dropped, moved away in confusion.

Cripples, both of us, he thought, wanting to reach out to each other, but not wanting to admit it, not able to admit it even in the face of destruction.

He knew each of them with an intimacy he had never thought possible. And if he knew them, then they knew him. The thought came as a shock. The idea that his privacy had been invaded as easily as theirs took away his breath.

What had they learned? What did they know? His hand sprang to his cheek, to the silver scar; his fingers traced it. Immortality. He saw his mother lying dead; he saw the futility of it.

Killer.

But he wasn't. He was giving it back. Giving back the stolen goods to the world.

Killer.

Suddenly he saw himself naked, every innermost feeling lying bare. Noble. How very noble he had felt. Gaining immortality not for himself, but for the world, for his sisters, his baby brother. But that wasn't the reason, that had never been the reason. He had only wanted to see respect in the eyes of strangers when they looked at him. He had only wanted to see the old prejudices fade away. He had believed they would, like magic.

Fool. Because he had reached a moment's equality in a transient beam, he believed it could happen. But it wasn't going to. It wasn't ever going to. If tomorrow came, it was going to bring the same looks, the same feelings it always had.

The thought stung deep: He was a Tatter and the world would always see him so. No matter what went on inside his head, inside his heart, he would always see the stranger's casual contempt.

And why not? came the harsh thought. Hadn't he had those thoughts himself? Hadn't they been bred into him, bone and flesh? He thought of Zoppa—Zoppa using humor as a shield for her soul. If only she could see that she was someone special. Wouldn't she believe it? Wouldn't the world believe it, too?

And then he saw what he had never seen before: If he could allow himself to be himself—if he could know inside that he was someone—then maybe, maybe....

The scar was hard beneath his fingers, and warm as flesh. He had thrust it there blindly, without thought, and it was a symbol that he could not read till now. He had seen it only as a pain that he could not bear to hold inside any longer, and it was that, but it was something more: It was the surfacing of the wound that festered in his soul, and the beginning of its release.

He touched the scar again, and when he did, it was with a faint trace of wonder. He had mindlessly placed it there without once realizing that a scar, even one of metal, meant a healing.

In the windswept dark, Shawm reached for Zoppa's hand. It felt cold in his, and small. His voice when it came was low and tentative. "We could help each other."

"If there's time." Her fingers closed over his, clutching, gripping, as if they caught a lifeline. "If there's time," she whispered, "we can try."

They stood in the rushing water, hands clinging, eyes fixed on the sky as dark clouds raced across the stars to the sound of distant thunder.

*   *   *

Kurt felt Ooberong steal away. The pain and the cold numbness left with her, and he felt strength flow back into his body.

He raised his eyes from the lens. The scout was an island, a speck in a black sea spangled with luminous ghosts. The distant lights of Alani's skimmer flashed, died, flashed again. A lighthouse, he thought, a beacon that steered him away from the shore.

He touched his cap, setting it for navigation. The skimmer was slow. He would have a head start. Jacoby would know that and not try to follow.

The scout spoke:

REMAINING OXYGEN SUFFICIENT FOR 15 RAMINS. RELAX NOW. ALL WILL—

The warning voice fell silent at his touch. He spoke quickly to the navpanel. Responding, the little ship chose a path and leaped.

He was heading on a random path toward a rendezvous with the ghost of a starship, and he knew it did not matter which of the ghosts he chose.

Moments later, as he knew it would, Jacoby's voice came on.

Kurt stared at the image of the man. Friend, he thought. Anchor. Friend. He wanted to reach out and touch this man one last time, grasp his hand, feel the steady warmth of him. He wanted to speak, to tell him what he had meant to him. Instead, he said: "I made a promise. Help me keep it. They've lost the process down there. I want you to see that they get it back."

Jacoby's eyes searched his. He did not speak for a long moment; then he nodded. "You're going alone."

Kurt heard a faint gasp. Then Alani's face appeared. "No, Kurt."

"It's all right." Wanting to say more, he looked at the two of them. And all he could say was, "It's all right."

His hand rose in a fleeting little gesture, and

then he shut off the connection between them, staring as their faces faded into phantom mists and phosphors. He reached out then, fingers stretching toward them, touching nothing. "Friend," he whispered. "Goodbye."

He sat staring at the darkened lens while the scout surged through the blackness toward distant lights that grew into a fleet of silver ships, until at last only a single starship filled the port of the tiny scout.

Distant lightning shot the bay with silver. Low thunder rumbled over the drowned island of reeds. Clarin trembled in Picardy's arms.

They had not moved. They could not move. They stood in the swirling black water and stared up at the sky.

"Cold?" Picardy whispered.

A slight nod.

She held the girl closer and found that she was trembling too. So much. She had learned so much, yet she didn't understand at all. Why? Why was it happening? She wanted her safe little world back; she wanted yesterday.

Like Dorian, she thought. He had locked himself into the old ways of Anche. He had kept his emotions tuned to Anche and found a war inside himself that he couldn't control.

A raindrop stung her face and began to course down her cheek. She wanted it back. She wanted it all back the way it was. But now, no matter what happened, it was over. And it wasn't fair. It wasn't fair to take it all away. It wasn't fair to make her know what a short time was left. Maybe just minutes. Maybe longer. But only a short time, only a short time either way.

She stood in the swirling tide and clung to Clarin while the rain fell faster to the rhythm of the surf.

Chapter 30

The giant bays of the alien Ram slid open in the silence of the night. The scout hovered for a moment like an insect at the throat of a pale flower. Then at a touch of his hand, it entered.

The firefly lights of the scout flickered over smooth, featureless walls. Although Kurt did not look, did not hear, somehow he knew that the bays were sliding shut behind him. Not looking back, he guided the scout toward a central port until he felt the tractor take control.

The scout slid into its berth. Instruments glowed, and a silent display flashed on its ready light. Kurt stepped out, and the conveyor under his feet began to move. He glided toward the door, which led to the heart of the alien ship.

He had invited it when the Ram was born, he thought. He had enticed the alien with a siren song ten thousand years old. Now it had come, and he had to meet it. He had to fly....

Blinking, Kurt considered the thought. For a moment, he could see Ooberong again, arms extended, flying, controlling every movement. Controlling...

Control... The illusion of control. The thought, when it came, was shattering. Control. It had been his way of dealing with a universe that he had perceived as hostile since he was a child. And until this moment, he had never known that he was driven by the need for it.

It seemed impossible to comprehend. How could he live within himself for millennia and never suspect that this was in him? How could he sound a mind for ten thousand years and find only the scattering layers of deception?

Was he so different from the men he had called enemy? They had tried to create their own brand of order out of chaos. So had he. And that was why he had governed the Ram for ten thousand years. He had never let go, because to let go would be to admit he was powerless in the face of a random, impersonal force that wore the mask of destiny.

The conveyor moved in silence. He grasped the railing, his hand quite still except for the almost imperceptible movement of tendon gliding over bone.

A part of him had always known that the time would come when the illusion would crumble. The greater part had denied it. The greater part had fashioned him into a little god in the microcosm of the Ram. A puny god, he thought. Safe in a closed little room, snug in the bed he had made, shutters closed against the storm.

The conveyor moved and reached its end. The waiting door slid open.

He stepped into a featureless corridor, white, deserted. As the door closed shut behind him, he felt the overwhelming loneliness, the emptiness of the Ram. It was an emptiness so complete it sucked out the marrow of his soul and he was left with nothing but a shell. He cried out with the loss. And then with mounting rage he railed at the silent ship: "Show me your face."

There was no answer. Nothing. Nothing.

"Let me see. Damn you. Let me see!"

Nothing.

He cried out then to Ooberong, wanting her there, wanting her pain there too because it was better than the emptiness.

Somewhere in the distant hollow of his mind he felt her tremble. Slowly, with great effort, she crept toward him; and as she did, he felt the numbness creep into his body. With it came an overwhelming fatigue, gray as winter, gray as the pain-glazed eyes that met his.

He heard her voice, faint as a whisper. "Minutes... no time, no time." He looked through her eyes....

Through her eyes he saw the Ram as a ghost of white mist, and he knew that he was seeing, from moment to moment, its continuous creation. The mist seeped through every seam and pore of the passage. Ahead, it curled its plumes around the startling blue of the hemichute and the car faded, wavered.

Fighting against fatigue and the anchoring drag of bone and muscle, Kurt reached out. He grasped a rail that faded to nothing in his hand and shimmered back again. He forced his body onto a flickering car and touched a dimming panel.

He felt a surge, and he was riding an illusion toward Ram Control.

His left arm hung uselessly at his side. His left leg was a cold weight, dragging behind him, slowing him. He reached out with his good right arm and grasped for support.

The room was empty. No one. No one.

The horseshoe console of Ram Control shimmered in white haze. He blinked. It wasn't a horseshoe, not a horseshoe at all, only a curving line edged in blackness. He blinked through the narrowing window of his vision. Blind, he thought. Half blind, like she was now. Slowly, he forced his head to move. Another portion of the console slid out of blackness: Star drive.

Amber lights flickered in mist.

Half-falling, he caught himself, steadied himself. His hand crept forward. "Status," he said and his voice echoed in the emptiness.

The companel spoke:

SMEAR. STAR DRIVE DEACTIVATED.

His voice was a whisper, "Ready star drive."

Lights flashed in an angry, blinking code.

SMEAR INCREASING WITH COMPENSA-
TION. STAR DRIVE DEACTIVATED.

"Override."

Red lights flared. Alarms blatted.

WARNING! COMPENSATION CRITICAL.
WARNING! ACTIVATION WILL DESTROY THIS
SHIP, DESTROY ALL PERSONNEL, THIS SHIP

"Priority override."

A thin shaft of light shot into his eyes.

RETINALS ACKNOWLEDGED, KURT PRIME.
ACTIVATING STAGE 3.

STATUS: MANUAL CONTROL. READY

He tried to focus; the override lever wavered.
So far away... He had to do it, redirect it, set the
alien free.

Cold drifted through his body. Rags of black
fluttered over his eyes. He caught his breath.
Ooberong!

Blackness. Black—and the distant, slowing flutter of a dying heart. His hand crept over the console,
touching, feeling for the lever. *Ooberong...*

Slowing. Slowing.

"Come with me," he cried, and his voice was
anguished. So far, so far. "Come with me."

"I can't...." A whisper. An echo. Dying, fading
to nothing. "...can't...can't...can't...." And she was
gone.

She had to do it alone, he thought. She had to
die alone as if it were too intensely personal a thing
to share.

And so now would he. He would do it alone, in
the final shuddering agonies of the ship, in the final
desperate hope that his death had meaning.

His hand closed over the lever. In a thousand
linked and phantom ships, a thousand hands closed,
pulled back, released.

In the offshore dark, Picardy stared up at the
sky. Dark clouds scudded before the wind and the
last of the storm. "Look!"

A thousand stars shivered in the night. A thousand starships trembled, vanished. Then there was only one pale distant Ram dimming in the light of the moons.

Tomorrow was coming, she thought, and a shiver ran through her. No turning back now.

She looked at Clarin. She was young enough, she thought. Maybe the only one of them young enough to be immortal. Clarin was going to have all the tomorrows. All that was left for her was now.

And then she knew that was all she had ever had, all any of them had ever had: a now, a succession of single moments. And it was enough.

She tried to imagine Clarin in a million years, still the same, not changing. She saw her leading a group through a museum filled with dry and dusty bones:

"To the left, a tri-tail."

And the group nodded and smiled its approval.

"To the right a Picardy. Picardies were tool users. Note the long, needlelike object clutched in its fingers."

Picardy laughed, and suddenly the others laughed, too. Then they were hugging, laughing, crying all at once, while a phosphorescent tide boiled around their knees and night winds swept the tattered clouds from a rain-washed sky.

Kurt felt the pull of the Ram in every bone, every fiber, every cell.

He raised blind eyes; he cried out. "Show me your face."

He sensed the great ship's star drive. He saw it as a golden plane, dipping under time, burrowing through blackness, plunging toward a point so distant that it had no meaning.

A billion twistors followed...a billion more....
More...more...

The Ram surged, and curiously, vision flooded back: circumscribed, flat, devoid of color.

"Show me your face," he cried again and again. "Show me your face."

And then he realized that it had none.

It was alien and utterly unknowable. It was an indifferent force plunging forward in its own time, backward in his. And in despair, he knew he would never know it, never understand it, never fathom its quest. He was riding its current with no more comprehension than a piece of flotsam riding the sea.

"No," he cried. "No." It couldn't be. It had communicated. He had known it, been sure of it. It was following the Earth's song. It had to be.

He listened, straining for overtones, undertones of meaning. When none came, he began to walk.

He walked aimlessly. Tall and straight, he walked, and the crystals he wore trailed and fluttered with the movement. He found himself on a colorless hemichute staring out onto a pale, empty world. Ahead, the forest of the Ram was silver and strangely translucent.

He stepped out onto the shore of a white, shimmering lake. Circling it, he walked over low hills until he came to the place of his retreat. Cycles, he thought. When the alien came, it was here they had found him, told him. It was here he would remain, he thought in desolation. Because it wasn't a cycle. Not at all. It was an entropy stretching out so far that it seemed like eternity before the final ebbing and dissolution.

He raised his hands to his head. The cap was almost weightless. He took it off, and its crystals flowed through his fingers like light. He laid it down; he had no need of it now.

He sat on the ground and leaned his back against the bole of a tall mahogany as pale as stars. On the rise above him a young gumbo limbo drew its sustenance from its fallen parent tree. Struggling toward a false silver sun, it carried destruction with it. The broad pallid leaves of a strangler fig showed in its crown, its knotted roots coiling like garrotes around the smooth blanched bark.

Cycles, he thought, and the thought was bitter. Bitter and pale as alkaline sand. He could see it, see the thought in his mind, pulsing, moving like a cloud of white flies—a cloud of colorless cylinders, pinched in the middle with fat curving ropes of glass. Twistors. . . .

Staring, he saw the pale cloud move. He saw it soar and bank; he saw it fly toward the center of the ship and join the others there. Staring, he thought he heard its voice: the faint tinkle of moving glass, the murmur of crystal rustlings, the distant echo of windblown sand.

Echoes.

Distant, alien echoes of a billion' thoughts, a billion shining thoughts.

He looked around and saw them everywhere, heard them everywhere. He looked and suddenly he knew them, knew what they were, and where they came from: *They* were the alien. They were the thing that had communicated. And they weren't from another universe at all. The whirlpool in time was only the vehicle—the tide they rode.

They were the questing, curious thoughts of a people from the edge of time, descendants of a human race so changed he had taken them for alien.

They were the people of the Ram.

He tried to comprehend it. A Ram so far in the future that its people had changed into something different, something more—the product of an evolution that was only beginning in his time. And it was then—in their time—that the fistula between the universes had opened.

They must have known it was coming. He tried to imagine them huddled in that future Ram, waiting for the cataclysm that changed them from flesh to energy in a moment.

They were pure energy now, caught in a rushing whirlpool.

And so, he thought in wonder, so was he.

With eyes that were not really eyes, he saw them. They were riding a current beyond understanding, and as they rode, they shaped it.

He laughed out loud at the wonder of it. And his laugh, his wonder, swirled in a cloud of crystal

movement. They were riding a tidal wave of time
back to their own beginnings.

Cycles.

He looked at the gumbo limbo again, and suddenly he was in it, of it. He was locked in mortal
combat, and there was nothing else in the universe
but a silent battle against the deadly coils of a strangler
fig.

He emerged at last, fatigued, shaken. And it was
only then that he saw that the fig, the gumbo limbo,
had sprung from a million thoughts—a billion twistors
generating infinitesimal particles that, joining, formed
that frozen battle. Mist. White mist. Continuous creation of matter from thought alone.

Immortals. All of them. Rushing back to an old
shore, rushing back to the origins of Earth.

True immortals. Energy, not flesh. He saw them
riding an endless tide, ebbing, flowing forever, and
he knew that somehow they had always existed, just
as time had always existed. It was only his sensing of
it that was linear. He could see it now, nested, linked—
boxes from a magic show, now empty, now full.
Building blocks. Twistor thought.

They're like gods, he thought. And the alien
tide they rode—did it have a name? A meaning? Was
it the guiding force that made them possible?

He could sense their thoughts now, sense that
his were linked to theirs, and he wondered if it
always had been so. He thought of a tide washing the
shore of a little planet. He thought of it touching
human lives with wisps of a future that would seem
to them to be the touch of inspiration.

Thoughts. Making the stuff of the universe.
How many did it take to dream Olympus? How
many more did it take to dream a world?

He stared at the gumbo limbo again and remembered the struggle with the strangler fig. Nothing else had been real then but the life of that single
tree, and he knew that if he had stayed there, made
that choice, with its death there would be an ending.

How do you choose, Kurt Kraus?

He stared at the tree and he thought, could it be possible? Could it be possible to try again? To have a choice?

The image of an infant came to him then. A new and mortal infant, not yet born...created whole.

The child's eyes opened, and he saw that they could be his own.

He thought of a curving golden figure eight with a break along its path.

How do you choose, Kurt Kraus?

Do you choose to deny your immortality? Do you choose your art?

He knelt on the silver soil of Earth below a silver tree. He reached out and felt the presence of a multitude; he held their thoughts in his hand.

He looked down at the ring that now lay in his palm: a simple ring of antique design. And on its face a line of gold traced a lazy eight on a field of black, a backward curving line with a single break.

"I choose to deny," he whispered. And when he slipped it on, he thought he heard the distant echoing of music.

ABOUT THE AUTHOR

A native of Tampa, Florida, Sharon Webb now makes her home in the Blue Ridge Mountains of North Georgia. The *Earth Song Triad*, which includes the novels EARTHCHILD, EARTH SONG, and RAM SONG, had as its genesis the novelette "Variation on a Theme from Beethoven" (chosen as the lead story for Donald Wollheim's 1981 *World's Best SF*). Sharon Webb is also the author of THE ADVENTURES OF TERRA TARKINGTON.

The Magnificent New Novel
by the Hugo and Nebula Award-Winning Author
of Startide Rising

THE POSTMAN
BY DAVID BRIN

Set during the long decline after a cataclysmic war, THE POSTMAN is an urgent and compelling fable for our times, a universal work in the tradition of ALAS, BABYLON and A CANTICLE FOR LEIBOWITZ. A chronicle of violence, brutality and fear, but also of hope, humanity and love, it is a moving, triumphant story of an individual's dream to lift mankind from a new dark age.

Buy THE POSTMAN, on sale October 15, 1985 wherever Bantam Spectra hardcovers are sold, or use the handy coupon below for ordering:

SPECIAL MONEY SAVING OFFER

Now you can have an up-to-date listing of Bantam's hundreds of titles plus take advantage of our unique and exciting bonus book offer. A special offer which gives you the opportunity to purchase a Bantam book for only 50¢. Here's how!

By ordering any five books at the regular price per order, you can also choose any other single book listed (up to a $4.95 value) for just 50¢. Some restrictions do apply, but for further details why not send for Bantam's listing of titles today!

Just send us your name and address plus 50¢ to defray the postage and handling costs.

BANTAM BOOKS, INC.
Dept. FC, 414 East Golf Road, Des Plaines, Ill 60016

Mr./Mrs./Miss/Ms. _____
(please print)

Address _____

City_____ State_____ Zip_____

FC—3/84